It's <u>Not</u> Me, It's You

Also by Alex Light
The Upside of Falling
Meet Me in the Middle

It's Not Me, It's You

ALEX LIGHT

HARPER

An Imprint of HarperCollinsPublishers

Typography by Jessie Gang
24 25 26 27 28 LBC 5 4 3 2 1
First Edition

To Alessia.
You're all the best parts of Julie and Jillian.

CHAPTER 1

"WHAT ABOUT *THE SECRET* *Life of the Teenage Amphibian?"*

I lift a hand to block the sun from my eyes. "No offense, but that may be the worst potential title I've ever heard," I say.

Suzy sips very loudly on her iced latte. Her video camera sits abandoned on the picnic table between us. "You haven't given me any better ideas, Jackie."

"*I'm* not the filmmaker in this friendship. *You* are," I remind her. "Plus, I'm the talent. And the talent doesn't get paid to think."

"Technically, you're not getting paid at all," she says. Right. I'm doing this out of the goodness of my heart.

This day is teetering on a billion degrees, so taking my lunch break outside of Monte's Magic Castle during the dead of July may not have been the best idea. "I'm sweating through this costume," I say. The pepperoni pizza on my plate is beginning to look more like soup.

"Welcome to summer in New York," Suzy says, her gold *S* necklace catching the sunlight. It's a conversation we've had every summer for the past ten years: I complain about the heat, Suzy reminds me that we've lived here our entire life and, well, what else did I expect?

And by New York, I don't mean glamourous New York *City,* with Broadway and Michelin star restaurants, where every corner is stuffed to the brim with people's hopes and dreams. No, no, no. We mean New York *State,* baby. Ridgewood, New York, to be exact, where our equivalent to Broadway is a run-down community theater and our top-rated restaurant is—you guessed it—a McDonald's off the interstate.

"But seriously," Suzy continues, "my school project needs a name. We can't keep referring to it as 'that documentary you're making.'"

"I think that has a nice ring to it," I say, staring bleakly at the mess on my paper plate. On one hand, I'm starving, and pizza soup sounds better than no food. On the other hand— Ugh, yeah. I can't do it.

Suzy continues. "What about *The Untold Story of Jackie Myers?*"

It sounds like an episode of the crime podcast my older sister Jillian loves. "That makes my life sound like a cold case," I say, shuddering.

Fresh out of ideas, Suzy collapses on the table. You know

what they say about art students—the *dramatics*. Sheesh. "This title is haunting me, Jackie." She sits up abruptly, her eyes wide with a new idea. "Maybe I can talk to Jillian? She always comes up with the coolest titles."

It's true, she does. Jill is a journalist at *The Rundown*, a local magazine owned and run by women. And Suzy is one of the rare people she actually likes. "You can try," I say. "She's pretty swamped with work."

Suzy tries again. "*Frog Fun and Freshman Frights?*"

I make a face. "Can we stop with frog-related titles?" Not to mention that everyone is starting college in September and I have yet to send in a single application. It was the result of great procrastination, living a life with no direction, and trying one too many clubs during high school and coming to the slightly disturbing realization that nothing seems to pique my interest. Not even the Culinary Club, which Suzy was certain I'd enjoy. Turns out eating food is a lot better than making it.

Suzy hides her laugh behind her drink. "How can I *not* resort to frog-related titles when you look like that?"

"Don't come see me at work if you're not prepared to handle all of this." By *this*, I mean the fact that from neck to toe I am literally stuffed into a frog costume. My frog head sits next to me on the bench, taunting. Haunting. I see it in my nightmares.

Looming behind us is Monte's Magic Castle, where I work and host kids' birthday parties. My official job title is entertainer.

My unofficial title is Frog—one of the woodland crew. Is it my dream job? No. Is the pay good? No. Do I enjoy working there? No. Did I forget where I was going with this? Yes.

Suzy reaches for her camera and begins recording. "Stoooooooooooop," I groan, shielding my face with my hand.

"Just a quick clip of you in costume!"

"Ughhhhhhhhh." I shrug off the embarrassment and let her do her thing. Who am I to question her creative vision? Not that I know what that vision *is*.

For the past month, Suzy's been carrying that camera around every single day, recording snippets of me here and there. When I ask what it's for, she says she's getting a head start on a school project. When I ask what the plot is, she responds that it's a study of the teenage American girl. As if there aren't billions of books, movies, and television shows about that *very* unique experience. But she is my best friend, immensely talented, and I would quite literally do anything to help execute her creative vision. So.

"You know you already got into one of the most prestigious film schools in the country," I remind her. Cornelia Film Academy has been all Suzy has talked about since she took a film class sophomore year. In a split second she found her calling: a director. When the acceptance letter from CFA came in the mail, we both cried for different reasons. Suzy cried because she got in; I cried because the school is in California, on the opposite side of *the country*.

Even now, when Suzy talks about leaving and starting a new life at CFA, it's like my emotions are split in two. Part of me is so unbelievably happy and excited for her, while the other feels like one gigantic bruise.

I am hyperaware that this summer is our final countdown. The last few grains of sand are draining through our friendship hourglass. Anything beyond August feels like uncharted territory.

Suzy brightens, in a very specific way that only happens when discussing film. "I may have already been accepted at CFA, but that doesn't mean I can't get a head start and be at the top of my class," she says.

"Well, save some storage space for our end-of-summer road trip," I remind her.

Suzy snaps the cap on the camera lens and snorts. "We have the *idea* of an end-of-summer road trip."

We've been planning it since we were kids—one summer, we'd drive straight to California. We'd have a yellow Jeep Wrangler, drive down the Pacific Coast Highway, and blast Katy Perry's "California Girls" because . . . duh. It was a dream we put off every single year—until now. This is kind of our last shot. And with Suzy heading there for college, it's the perfect excuse to make one final core memory as I drive her there instead of crying in the airport as her flight boards.

Not to mention that I've never left the state of New York. A very large part of me has the sneaking suspicion that life may become infinitely better once I leave Ridgewood in the rearview.

"But we don't have a car," Suzy points out, "which is kind of crucial when planning a road trip. We're already using the little cash I have saved up for gas, but we still need, you know, a *vehicle*."

I wave my hand in the air, dismissing her concerns. "I told you what happened with my parents. I'm working on it." Initially I asked my family if I could borrow one of their cars, and it was a hard *no*. But my parents promised that if I could save up twenty-five hundred dollars by the end of summer, they would chip in the other half so I could buy a used Nissan that's for sale at a dealership in town.

Plus, diving headfirst into planning this road trip helps take my mind off the gigantic question mark that is my future.

Suzy clears her throat. I stare down at the table, suddenly very interested in the grains on the wood. Is this oak? Maple? Cedar? Maybe I should Google it.

"And how much money have you already saved up?"

"What was that?" I ask. "Sorry, I couldn't hear you."

I yelp when her foot collides with my shin. "Answer the question, woman. How much money?"

"That's confidential."

"More than a thousand?"

"Suz, I get paid to dress up as a frog. What do you think?" Whoever said money can't buy happiness was insane. Like, I'm pretty positive I'd be *quite* happy with a few million dollars lying around. Or even just twenty-five hundred dollars, to be exact.

"I can't believe our dream of a yellow Jeep is turning into a beat-up Nissan." She groans.

Picking my phone off the table, I pull up the *iDiary* app. My blog loads, and I type out a quick text post: *anyone know any good get-rich-quick schemes?* I post it to my two hundred followers. I pretty much use my blog to shitpost whatever thoughts come to my head. I mean, my account name is @shitjackiesays, so it can't be taken *too* seriously.

"What are you doing?" Suzy leans across the table to peek at my phone. She shakes her head like a disappointed mother. You're way too obsessed with that app." She undoes her long black braids and begins retying them as I watch with envy. My wild brown curls could never do that.

"Am not," I say, attention back on *iDiary*. I refresh my activity section, checking if there are any new notifications—comments, followers, messages, that kind of stuff. There's nothing. Typical.

"I got a notification last night when you posted at three a.m.," she says matter-of-factly.

"I couldn't sleep."

"Yes, *because you're on your phone all night.*"

"I have two older sisters and parents who regularly enjoy shoving their noses in my business. I don't need any additional judgment, thank you very much," I say. As I'm about to close the app, the alarm I set goes off, signaling that my lunch break is over.

"That extra-long break went by oddly fast," Suzy says, slurping the final dregs of her latte through the straw.

Technically, my lunch breaks are a short fifteen minutes. But my manager, Monte Jr., is so laid-back he's practically a beach chair. Well, that, and he's carrying the weight of running his family's business on his shoulders. The man is so perpetually stressed, I swear he develops a new wrinkle every week. On the bright side, he's so busy running around that he barely has time to actually, you know, *manage* his employees. It's been said that we may take advantage of it.

Which is why tomorrow being his last day is soul crushing. (And why I need to make the most out of my extra-long breaks while I still can. For example, today's fifteen has turned into a forty-five.)

"You know how Monte Jr. is," I say. "He won't even notice I was gone."

"I wasn't talking about Monte Jr. I'm talking about Wil—"

I cut her off before she can so much as speak his cursed name. "We don't talk about *him* on break. Remember?"

Suzy smirks. "How could I forget. Sorry."

Ignoring that, I stand up, dust the crumbs off my costume, and tuck the frog head under my arm.

Suzy pops the lens off the camera. "Let me get one last shot of you walking inside."

I've been embarrassed enough today. "Not a chance. Stop profiting off my misery."

"But it's so fun," she whines.

I make it halfway to the door when she calls, "Jackie—put the frog head on!"

With nothing else to lose, I do.

CHAPTER 2

FRIDAYS ARE OUR BUSIEST day at Monte's. There are three birthday parties booked, and it's a zoo of screaming kids running around, fighting over the arcade games, leaving a trail of tickets all over the floor, and eating too much pizza before throwing it all up. I pose for a photo with Anita, my coworker, who rocks a very adorable squirrel costume, and the birthday girl, who just turned six and wears a bubble-gum pink dress with puffy sleeves and a hemline covered in ruffles.

"Can we get one with just the frog?" the mother asks, her face half hidden behind a very expensive camera.

Anita whispers, "Clearly she finds you *ribbit*ing," and giggles as she walks away.

I snap a couple more photos before I'm finally released. I spot Anita hovering near the air hockey machine, watching two young boys locked in a very intense battle.

"Don't go into the break room," she immediately says without tearing her eyes away from the match.

"Why?"

"Justin and Margaret are making out."

It's not the first time Monte's prince and princess have been caught in a compromising situation.

"That's not very royal of them," I say. One of the boys scores and lets out a scream.

"If I have to see that girl's boob one more time, I'm calling HR."

"We don't have an HR team," I remind her.

She turns to me and says, dead serious, "Then I'm calling the police." Anita tucks a few pink hair strands beneath her costume.

"Maybe our new boss will have less of a tolerance for rule breaking." A bit ironic, coming from the girl who sneaks away every thirty minutes to smoke.

"Speaking of . . ." I say. "Who do you think it will be?"

"No idea," Anita says. "Before Monte Jr. stepped in, his brother ran this place. Before him, it was their dad. I wonder if they'll try to keep it in the family."

I've heard the story too many times to count. Seven years ago, Monte Sr. passed away unexpectedly of a heart attack. He had built this business from the ground up, named it after himself and everything. After he passed away, his eldest son took over. Then it got passed on to Monte Jr., who's been running it ever since. It's practically been a Ridgewood staple for decades. As much fun as it is to poke fun at it, there isn't a child who hasn't celebrated at least one of their birthdays at Monte's Magic Castle.

"I wonder if our new boss will give me my old job back," I grumble.

Long story short, I started working here as a waitress last summer. The tips were decent and the job was fairly easy, since our menu consists of maybe ten items that are all deep-fried. Then six months ago, the world collapsed around me as I was demoted to frog duty.

Those waitress tips would really help with this car dilemma. And solving the car dilemma would really help get me out of this town.

"How long are you stuck in frog purgatory?" Anita asks. "It feels like forever ago when that whole situation went down."

Just the brief mention of my villain origin story conjures up memories of *him*. Shaggy brown hair and a stupid, perfectly ironed button-up shirt. The storage room in the back of the building, where I was perched on a stool, hiding away on my phone instead of working. And *him*, barging through the door, catching me red-handed, and ratting me out to Monte Jr. That day, I lost my job and gained an enemy.

Anita lets out a low whistle, giving me a look. "My bad," she says, her hands up in surrender. "I should know better than to mention Wil—"

"Please don't say his name," I beg.

"Fine. Let's change the subject— How's your hot sister?"

This topic is somehow worse. "My *what*?"

"Your hot sister," Anita repeats casually. "I saw her drop you off at work today. What's her name?"

"First of all, gross. Second, I have two sisters."

"Well, which is the hot one?"

"You must understand why I can't answer that."

Anita just laughs. "She had a shaved head and was blasting old rock music."

"Oh, that's Jillian," I say.

"Is she single?"

"Anita, you're not dating my sister."

"Who said anything about dating? Dating sucks," she says. "After I broke up with my ex, I swore to myself there'd be no more commitment until I hit thirty-five. Maybe even fifty."

Since I grew up with two older sisters who dished out their fair share of heartbreak, that sentiment comes as no surprise to me. I was nine years old, tucked into bed with Julie and Jillian, listening to the ins and outs of their relationships—and believe me, there was a new one every week. When it comes to dating, there really isn't much that can surprise me now. What I lack in dating experience, I make up for in secondhand knowledge.

"Jillian's the same," I say. "She's not the dating type."

Anita grins, like that's exactly what she wanted to hear. "Interesting."

I'll ignore that. For now.

When the air hockey match ends, Anita turns her large squirrel head to me. "I'm going for a smoke," she declares, undoing the Velcro strap of her squirrel head and marching outside.

To my left, a child throws up.

If there is one thing this job has given me, it's killer reflexes for moments like this. I jump back before the spray hits my costume. The boy who lost the air hockey match is wiping vomit off his mouth with his shirtsleeve.

I should call for help. I should grab a mop. I should most definitely help this kid find his parents. But today's vomit count is a mind-blowing four, and I still have three hours left in my shift.

So instead of helping, I run in the opposite direction and hide.

Monte Jr. finds me minutes later, crouched behind the ball pit.

"Sorry, Jackie." He visibly winces as he hands me a mop. I take one glance at the stressful shade of red blooming on his cheeks and the permanent frown lines on his forehead. His hairline has receded so far it looks like it too is running away from this place.

Tomorrow, he'll finally have a taste of freedom.

The mop hangs between us.

"I've cleaned it three times today," I whine.

A baby's scream pierces my ear. Monte Jr. cringes. There is a flash of something in his eyes. Regret? Terror? The sudden desire to sell this place to the highest bidder? He blinks, and the usual exhaustion is back. He holds the mop higher.

"Please," he begs. "No one cleans vomit quite like you do."

The worst part is that he's right. No one does clean vomit like I do. I wear my vomit-cleaning talent as a badge of honor.

Then I remember what Anita said about my frog purgatory. This could be my last chance to leverage my skills for a promotion. To reclaim what was once rightfully mine and get my old job back before Monte Jr. is no longer in charge.

I grab the mop. "I'll clean it—"

"Oh, thank *God*."

"On one condition. I want to talk about this," I say, gesturing at my frog costume. "I've been stuck in this costume for two months now. I want to be a waitress again."

"Oh," Monte Jr. says. He scratches the top of his head. "I thought you were enjoying this new role."

"Uhm, what on earth made you think that?" Does the permanent scowl on my face radiate joy?

"Look, Jackie." He looks behind both shoulders, scanning the area before lowering his voice. "You're aware there is going to be some . . . restructuring happening within the company. New management is being announced during that private event we are hosting tomorrow. I won't say too much for now, but I'm sure we can discuss altering your job title."

Like the sky after a storm, the clouds over Monte's Magic Castle part and sun bursts in through the windows. I hear birds chirping, angels singing. I envision a future where the color green ceases to exist and I never have to wear this horrific costume again, a future where I'm making enough money to give Suzy the send-off she deserves, road trip style.

Altering your job title.

And just like that, the chaos quiets for a moment and life feels exciting again.

"Sounds good," I tell Monte Jr., flashing him a rare smile.

"Vomit's in the dining area. You got this!"

I locate the mess and begin cleaning the floor with a new vigor. Wait . . . Am I *actually* excited for work tomorrow? That has never—

"Why are you smiling?"

Ughhhhhhhhhh. I'd rather clean vomit indefinitely than deal with him.

I focus intensely on the floor, hoping that, if unacknowledged, Wilson will go away, kind of like a bumblebee.

"I know you can hear me," he says.

If there is one thing Mr. Bossy Know It All hates, it's being ignored.

"Unfortunately, yes," I say. Prepared to tear through this entire interaction as quickly as possible, I meet Wilson's gaze. He is seated at an empty table, spawning there like the devil himself and flipping through an enormous book.

"*Employment for Dummies*?" I ask.

As usual, he doesn't crack a smile. Instead, he watches me with that intense, steely glare, his pristine white shirt buttoned all the way up to his neck. Today he wears his green Monte's Magic Castle vest over it. My attention snags on his name tag: Wilson, Assistant Manager.

There has never been a title so wrongfully given.

Wilson slams the book shut and shows me the cover. *Understanding the Ins and Outs of Corporate America*. So just some light reading. Lovely.

"Hate to break it to you, but this job is the furthest thing from corporate America," I say. "Plus, don't you learn about that at your fancy business school?" When he isn't spending his summers haunting these four walls like a poltergeist, Wilson goes to a business school in New York City. I'm not sure which, but I suspect it has a very high acceptance rate.

He straightens up in his seat. Going to business school is practically Wilson's entire personality. "I do," he says proudly.

"It's summer break," I point out.

"I'm aware," he says.

Understanding that this conversation's pulse has flatlined, I continue scrubbing the vomit off the floor. Actually, I sort of forgot that's what I was doing to begin with. Now, the water in the bucket has turned a murky brown, and it's beginning to smell. At this point I'm basically making a bigger mess.

"Why are you studying in the summer?" I ask. Just then I remember the half-eaten Twix I shoved into my pocket earlier today.

Wilson watches me eat with nothing but sheer disgust on his face. "How can you possibly eat that while you're cleaning up vomit?"

My teeth sink into the chocolate-caramel goodness. "Look where I work, Wilson. If I struggled to eat near gross smells, I would have died from starvation months ago." I peel off the wrapper and attempt to fling it at Wilson's head. It lands about eight feet to his right.

He sighs.

"You didn't answer my question," I say to distract from my terrible aim.

His fingers skim through the textbook pages. "I'm not studying. I'm reading this for fun."

"*That's* what you read for fun?"

"Yes, Jackie. Not all of us are illiterate." Wilson stands, tucking in his chair by lifting it off the ground so it doesn't make a scratchy noise. With his book in hand, he takes a few steps toward me.

Accepting that the floor is not getting any cleaner, I stop mopping. "I'm not illiterate. I can read your name tag easily." I tap the cool metal pinned to his shirt. "'Wilson Monroe, Assistant Dickhead.'"

He makes a big show of examining my costume head to toe. "Right. And you don't wear a name tag, because you're a frog."

"Actually, it's because it clashes with my look."

"And what look is that?" he prods.

"Amphibian chic," I say, squaring my shoulders like one dignified lady.

"Not the word I had in mind."

I have to actually force myself to breathe out through my nose so I don't combust from anger. And he knows it, too. From the way that stupid grin splits across his ridiculous face, Wilson knows *exactly* how to get under my skin. The easiest way? Mentioning the costume. Why? Because I am staring at the man who did this to me.

You see, two months ago Wilson walked through the doors of Monte's Magic Castle with a briefcase in hand and a mission to ruin my life. And actually, what nineteen-year-old carries a briefcase? Like, just say you've never been kissed, and—

Anyway. Wilson is Monte Jr.'s nephew, hence he was able to strut in here with a cozy little job title and an ego the size of a freaking blimp. On day one, he was bossing people around. It was "clean the bathroom" and "try to look a little happier when talking with guests." How about you try to remove my foot when I shove it up your—

What was I saying? Oh yes. That first day. Wilson was not a fan favorite around here with the other employees. He just didn't fit in. Like, everyone who works here is bonded by two things: a deep hatred for this business and the fact that we are broke teens struggling for a minimum wage paycheck. So for Wilson to not share any of those qualities? Yeah, he stuck out like a sore thumb.

But *whatever.* That's cool. Hey, it's not your fault you were born into generational wealth. I would have been all fine and dandy to coexist with him, sharing the occasional glare and "good morning" grunt.

Wilson, on the other hand, had something much different in mind.

Treachery.

He was a treacherous little traitor.

Only a month after he started working here, he caught me doing what he refers to as "time theft." It was the day that Julie and her fiancé, Massimo, got engaged. My phone was blowing up—missed call after missed call. I was in the middle of serving four tables, but I couldn't focus. In an anxiety-ridden rush, I hid in one of our storage closets, perched myself on a stool, and *finally* checked my messages. I quickly realized the good news and sent appropriate—and slightly unhinged—memes to the family group chat and a long text to Julie about how happy I was for her, adding that I absolutely refused to wear a pink bridesmaid dress.

Then the storage room door burst open. There stood Wilson, looking ten different shades of angry. And there I sat, tucked away in the corner of this darkened room on my phone, having completely lost track of time.

Long story short, Wilson ratted me out to Monte Jr., saying that I wasn't fit to be a waitress.

Apparently, my four tables all complained and threatened to never return.

Apparently, I was the worst waitress in the great state of New York.

In an extremely hasty decision, Monte Jr. stripped me of my apron and sentenced me to amphibian jail. The next day I was given my new costume and job title: entertainer. Every day since, Wilson has had the satisfaction of seeing me like this—parading around kids' parties in this green outfit, carrying my shame day after day.

I've contemplated quitting, but we are too far into the summer season now for me to find a new job. New positions won't open until the holidays, and I can't possibly go that long without a paycheck, not with Suzy and our road trip on the line.

"What are you doing?" Wilson asks.

Snapping back to reality, I realize I've been glaring at him while leaning against the mop. "Thinking," I say.

"Huh, didn't know you could do that."

I clench my jaw, breathing out through my nose like a furious dragon ready to blow flames. "And I didn't know you could read," I grit out. "When'd you learn that?"

"Shortly after I became assistant manager and you turned green," he says.

And then he does the most insane, humiliating thing possible. Wilson pats the top of my froggy head with his hand, all while his face is home to the most bloodcurdling smile I've ever seen.

As he walks away, there is one thing I'm certain of: in a world with infinite timelines, I hate Wilson Monroe in every single one of them.

CHAPTER 3

SATURDAY MORNINGS AT THE Myers house are home to my most chaotic memories.

Growing up with two older twin sisters who suffered from severe commitment issues was eventful, to put it lightly. They are experts in heartbreak—both having a clean breakup record; they've always been the dumper, never the dumpee. And an extraordinary amount of dumping has gone on in this house. For some reason, it always happened on a Saturday, when a new character would join the Myers family—only to never be seen again.

Saturday meant hobbling downstairs to the most awkward family breakfast imaginable. There was always a new addition to our dining room table: a guy named Matt eating a breakfast burrito and not leaving any eggs for the rest of us; a girl named Nadia who, after my mom brought out honey for her tea, would not stop talking about how we need to save the bees; or even poor Peter, who was so scared he went straight out the door after witnessing my dad's prebreakfast stretching routine right in the middle of the living room carpet.

Then there are my parents, two easygoing, life-loving hippies. They spent their twenties traveling through Asia in a van. My dad was briefly in a band during the eighties, and they had a huge radio hit in the summer of '85. My parents retired early with the money they still rake in through royalties. Once they had children, they enforced absolutely no rules in this household—hence Julie's annoying tendency to take on the mother role.

I'm fairly certain the reason I've steered clear of relationships for eighteen years is because of the chaos I witnessed as a kid. I mean, you can witness your sisters breaking only so many hearts before you start to realize that love is crazy, messy, and maybe safer to stay away from entirely. There's also the fact that there is truly no guy even slightly desirable in all of Ridgewood. You're choosing between Billy, who you watched pee his pants in third grade, or Steve, who drove his daddy's truck into a pole one summer 'cause he was tipsy from too many keg stands.

Still, what this town lacks in excitement is made up for in our singular household. This Saturday, like all others, starts off with a healthy dose of mayhem.

My eyes open, and I wait. I wiggle my feet, admire the sun cutting in through the slit in my curtains. I listen to the faint sound of pots clanging from downstairs in the kitchen. I try and I try and I *try* to resist, but Suzy was right: I'm obsessed with my phone.

Declaring defeat, I grab it from my nightstand, open *iDiary*, and disappear into this little online space that is solely mine.

In a house with no boundaries and a town where everyone knows everyone, having something that belongs to me and no one else feels precious.

I'm scrolling through the app's home page when my bedroom door bursts open. In walk Julie and Jillian, polar opposites in every way. Julie is in a light pink, button-up pajama set that has tiny embroidered strawberries. Jillian wears an oversize Fall Out Boy concert tee and crew socks.

Jillian tosses my laptop on my bed. "Took it again by accident," she says. We have the exact same laptop, same color, same case—everything. The two of us are always accidentally grabbing the wrong one.

"We made you breakfast!" Julie declares. She carries a large wooden tray that holds a tall glass of orange juice and a plate of pancakes smothered in whipped cream.

"*Mom* made you breakfast," Jillian clarifies, making herself comfortable on the edge of my bed. Julie places the tray on my lap while I quickly close *iDiary* and hide my phone under the covers.

"Great," Jillian says. "Jackie's watching porn again."

My cheeks flare. "Am *not*."

Julie's hand grasps my shoulder. "It's nothing to be ashamed—"

"*I wasn't*. Shut up. Both of you."

Jillian is cackling like an evil witch. Julie's face is so concerned she looks like she may burst into tears. Desperate to change the subject, I grab the fork and dig in. "What's the occasion?" I ask. The pancakes are as fluffy as ever, with just the perfect dash of vanilla—Mom's signature touch.

Jillian shrugs, already distracted by her phone. Julie is walking over to the large floor-to-ceiling windows that take up an entire wall of my bedroom. She pulls back the blackout curtains, allowing the morning sun to find its way into our Saturday. Her gigantic engagement ring catches the sunlight, casting rainbow fragments over the white walls.

"Much better," she says. Then she is shoving me over in *my own* bed, cozying up under *my* blanket before her head rests on *my* shoulder.

"We know today is going to be rough for you," Julie says. Her voice is feather soft, like I'm a piece of glass that will shatter beneath the slightest pressure. "Mom remembered too. We thought maybe this could cheer you up a bit."

"Is it working?" Jillian asks, typing furiously on her phone. "Do you feel the *cheer*, Jackie? Are you now *cheerful*?"

"I don't understand," I say over a mouthful of pancakes. "What exactly do I need cheering up from?"

"It's your boss's last day," Julie shares.

"*That's* what you're worried about?" I ask in disbelief.

Jillian snorts. Her hair this morning is definitely a sight. It's in the process of growing back from when she shaved her head last summer. Now, short curls stick up in all directions like she's been electrocuted. "I told you she'd be fine," she says. "Jackie isn't a

25

sentimental crybaby, like *some* people in this house."

I stuff more pancakes into my mouth to hide my giggle. Jill and I definitely inherited more of our personalities from Dad, while Julie is a carbon copy of Mom. They excel in baking, wearing the color pink, and diving so deeply into their feelings they may as well be ocean explorers.

Julie silences her twin with a glare. "Jackie," she says, talking to me like I'm one of her students, "when the principal at Ridgewood Elementary quit last year, you saw how devastated I was. It was so much more than losing a boss. It was like losing a friend."

"Guys, I'm completely fine." Over a mouthful of food, the words come out barely audible. Truthfully, these pancakes are doing more for me than they are.

Julie squeezes me into her side. "You're so strong," she says. "Honestly, you're handling this so much better than I did." Probably because her boss was a fifty-five-year-old woman who baked her pies. My boss is a balding man in his thirties who makes me clean vomit three times a day.

"I'm fine," I say again. "Seriously, your concern is not needed."

While my sisters argue, I eat a spoonful of whipped cream. The years they spent off at university turned the house a dull, sad gray. It wasn't until they were gone that I realized how much I needed them around. Dinners weren't the same without the three of us roasting my mom; weekend breakfast sucked without Jillian there to list all the reasons why my dad should stop eating meat. Their bickering was my favorite background noise.

My dad appears in the doorway. His white T-shirt is covered with flecks of paint, and he is wearing the ultimate dad jeans, with little holes in the knee from decades of wear. The length of his goatee has doubled, and there is pink polish covering his fingernails—undoubtedly Julie's doing.

"What are you three scheming about?" he asks.

"Your daughter is mothering me," I say.

"Jules, let's leave the mothering to your mother," Dad says. He heads downstairs, leaving us to our usual mess.

Beneath the covers, my phone begins to ring. Julie lunges for it. "*Ohmygoshcanyoustop,*" I say, tearing the phone from her fingers and accepting Suzy's call. I put it on speaker, since she's basically the fourth Myers child. "Good morning," I say.

We all jump when Suzy's voice booms from the phone. "CAN WE KEEP THE FAMILY BONDING TO A MINIMUM WHEN THE CAMERA IS NOT AROUND."

"What are you—" I hop out of bed and run over to the window. Next door, Suzy stands in her bedroom, glaring right into *my* bedroom. Jill joins me at the window and bursts out laughing.

"That's hilarious," Jill says.

"Cut it out!" Suzy says. She is all kinds of serious, standing there looking comically grumpy in her button-up pajamas. Still, her threats are way less scary when she's fifteen feet away and we're separated by two brick walls.

Jillian takes the phone from me. "Oh, we are going to bond *so hard.*"

Suzy gasps.

"Harder than ever before," I add.

"I'm coming over right now—"

"Mom, lock the doors!" Jill yells downstairs.

"Bye, Suz!" I singsong, hanging up the phone just as she begins to threaten me.

Jillian shuts the curtains. Behind us, Julie is very confused. "What was that all about? What camera?" she asks.

"You don't want to know," I warn.

When Jill begins walking out of my room, Julie says, "Where are you off to?"

"Work," Jill answers.

Julie doesn't buy it. "It's Saturday."

"And? Just because you have the weekend off doesn't mean everyone else does, Julie." She leaves, taking her attitude with her.

Still tucked into my bed, Julie releases a loud sigh. "I don't like her working with Camilla," she says. The mention of Jillian's ex-girlfriend quickly changes the mood in the room. "I'm worried about her. We both know how that ended last time."

Camilla is Jillian's boss at *The Rundown*, who also happens to be her ex-girlfriend. Not just any ex either—*the* ex. Camilla and Jill dated for two years when they were eighteen. When Camilla cheated on her, there was a solid month where my entire family didn't see Jillian. The door to her bedroom was permanently locked. I'd hear her window opening at night and spot her climbing down the trellis, hopping into some sketchy car that

28

waited at the end of our driveway. That heartbreak kicked Jill's ass right into a No Commitment Zone. She hasn't been the same since.

"She seems okay to me," I add. By which I mean she's been her usual sarcastic, irritable self. "She said they were on good terms when she took that job."

Julie shakes her head. I notice that one of the buttons on her pajama shirt has fallen off. "I don't want her getting mixed up with Camilla again, Jackie. And she seems more like, moody lately."

"She lives in a constant state of annoyance, Julie. Irritable is her only mood." If you even look her way before ten a.m., she will tear you in two.

Julie collapses on the pillow.

"What are you up to today?" I ask to change the subject.

"Massimo is coming by," she says, her face taking on that dreamy, faraway look that only happens when she's thinking of her fiancé. Julie's heartbreak era ended two years ago, when she met Massimo while grocery shopping. The handsome—and insanely rich—Italian chef quickly swept her off her feet and managed to lock down her untamable heart.

"We're looking at another wedding venue," she continues. "The last few didn't live up to that fairy-tale idea I have in mind, you know?"

No, I don't know. But when your wedding doesn't have a budget, I'm sure achieving fairy-tale status is possible.

Finally, Julie vacates my bed. "Well, I should get ready. Oh! If you want to skip the bus today, you can take my car to work." Seeing the look in my eyes, Julie says, "Only for today, since I don't need it. This is a onetime thing. Got it?" I nod. "And for the love of Taylor Swift, check the freaking camera when you reverse out of the driveway. I won't have you nearly running anyone over in my car."

"It was one time—"

"Too many," Julie finishes. "You know where the keys are." After blowing me a kiss, she leaves, closing my bedroom door behind her.

I call Suzy, who picks up on the first ring. "Wanna go for a drive?"

"Why can't we just take this car on our road trip?" Suz asks as we get into Julie's Volkswagen Tiguan, my bare legs sticking to the hot leather seat. "It would make things a lot easier."

I turn the engine on and immediately blast the AC.

"Because I've been indefinitely banned from driving my family's cars," I say. After I very carefully reverse down the driveway, we are cruising down the road. Suzy reaches for the aux, playing the *La La Land* soundtrack as per usual.

"Because of what you did to Mrs. Clemens?"

"I didn't *do* anything to her—"

"You reversed your car into her," she says like a lying liar.

"I *gently* nudged her—"

"Hit her," Suzy says while clearing her throat.

You have one incident when you're sixteen, and suddenly you aren't trusted to operate a motorized vehicle. Wow. "She shouldn't have been standing behind my car," I say.

"She was on the sidewalk. You know, that area meant for *walking*."

"That's not what happened." It is in fact exactly what happened. "She shouldn't have been behind my car."

In the passenger seat, Suzy snorts. "Don't victim blame."

"It's not victim blaming if the victim was actually at fault!" I pull out of the neighborhood extra carefully. "Can we change the subject, please," I beg. "Why exactly am I dropping you off at Bee's?" Bee's is our favorite café in town that's conveniently in the same plaza as Monte's.

"Course selection opened today," she says. "I have to finalize my schedule before all the good classes are full."

The mere mention of college makes me clam up. Partly because thinking about Suzy leaving places a giant question mark on my life. The other reason is, simply, that I didn't apply to any. Through four years of high school, nothing clicked. No subject stood out, no career path felt possible or even somewhat exciting. When I start to think about my future, all I can see is working at Monte's and Suzy being on the other side of the country. Which is very, very bleak.

Suzy swats my arm, which is very unsafe since I'm driving. "Stop spiraling," she commands.

"Am not."

"Are too. I can see it on your face."

Chewing on my bottom lip, I brake as we approach a red light. This isn't a full-blown spiral like normal. This is, like, a semi-spiral. Much less dangerous and easier to snap out of.

"*Stop*," she says again, reaching over and pinching my leg.

"What if I'm just stuck at Monte's," I say. "What if that's all I'm destined for?"

"I won't let that happen," Suzy says.

But you won't be here.

It feels like I'm walking a tightrope, constantly torn between being a supportive friend and wanting to be a selfish monster who asks Suzy to go to school in state so our futures can stay intertwined.

Thankfully, we arrive at Monte's and I can stop worrying about my what-if future and start focusing on the present—which, to be honest, isn't much better. Suzy runs over to Bee's, and I take out my phone and open *iDiary. do you ever wish you could hit pause on the future?* I write. *just prolong it for a little while longer? not to be too emo on a saturday morning, but I've been feeling like that a lot lately.* When it's posted, I start walking.

Standing below the gigantic MONTE'S MAGIC CASTLE sign, with a generic fairy-tale castle and a princess in front, waving a magic wand, is Anita, smoking a cigarette. She is the complete opposite of this fairy-tale image, with her Dr. Martens (mind you:

in the middle of summer) and her short hair tied up in two little space buns. She flicks her cigarette ash onto the grass and nods as I approach.

"Steal someone's car?" she asks.

"I'm not that cool," I say. "What's going on in there?"

"No idea. I think Monte Jr. was intentionally vague about today's private event so he wouldn't scare us away."

She's not wrong. The text he sent out in the work group chat gave no details whatsoever. Just that we would be closed today for a private party, but we needed to come in anyway.

Anita's phone chimes. She glances at the screen and groans.

"Everything okay?" I ask.

"It's this girl I went on a date with last night," she says, tucking her cigarette between her teeth before furiously texting. "We're going on a second tonight, but I'm not feeling it. Like, at all."

"What happened?"

"The chemistry was kind of off," she says, the cigarette muffling her words. "And she went into a kiss with full-on tongue. What kind of sicko does that?"

"Gross."

"I'll give it one more shot I guess," she continues, her fingers flying across the phone screen. "I just don't want to get stuck on a date with no escape. I have to be able to flee at a moment's notice."

A bead of sweat drips down my neck, the summer sun melting

me like a Popsicle. "Take separate cars," I suggest, remembering a time when Jillian ran into this exact dilemma. "So you're not stuck driving home together if it ends badly."

Anita stops texting. "That's . . . actually very helpful," she says, her eyes on mine. "What other advice you got?"

"Uhm . . ." I scramble. "Obviously go somewhere public. You know, like a coffee shop or something. That way you can get up and leave whenever you want. If you hang out at your house, she's there for as long as she wants."

Anita stares at me like I just offered her the solution to world peace. "Jackie, you're a genius."

"No," I stress. "I just have two older sisters."

Back to furiously typing on her phone, Anita says, "Whatever the reason, that's great advice. Like, you should sell it or something. You probably have way more where that came from, right?"

I nod. I could fill a textbook with it.

"Geez, you're some sort of heartbreak expert. I wish I'd known that sooner," Anita says, tucking her phone into her pocket. "And don't think I've forgotten about Jillian. I'm still working on a way to get her number that doesn't involve breaking into your phone. All right—ready to get in there?"

I ignore the first half of that sentence. "You head in. I need a second."

Anita stubs out her cigarette and flicks it to the ground before heading inside. I pull out my phone and open *iDiary*, creating a new text post. *was just called a "heartbreak expert,"* I write. *have*

I finally found my life's calling . . . ?

Unprepared for the day, I head inside Monte's and get blasted by the familiar gust of air-conditioning, but that's the *only* familiarity—because Monte's Magic Castle has been given a much-needed facelift.

The fifty-something arcade games are literally sparkling in the light, as if they've been scrubbed, waxed, and polished. We wander over to the pinball machine. Anita runs her finger along the glass cover. "This was covered in dust yesterday," she says.

I point at the floor. "I watched two kids throw up on this exact spot just yesterday." Now the red carpet looks clean enough to sleep on.

Anita whistles. "Geez. Who the hell is this party for? The president?"

I follow Anita to the right side of the building, where a dozen self-serve ticket kiosks line the walls beside the Prize Hut—where you can trade your tickets in for stuffed animals, candy, bouncy balls, or the higher-ticketed items: headphones, a Nintendo Switch, and a pack of signed baseball cards. The rows of prizes lining the walls and stuffed into display cases have been completely reorganized, now arranged from smallest to largest, color coordinated.

Justin and Margaret, Monte's prince and princess, are standing inside, reorganizing the shelf that's filled with different candies and chocolates, all worth the low price of one hundred tickets.

Anita grabs a pack of Starbursts and rips it open. "All right, you two. What's going on here?"

I follow her lead and grab a Twix bar, stashing it in my pocket for later.

Margaret, focused on bags of Sour Patch Kids, looks up at us with her big blue eyes. Her skin is milky white and covered in soft matte makeup that makes her look like a doll. "What do you mean?" she says.

I stare at her pretty pink princess dress with envy.

"I haven't seen Monte's this clean since there was that lice outbreak three years ago," Anita says.

"Has Monte Jr. said anything about who's coming?" I ask.

Justin and Margaret shake their heads perfectly in sync. "No," Justin says. "He's been running around all morning. He hasn't gotten off the phone."

"Whoever our new boss is, they're coming in hot," I say.

Anita offers me the roll of Starbursts. I grab the orange one. All orange-flavored candy is the safest bet. It always tastes good, never too artificial, like strawberry or lemon.

"I still can't believe he's actually leaving," Margaret says.

"Same," Justin says. "Dude's got a permanent hard-on for this place."

"I thought he'd die in that ball pit," Anita adds.

That makes me laugh. "As if it could smell any worse."

A voice comes booming from behind us. "ATTENTION!"

Monte Jr. is standing on a chair. He speaks into a megaphone, which is somehow the strangest and most on-brand thing I've ever witnessed.

"It's finally happened," Anita says. "He lost his mind."

"CAN EVERYONE PLEASE FORM A CIRCLE AROUND ME! EVERYONE PLEASE GATHER AROUND."

Monte Jr. steps off the chair and lowers the megaphone. Beads of sweat drip down his forehead, and half-moon circles dampen the fabric beneath his underarms. He lets out a long, long breath. "Thanks to everyone for being here today," he begins. "I know you all have questions as to who this event is for—"

"Who's our new boss?" someone yells.

Monte Jr. scratches his head. "A lot of work has gone into prepping for this party today," he continues, entirely avoiding the question. "The guests we are hosting will be the Monroes—my entire family. And they will be arriving within the next half hour."

At that, I groan. If we're hosting the Monroes, that means we're hosting Wilson. I think the only thing worse than working *with* him would be working *for* him. Dammit, I need to find a way out of this.

"To thank you all for being here, you will be paid time and a half today." At that, everyone cheers. "And," Monte Jr. continues, now smiling, "a one-hundred-dollar bonus for all your hard work."

And just like that, I know I'm not going anywhere.

CHAPTER 4

IT TAKES APPROXIMATELY FIFTEEN minutes for Monte's Magic Castle to descend into chaos.

Waiters are running around, lighting candles on the center of each table, as if this is a five-star restaurant and not a three-star business on Yelp with a review that literally just says "Absolutely not."

Monte Jr. frantically tasked me with assembling the wood-land crew and greeting all the guests at the door, which is exactly what I do. Kind of. As we wait for everyone to arrive, I drift off to the arcade area and open *iDiary*. I'm about to type out a new text post when a tiny red number catches my eye. I have three new notifications! Which is kind of a big deal, considering I usually have zero.

Clicking on the alert, I see that three people have interacted with my heartbreak-expert post. Two people liked it, and one person commented, *Share the knowledge!*

Not me being validated by strangers online and instantly feeling my ego swell.

I'm typing out a response to the comment when I hear my name being called.

No—*screamed.*

"Oh, no," I whisper.

Monte Jr. has returned to the megaphone.

"OUR GUESTS ARE ARRIVING. ALL WOODLAND CREATURES REPORT TO THE FRONT DOOR TO GREET OUR GUESTS. AND GET OFF YOUR CELL PHONES THIS INSTANT. I AM SPEAKING DIRECTLY TO YOU, JACKIE MYERS." His voice booms through the building, practically making the floors shake.

I run to the front door and stare out the floor-to-ceiling windows. Dozens of cars are pulling into the parking lot. It's a never-ending stream of Lexuses, Mercedes Benzes, and Porsches, with a shiny black Rolls-Royce leading the way. In seconds, the entire parking lot is full. Car doors pop open and slam shut. A mob of humans walks toward us. I have a random flashback to when Suzy and I watched *Shrek* last week. More specifically, when the village people charge Shrek's swamp in full outrage, armed to the teeth with pitchforks and torches.

"SHIT." Monte Jr. forgets his megaphone is on and says exactly what we are all thinking.

I stand beside Anita the squirrel, Olivia the beaver, Shauna the rabbit, Paxton the fox, and Davis the bear. We all share the same look of terror.

The bell chimes, a cute little *ding*!

Then the rest is a blur of Chanel perfume and the sound of heels click-clacking against linoleum. In seconds, Anita has turned into a coatrack and Paxton is rocking a newborn baby in his arms.

Anita peers up at me from beneath a brown fur coat. "Help," she gasps.

They won't stop coming.

Cousins and nephews and nieces and great-aunts and regular aunts and great-uncles and family friends and This Person's second cousin and That Person's mother-in-law and the wife of Some Man and the ex-husband of Some Other Woman. Monte Jr.'s family pours in like a freaking dam on the verge of collapsing. There are so many of them, and we barely manage to get a "Hello!" out of our mouths before they are storming past, ignoring us like overlooked statues in a museum.

Throughout all of it, I search every face, every group of people, waiting for Wilson. I need to be prepared for his entrance. I need to know the exact moment to *run*.

Finally, the last members of Monte Jr.'s Largest Family in the Entire Freaking World pile into the building, and the door shuts. I feel a slight pang of guilt for whoever broke their back cleaning these floors overnight. All that hard work, demolished in seconds.

"He's not here yet," I say to Anita. All the other woodland crew members have dispersed, leaving the two of us standing like weirdos by the door.

"Cool, cool," she says. "Great observation. Hey—could you help take these insanely heavy and very inhumane jackets off of me?"

"Right. Yes. Of course. Who even wears a coat in this weather?" I have never seen this much fur in my life. I begin piling them in my arms. "I hope this is faux."

"We both know damn well these are real," Anita says, looking utterly disgusted.

"If Jill was here, she'd call PETA."

Anita holds up a cropped fur coat that looks hauntingly like a zebra. "Where are we even supposed to put these? Other than the dumpster."

"Definitely *not* that. I can stash them in the break room?" I offer.

"Great idea," she says. I hold my arms out, and Anita piles the rest on. "I'll stay here and continue greeting. Go, Jackie, go!"

I quickly disappear through the Employees Only door and head straight for the break room. I dump half the coats on the table, covering it entirely, then stumble down the hall with the rest to Monte Jr.'s office. A large wooden desk takes up most of the space, with two armchairs positioned in front, and floor-to-ceiling shelving that's covered in mostly black-and-white photos of Monte Jr. shaking hands with various men and a few photos of Monte's Magic Castle back in the day, before it crushed the hopes and dreams of so many young teens. Ugh— I take a moment to pay my respects.

The moment ends with a *thump!* My arms finally fail me, and the coats pile onto the top of Monte Jr.'s desk like an avalanche. With that, I decide I'm due for a little break. After making myself cozy in Monte Jr.'s chair, I pull out the Twix bar and my phone. I'm mid-bite when the office door is pushed open. I shriek, my phone crashes to the floor, and Wilson stands in the doorway. Once again, catching me in a bad situation.

Can this day get any worse?

Then Wilson steps into the office and— Yup, turns out it *can*, because behind him is the most gorgeous girl I have ever seen. To my absolute shock, she's holding Wilson's hand.

"Hey, Froggy," he says, because calling a gal by her legal name is apparently overrated.

I eye their intertwined fingers.

No. That can't be right.

"Hello, William," I say, purposely using the wrong name to both annoy him and undermine his authority. "Step into my office."

"You know my name is Wilson," says the worst person in the world.

"Whatever, Wilfred. What are you doing here?"

Since we are openly staring at each other, I take a moment to note how different he looks. His usual wavy hair that falls both this way and that has been tamed with gel, and he's wearing dark denim and a black polo. He looks a *bit* better than normal. Like, if I had a gun to my head, then, yeah, I'd admit that.

His girlfriend easily outshines both of us, looking like a young Halle Berry. She stares at my costume, grinning. But not in the mean way Wilson does.

"Does my uncle know you're in his office?" Wilson blabbers on.

"I thought this was your—" his girlfriend begins before he cuts her off.

"Jackie?" he prompts.

I ignore him entirely and take the liberty to introduce myself to this girl. "I'm Jackie," I say, smiling. "I'm the assistant manager here."

"No she is *not*," Wilson says.

I ignore his frustration. Annoying him is just *so fun*. "No, he's right, I'm not. I declined the position because it was just too easy, you know? Good thing Wilson was the second pick."

Wilson's face is a fantastic shade of red. "That's not true," he says, forcing each word out between clenched teeth.

"Is true," I chime, taking another bite of the Twix. My teeth sink into caramel chocolatey goodness.

"Is *not*," he fires back.

We are children on a playground, fighting over who gets to go down the slide first.

Wilson's girlfriend laughs. Even her laugh sounds like it should come out of a Disney princess. "Woah. The infamous Jackie. I've heard *a lot* about you."

That . . . Well, that entirely catches me off guard. From the look on Wilson's face, I don't think he ever intended for me to know that.

I smile sweetly at him, basking in his discomfort. "You talk about me outside of work? I'm so flattered, Willy."

"I *complain* about you outside of work," he corrects.

"Doesn't matter. My presence still takes up a tiny part of your brain at all times. How sweet," I say.

"See what I mean? She's impossible," he says, shaking his head.

The girl's smile doesn't waver. "He definitely didn't overexaggerate. I'm Kenzie, by the way," she says, giving a wave. "Wilson's girlfriend."

"You can blink twice if you need help," I say. "There must be a panic button in here somewhere."

When she actually blinks twice, we both laugh out loud. "Kidding," Kenzie says.

No—she's amazing.

What on earth is she doing with *him*?

Wilson looks as if he is witnessing the downfall of society. But when he turns to Kenzie, his entire face softens, like an ice cube melting in the sun. The tension is gone, replaced by a look filled with so much adoration it's entirely foreign on his face. "Could you let my uncle know I'll be out there in a minute? He's probably looking for me."

"Sure." Kenzie says goodbye to me, pressing a quick kiss to Wilson's cheek before leaving. He watches her go, a tiny smile playing on his lips. It's like in the movies, when the monster takes their mask off and there's a real person underneath. Who knew that beneath Wilson's cruel remarks, superego, and tyrant-like tendencies, he actually had a heart.

"Have you walked along a yellow brick road lately?" I ask.

When he turns to me, his entire face has hardened right back up. "What? No. What are you talking about?"

"Just wondering if you've run into any wizards? Perhaps behind a curtain? That give out hearts . . ."

I see the moment the joke clicks. "*The Wizard of Oz*. Hilarious."

"I watched it last week," I say. Suzy and I made our usual popcorn concoction—a bowl of popcorn with a minimum of two sour candies and two chocolates mixed in—and spent the night on the couch.

"Let me guess," Wilson says, leaning against the doorframe now. "Did you watch it on your phone in the storage room? On company time?"

"That's so rude of you to say. I watched it in the *break* room on company time, obviously. The lighting is way better in there." Wilson rubs at his eyes, like I'm a strange hallucination that will disappear in three, two, one . . .

"If you're so annoyed by me, feel free to leave at any time," I say.

"I'm not leaving you alone in here," he fires back.

I'm fully aware that his entire family is a few feet away. There are definitely a dozen people he should be talking to, and yet he chooses to be in here, heckling me.

"So . . ." I continue. "What else do you say about me to your girlfriend?"

He bangs his head against the door.

"I only ask because you apparently talk about me *so much*—"

"How does so much sarcasm fit in such a small person?" he asks, looking genuinely confused.

Hey, I'm only five three. I shrug. "No idea. I'm, like, fifty percent Diet Coke and fifty percent wit."

Wilson walks toward the desk, and the entire space seems to shrink. I don't like the way he towers over me, looking down on me. "You really shouldn't be here."

I ignore that. "Your girlfriend is gorgeous."

"I know."

"She's way out of your league."

At that, he actually laughs. "I know that, too."

"Where'd you two meet?" I'm not entirely sure why I'm asking

46

about their relationship. Probably because I'm so shocked there's someone out there who could actually tolerate him, so, naturally, I need to learn all the details to see exactly how this pairing happened.

"School," Wilson says. "Can you get out of that chair?"

Instead, I do a little spin on it. "How long have you been together?"

He sighs, like he is resigning himself to my questioning. "Seven months."

I whistle. Dang, that's a good chunk of time. "And she hasn't gotten sick of you yet?"

"Apparently not."

"Does she live here?"

"No," Wilson says. "But Kenz has some family here that she's staying with for the summer. Why do you care?"

Kenz. Every attempt I make to imagine Wilson not only coining a nickname for his girlfriend but maybe whispering it gently in her ear before kissing her, comes up empty. It's like if you threw Wilson and romance into a math equation, the answer wouldn't exist.

Yet here I am realizing that, somehow, it does.

"No reason," I answer.

"What are you doing in my uncle's office?" he asks again. He shoves his hands into his jean pockets, probably to hide his fingers as he flips me off.

I'm starting to think there's a specific reason he doesn't want me in here. Something to hide, maybe? I lean back in the chair, cozying up. "I don't know," I say. "I could be working. I could be taking a break. I might be hiding from your family— Hey, maybe I'm planning a hostile takeover."

"Hostile takeover? That means you'd be spending even more time here," he says.

"Oh, gross. I definitely don't want that." Even with every aspect of my life feeling like a gigantic question mark, the one thing I know for certain is I am not making a home out of this job.

"What do you and Kenzie do for fun?" I ask, digging my nose a little deeper into their business. "Color-coordinate files? Rank your coworkers from most to least hated?"

"Yeah, and guess who's at the top of the list?"

"Justin?" I joke. "Don't worry. I won't tell him."

After a pause, Wilson huffs out, "We go on dates."

"I'd hope so." With a girl like that, Wilson better be pulling out all the stops to keep her eyes on him.

"Nice dates," he adds.

"Are you trying to prove something to me or yourself?" He looks completely exasperated with me. Welcome to the club, buddy. "Anyway, planning a cute date in Ridgewood must be a pain in the ass. This town is impossible to romanticize. You know what I would love? A cute picnic in a park or something. Have you guys done that?"

"Isn't there a mosquito warning in effect?"

Ah, shoot. "There is. I forgot about that. By the way, your family turned me into a human coatrack," I say.

Wilson's gaze searches the room, taking in every inch, like he's analyzing the square footage. "Sounds like something they'd do."

"Any chance those coats are faux?"

He snaps back to attention, his eyes landing on the coats. "Unfortunately, no."

"Don't tell Anita," I say.

He hits me with a confused look. "Why would I tell Anita?" This man has the sense of humor of a brick wall.

The fluorescent office lighting is beginning to give me a headache. I give up my power position in the chair and strut past Wilson, hitting him with a heavy amount of side-eye. "If anyone asks, I was never here," I say.

"I wish that were true," he grumbles.

After lunch is served, the chaos begins to dwindle. The second the last plate is cleared, Monte Jr. stands up and asks for everyone's attention. I feel the nervous anticipation build up in my bones. This is the moment when he announces our new boss—the person who can get me out of this frog costume and into my brand-new car.

When we have all gathered in a circle around Monte Jr.—Wilson, weirdly enough, stands at his side—he begins his speech by thanking everyone for coming. "As you all know," he continues, "my time managing Monte's Magic Castle is being put on hold. I have prided myself on running this business for the past decade. When my father, Monte Sr., passed away"—his mother, an older woman with a tuft of white hair, begins crying at the mention of her husband—"he trusted this business to my brother, and then to me. In the past ten years, we have taken Monte's Magic Castle and grown it into more than a business. It's a pillar in this community, where memories are made and life's biggest moments are celebrated. Today, I'm saddened to be taking a step away from the company, but I believe it is being left in great hands while I'm gone."

A hushed murmur falls over the crowd. Everyone scans the room, trying to spot the new boss. But my eyes land on Wilson, who looks like he's about to take a step forward.

And just like that, the events from today click into place. I understand why Wilson's family was so happy, why Wilson was showing Kenzie his uncle's office—he was showing her *his* future office.

"While I step away for an indefinite amount of time, my nephew Wilson will be taking over as the acting manager of Monte's Magic Castle." What Monte Jr. says next is drowned out with applause. People are standing up, cheering, clapping, whistling. I stand frozen, watching an unstoppable series of catastrophic events play out in front of me.

Beside Monte Jr., Wilson takes that step forward. His hair is perfectly in place, his face stoic and ready. In a room of seventy people, his eyes find mine. His smile is ruthless, like the first shot being fired.

I gasp. Wilson was right—this *is* a hostile takeover. Only it's not mine.

It's his.

CHAPTER 5

THERE IS NO ELOQUENT way to say this—I'm screwed.

Once champagne bottles were popped and the party got really crazy, I snuck out the front door and headed home. I highly doubt that anyone noticed. They were way too preoccupied kissing Wilson's butt and celebrating the end to my soon-to-be-promotion. With Wilson in charge, there is no way in hell he'll ever promote me back to waitress. Not after he went out of his way to make sure I was demoted in the first place.

This promotion was my last hope—my last chance at getting a raise, making more money, and affording that road trip with Suzy. Now our final memory together will be here, stuck in Ridgewood instead of driving down palm-tree lined streets. It was a dream so clear it nearly felt like reality. And now Wilson has stomped all over it, ripping it away before it even had a chance to happen.

At home, to mourn the loss of my future, I collapse on the

couch and never get up. My family passes in and out of the room like background characters in a television sitcom: Dad dropped off a bowl loaded with cookies-and-cream ice cream, Mom stopped by to watch the final fifteen minutes of a rerun of *The Office* with me, and Jillian came by to refill my bowl with two scoops of chocolate fudge brownie.

Thankfully, I'm six ice-cream scoops deep, and the sugar is perking me up a bit.

After I've watched two more episodes of *The Office* and skimmed through the Food Network, Jillian reenters the room. She looks ready for bed, her face scrubbed clean of makeup, and she's wearing an oversize Joy Division T-shirt.

"Name one song," I say in lieu of a greeting.

Jill gives my shoulder a shove and says, "Shut up." She tucks herself under the blanket with me, cozying up so we are pressed shoulder to shoulder. "What happened at work? By the look of this sadness cocoon, I'm guessing it didn't go well."

I rest my head against her shoulder.

"That bad, huh?"

"Yeah," I say, remembering the moment Wilson's eyes locked with mine. "I think I might be stuck as a frog forever."

Jill laughs. "I'm sorry. That sentence is just so ridiculous."

We stare at the TV for a few moments. I watch the colors change on the screen, not really paying attention. What I want to do is hit Pause on the turning of time so my shift tomorrow never comes.

When the show cuts to a commercial, Jill says, "So, who's the new boss?" She takes the ice-cream bowl, finishing off the final spoonful.

"Wilson," I grumble. The sugar high is wearing off, and the sadness is trampling all over my serotonin.

Jill pauses. "Who's that again?"

I groan. "I've told you so many times!" Julie would know exactly who he is. She would have done an extensive social media stalking campaign *and* memorized the name of his great-great-aunt.

But it's Jillian who pokes me in the ribs. "Tell me *again*, dork." When I finish explaining, she says, "I hate to break it to you, but having a boss you dislike will be a constant for the rest of your life. Ninety-nine percent of the time, bosses just suck. It's unavoidable."

Those are definitely not the words of wisdom I was hoping for. "Do you think your boss sucks?" I ask cautiously.

"My boss is my ex-girlfriend. It's different." She says it without a hint of anything—affection, anger, heartbreak. Nothing.

"I just really needed to save up money for my road trip with Suzy," I explain. "Now Wilson will never promote me, and without the tips from waitressing, I'll never be able to afford a car."

"Well, maybe if you hadn't hit Mrs. Clemens—"

"I didn't hit her!"

"—then you'd be trusted to borrow one of our cars," Jill finishes. "Actually, there was something I wanted to ask you."

"Ask away," I say, feeling defeated.

"Camilla wants to hire an assistant at *The Rundown*. Nothing glamorous. It'll mostly be getting coffee, answering phones, maybe some filing here and there. The pay is pretty decent, though. It's nineteen an hour."

I gasp so loud it sears my throat. "Nineteen *dollars*?" That's enough money for me to briefly overlook my hatred for Camilla.

"Yes."

"Like, one-nine?"

"Oh my God, Jackie. *Yes*. I take it you're interested?"

"Jillian, if I don't get this job, I very well may die."

She rolls her eyes. "I'll let Camilla know."

"Do I need to interview?" I ask warily. I get too nervous, and my hands get all clammy.

"Doubt it. Cami knows you. She'll hire you on the spot."

Before I can fully understand the situation I've gotten myself into—aka working with my sister and her cheater ex-girlfriend—the front door swings open. Julie walks in, her hands filled with reusable floral bags. Her eyes are wide with excitement and her hair is coming loose from its bun. It is immediately clear that she is up to something.

"What's going on?" I ask slowly. The last time Julie walked into the house like this, she announced that she had volunteered at a charity in town to bake three hundred assorted cupcakes for a bake sale. The bake sale was *the next day*. The five of us were up baking through the night.

Massimo walks through the door next, holding a—

"Is that a pet carrier?" Jillian asks. She says it in the same tone someone would ask *is that a dead body?*

Julie straight up drops the bags on the floor, turning to beam up at her fiancé. "Do you want to tell them, or should I?" Massimo, bless his shy Italian heart, smiles down at her. Jillian and I are quite literally on the edge of our seats when Julie turns to us, hands clasped under her chin, and shrieks, "We adopted a cat!"

"A what?" Jill basically hisses. I pry the ice-cream bowl out of her hands before her death grip shatters it.

"A cat!" Julie repeats, positively giddy. Massimo gently places the pet carrier on the floor. I spot a big pair of eyes between the metal bars. "We brought Massimo's dog to the vet today, and this little guy was *obsessed* with us. Like, he wouldn't leave me alone. I couldn't leave without him."

"You could've, and you should've," Jill says. She is now pressed back into the couch cushion, holding her knees to her chest, as if Julie is about to unleash a lion in our living room.

Something about seeing always-tough Jillian crumble to a cat is hilarious.

"I, for one, love cats," I say, earning a thankful smile from Julie. Suzy's family has two Bengals that I've practically grown up with.

"You're going to love him," Julie gushes. Crouching down on the floor, she jiggles the carrier's metal door. "He was *so* unbelievably sweet and cuddly."

The door pops open, and out stomps a—

I gasp. "That's a baby cow."

"Julie, that is the biggest cat I've ever seen," Jillian says.

We both stare in disbelief as this very overweight, black-and-white chunky cat runs over to the couch and, *somehow*, defies all laws of physics, squishing his big body beneath the couch like a slug.

A solid ten seconds of silence passes before a gentle "oh" leaves Julie's mouth. "He didn't do that at the vet," she says.

"Perhaps he is scared, my love," Massimo offers before walking back outside.

"Well, the vet did say it may take him some time to come around." Julie walks toward the couch. On her knees, she peers beneath it.

"What do we do now?" I ask.

Jillian sneezes twice in a row. Julie is plopped on the floor, snapping her fingers as if that'll coax him out. "We wait for him to come around," she says. "This is only his temporary home until Mass and I move out."

"What's his name?" Jillian asks. She sneezes again.

"Uh, Jill? I think we're finding out in real time that you're allergic to cats," I say. Her eyes are starting to water, too.

"Jillian isn't allergic to cats. And his name is . . . Well, I haven't decided yet," Julie says.

I hang upside down off the couch, peeking underneath it. There, pressed against the wall with these huge alert eyes, is the cat. He is staring right at me.

"What if he never comes out?" I ask.

"Oh, I'm sure he'll come out to eat," Jill says.

"Hey!" Julie cuts her a glare. "Don't fat-shame him."

"How much does he weigh?" I ask, having never seen a cat that big. I didn't even know they could *get* that big.

"Twenty-seven pounds," Julie says. "We're starting him on weight loss food. Apparently his old owners only fed him pasta."

It makes me giggle, imagining him slurping up a plate of spaghetti. With all the blood in my body now rushing straight to my head, I sit upright on the couch. Jillian is still sneezing, rubbing her eyes with her palms, when Massimo walks back through the door carrying two industrial-size bags of cat food in his arms.

"He's probably overwhelmed and scared," Julie is saying, now sitting cross-legged on the floor. She is speaking mostly like she's trying to assure herself. "He's in a new home, surrounded by all new people. It'll take him some time to come around."

Massimo walks off to the kitchen with the bags, leaving the three of us alone.

"I don't think this is what Mom had in mind when she asked about grandkids," I say, making both my sisters laugh. I take another peek under the couch. The cat is now sprawled out on his tummy, watching me like a hawk.

"What do we name him?" I ask.

"Please don't say Oreo," Jillian begs.

Julie is suspiciously quiet. "That's definitely not the name I had in mind." She says it in a way that makes it very clear that it is, in fact, the exact name she had in mind.

I snap a photo of the cat under the couch and post it on *iDiary* with the caption "name ideas?" just to see what happens. "I bet he'd go viral," I say, now texting the photo to Suzy.

"Very true," Jill adds between sneezes. "The internet loves a fat cat. We ran an article on it a few weeks back."

I prep for another photo when Julie smacks my hand away. "Sticking your phone in his face will only scare him more!"

Mom and Dad choose that moment to walk into the room. "Who's sticking what in whose face?" Dad asks. They hover in the doorway, hand in hand.

Massimo picks this exact moment to walk in from the kitchen holding a small metal bowl. "*Amore mio*, where should I put his weight loss food?" The thick Italian accent makes it a hundred times funnier.

"Whose weight loss food?" Mom interjects.

"Your daughter"—sneeze—"adopted a cat," Jillian says.

Mom and Dad share a loaded glance. "Which daughter?" they say at the same time.

"Julie, obviously," I say.

"He's stuck under the couch," Jill adds.

Julie's face puckers. "He isn't *stuck*." She takes the food bowl from Massimo and places it on the carpet. Then she turns to our parents, flashing her forgive-me eyes. "He was just abandoned by his family. I couldn't leave him at the vet. And it's only temporary until Mass and I get a house."

"I had a cat growing up," Mom says. "I miss that little guy."

"Fine," Dad adds. "But you're feeding him *and* cleaning up after him. I don't want to so much as smell his litter box, Julie."

Julie runs over and throws her arms around them. "You guys are the best ever."

Beside me, Jillian snorts. "They'd let her adopt a lion if she asked nicely," she whispers to me.

"Why didn't we inherit her powers of persuasion?" I grumble.

"Julie has something that you and I lack—a sweet, angelic soul," Jill says.

Then her entire face scrunches up. "What is that smell?" she asks. There's a trickling sound too, like a tap is leaking.

Then it hits my nose—a sour, pungent smell starts to fill the air. "Eeeeeeeew," I say, covering my face with the blanket. "What is that?"

Julie runs back over to the couch and sticks her head under it. When she returns, her lips are pressed into a thin line. "Uhm," she says, "he peed."

We all groan.

CHAPTER 6

WHEN IT'S PRETTY OBVIOUS that the cat is not leaving his new hiding spot, everyone calls it a night. Julie prepares a makeshift bed on the carpet beside the couch so she can "monitor his food intake." The joke Jillian made after that was "very inappropriate" Julie's words.

On a mission to not think about work and not individually examine every shattered piece of my life, I settle into bed and load up *iDiary* on my laptop. There are a few unread notifications on my "heartbreak expert" post, and one new message. I click on the unread message. It's from user @mirrorball03. They wrote:

> If you really are a heartbreak expert, can you give me some
> tips on ending things with a persistent partner who won't take
> no for an answer . . . ?

That is . . . not at all what I was expecting.

I stare at the message. Clearly, this person is desperate. Why else would you ask a stranger online for breakup advice? Let alone me—the person who has never actually, you know, broken up with someone.

But I did grow up with older sisters. I did witness heartbreak too many times to count. Maybe I *do* know a thing or two about relationships. Isn't that what Anita said earlier? That I gave her pretty good advice about that new girl she's dating?

Okay, Jackie, think. I can either try to say something useful, or do the smart thing and delete this person's message.

The cursor hovers over the delete button, but I can't quite bring myself to do it. This is the first real message I've ever received that isn't Suzy making fun of me. I have to answer it. I have to try.

Okay, I need to think this through. They said their partner is persistent and won't take no for an answer, which is problematic in itself. My first thought is to have a serious conversation with them, explicitly stating that the relationship is over, so there's no misunderstanding . . . But that sounds like the stupid, obvious answer anyone would give. And it sounds like their partner might ignore it anyway. Ugh.

Then it hits me. Jillian. Maybe five or six years ago. She was dating this guy who was *so* clingy. I think his name was Harvey? Harry? Henry? Definitely began with an *H*. She called him a stage-five clinger and tried to dump him for *weeks*. Eventually she managed to shake him, but I don't remember how.

Before I can talk myself out of it, I'm tiptoeing across the hall and into Jillian's room. I tap a quick knock, wait two seconds, then open the door. She is swaddled up in bed watching a true crime documentary. A bit of a weird choice to watch before bed, but I'm not surprised. There's a candle lit on her nightstand, too. I take a whiff, and it smells like . . . nothing.

"Is that an *unscented* candle?"

She responds with a glare. "Do you know what time it is?"

This feels like waking a bear from hibernation. "I know, but it's important," I plead.

I'm walking toward her bed when she says, "Do *not* sit on my bed." I take a seat anyway. Jill has one of those memory foam mattresses that feels like sinking into a cloud. Even after I up and leave, my butt print will be molded into the fabric.

I'm now realizing why she asked me not to sit down.

"What do you want?" she hisses. Some people are moody in the morning, but Jill is moody every second of her existence.

"Remember that guy you dated when you were, like, nineteen? Henry something . . ." When she shakes her head, I continue. "You said he was a stage-five clinger and wouldn't let you break up with him."

"Oh, Hugh," Jill says, her face taking on this reminiscent look. "I remember. The little shit wouldn't leave me alone. And why is this important right now?"

The candle on the nightstand flickers, casting orange shadows over Jill's face. "I need breakup advice," I say. "Not for me. It's for a friend. Who is in a . . . similar situation."

Jillian groans into her pillow. "Jackie, I don't want you sharing my personal life with your friends. I barely want to share my personal life with *you*."

"Okay— Ouch. And it's only one person, who won't tell anyone else. I promise." It's sort of a half-lie. Technically, I *am* telling this advice to only one person. Plus, I'll keep it super vague.

"If this gets out, you're dead."

"Works for me," I say. "So, how'd you get him to finally leave you alone?"

Resigned to my questioning, Jill sits up. "I don't remember. I— I *think* I showed up at his house one day and told him straight up to leave me alone. I didn't step foot inside or anything. Just right there in the doorway I told him that we were over, that I didn't want to hear from him again, and I handed him all his shit back." She pauses, as if in her head she is right back on that porch. "I might've also blocked his number and cussed him out."

"That's ruthless," I say in awe.

Jill shrugs, entirely unfazed. "Maybe, but he deserved it."

I commit everything she said to memory: show up at their house, don't go inside, dump them on the spot, give them all their belongings back. Cursing them out and blocking their number is optional.

I jump forward onto the bed and give her a big hug. "Thanks, Jilly!"

"Get off of me."

"Oops, yes. Okay. Sorry." I run out the door and whisper good night before closing it behind me.

"Jackie!"

I reopen the door a crack. "Yes?"

Her voice springs out from the darkness. "I just talked to Camilla. The assistant job is yours. You're coming into the office with me on Tuesday. Got it?"

I do a little happy dance as quietly as possible. "Yes! Thank you."

Well, consider that a successful mission! Killer advice and a new job? That end-of-summer road trip is calling my name—

Wait. It's past midnight.

It's extremely late, and Jillian is on the phone with Camilla? That doesn't exactly scream "healthy work relationship" to me. There's a sinking suspicion that something deeper is going on there. Something that my previously heartbroken sister definitely doesn't deserve to deal with *again*.

At least now that I'm their newest employee, I'll be able to investigate with my own two eyes.

Oh, Julie is going to *love* this.

When I'm tucked back into bed, I type out my response to mirrorball03. I fudge the details here and there and elaborate a bit, just to make it seem more relatable. After a minute or two of editing, I settle on this response:

Here's how to get rid of a stage-five clinger: Show up at their house and DON'T go inside. Right there in the doorway, you're going to tell them how you feel. No sugarcoating here. Honesty is key! Then, immediately give them ALL their belongings, so they know you mean it. For the finale, don't allow them a chance to manipulate you into staying. Say your piece and GTFO! (blocking their number is optional.) Hope that helps!

I chew on my lip, wondering if there are too many exclamation marks. Is it too casual? Too silly? Does it read too young? Should I make it sound more mature?

I groan into my pillow. Before I can obsess over it too much, I post the answer publicly. I doubt anyone will even read it in the first place, so why does it matter?

After putting my laptop to charge, I tuck myself into bed. Then it dawns on me—I have work tomorrow.

I have to face Wilson again. But now as my boss.

CHAPTER 7

"**TWO ICED VANILLA LATTES** for Suzy!" the barista calls. I grab our drinks and meet Suzy at the table we secured at Bee's, nestled in the corner between cozy yellow walls and chestnut bookshelves. She tinkers with her laptop, editing some footage of me for the doc that she refuses to let me see.

It's just past eleven, and my shift at Monte's was supposed to begin at noon. I called in sick the second I woke up, throwing in a few fake coughs here and there. Do I think Wilson bought the performance? No. He hung up on me mid-cough, which is incredibly rude on a multitude of levels. At least the anxiety that had been twisting my stomach into knots all night has settled down.

"Your latte." It barely hits the table before Suzy grabs it and gulps half of it down.

"I need this in an IV," she says, kicking at the chair across from her. "Sit down, I want to show you something." Suzy turns the laptop to face me, and I'm staring at some sort of online forum. The title is "Top Five Films of the Past Two Decades." There are twenty-seven comments.

I sip my latte. "What is this?"

"A film club I joined for school. I posted my top five movies on this thread, and look at the comment some moron left." Her finger taps the screen, pointing at a comment from user @shawnofthedead. They wrote: *ESotSM at #1? That movie put me straight to sleep.*

"What does that stand for?"

"*Eternal Sunshine of the Spotless Mind*," Suzy says.

Oh, right. We watched it a few weeks ago. "I thought it was a great movie."

"Because it *is* a great movie, Jackie. It's a heart-wrenching masterpiece that explores the intricacies of human nature—what it means to love someone and the bravery in experiencing heartbreak and still trying to love again afterward. It's one of the wisest, most self-reflective movies of our time, and this moron with a shitty username fell asleep during it!"

Suzy is smashing her fingers into the keyboard, undoubtedly firing back a very rude but grammatically correct response.

"There. That'll show him," she says, flexing her fingers when the damage has been done.

"What did you write?"

"I told Shawn that his *Dawn of the Dead* username is very

68

accurate, considering he would most likely survive a zombie apocalypse. Zombies eat brains, and he clearly does not have one."

I high-five her above the table. "Does this mean we both have mortal enemies?"

Suzy laughs. "Maybe. Let's hope the other students I meet are a lot better than this guy." She scans through the rest of the comments on the thread. "This one girl just listed the entire *Twilight* franchise."

"Valid," I say.

"This film club is kind of cool," Suzy continues. "They host weekly watch parties on campus and alternate snack days. One girl suggested marathon nights, where we watch as many movies as we can before everyone's asleep. I'm going to suggest we start off strong with the James Bond franchise."

I hate the way my heart plummets the moment Suzy gets excited about her future. To her, the idea of *someday* is exciting because she has a passion, she has goals. I can't wrap my mind around how comforting that must be, to know exactly where you are going to end up four years from now.

To me, *someday* just feels unsettling. It stops me in my tracks, makes it a little difficult to breathe if I spend too long thinking about it. It's the blinding reminder that I feel stuck in a world where everyone around me seems to be moving forward: Julie is moving out and getting married; Suzy is moving across the country; even Wilson is beginning his career. And I'm here, with no direction, no goals, nothing to aim for or aspire to be.

When everyone moves forward but you, isn't being left behind inevitable?

Suzy is snapping her fingers in front of my face. I've spiraled, and now she's reeling me back in. "Come back to me, Jackie," she says like a hypnotist.

"Sorry. Hi, I'm alive." I take a long sip of the latte, the coldness rooting me in place.

"Everything okay?" she asks, her face taking on the kind of concern I'm used to seeing from Julie.

"Just my daily existential life crisis. No biggie," I say.

Suzy frowns across the table. "No one has their life figured out by eighteen."

"I guess." The knowledge that millions of people also feel this way doesn't ease the anxiety. It doesn't stop *me* from not wanting to feel this way. I guess it's nice to not feel alone, but I'd rather not feel this at all.

"Would a chocolate chunk cookie make this better or worse?" she asks.

I pause. "Better. Definitely better."

She is up from her chair, ordering at the counter, and back with cookie in hand in under a minute. It's very impressive and makes me think that acquiring baked goods under a time restraint should be an Olympic sport.

I munch on the still-warm cookie as I skim through my emails. When I see an article Jill sent me about feminism in the workplace and how to "dismantle the patriarchy and be taken seriously," I remember the events that led up to me falling asleep last night.

"By the way, I got another job," I say.

Suzy nearly chokes on her half of the cookie. "We've been sitting here for half an hour, and you bring that up *now*?"

"I was distracted by caffeine, sugar, and existential dread. Sue me."

"What's the job?"

"Receptionist at *The Rundown*," I explain. "Jill said it's nothing glamorous, but the pay is good and it's extra money toward our road trip."

Suzy grins. "California, here we come."

We settle into a few more minutes of quiet work. I received an email from Jillian with a few new-hire forms I need to sign. There are a few documents attached that explain office protocol in fancy cursive fonts and an array of pastel colors. Even the dress code section is crossed off, replaced with "freedom of self-expression is our highest priority." I'm skimming the rest of the document when an email comes in from *iDiary*, reminding me that I have new notifications to check.

"I forgot to tell you," I say while the site loads. "I got the weirdest message last night on *iDiary*. Someone asked me for advice on breaking up with their boyfriend."

"Breakup advice? Isn't it usually the opposite?"

"I think so— Hey!"

Suzy grabs my laptop and begins tapping away. "I have to see this for myself."

"There's nothing to see. The person who asked the question probably already forgot about it and—"

Suzy's eyes widen. "You have thirty-seven notifications."

I scoot my chair to Suzy's side of the table so quickly I nearly tip over. People have been liking my response to @mirrorball03, leaving comments, and have even started following me. "They loved your advice. One girl called it 'low-key good.'"

"It wasn't even *my* advice. It was Jillian's." But Suzy is right, people did seem to love it. I've never posted anything that has gotten this much traction. "It doesn't even matter. It was a onetime thing. No one is going to ask me for breakup advice again."

Suzy points at the screen. "Someone else just did."

"No way."

A new message appears from user @livelaughloathe. I read it out loud.

Last week, my boyfriend came over and flooded my toilet. It gave me the biggest ick, and I literally cannot look at him the same way anymore. Everything he does is so gross now! Is it insane to dump him over this?

Suzy and I burst out laughing at the same time.

"I have so many questions," Suzy says, gasping for breath.

"How do you tell someone you're breaking up with them

72

because they *pooped*?" I say, causing us to giggle all over again. "I'd never go to the bathroom again."

When our laughter subsides, Suzy asks, "So what do we respond?"

"*Should* I even respond?" That earns me a gentle slap on my upper arm.

"Of course you should, Jackie! These people clearly need you. You can't leave them hanging. Geez, you're always so *iDiary* obsessed. Now, the second it actually gets interesting, you want to quit?"

"The advice I gave last night was from Jillian," I repeat, pretending to look around the café. "As far as I can tell, she isn't here right now to ask again."

Suzy taps on my head. "We don't need Jillian, goof. Everything Jill went through lives right here in your head. You're always saying how your sisters overshared all their relationship drama with you over the years. What advice can Jill offer now that she hasn't already told you?"

That makes me pause. Suzy is right. The original advice I gave Anita came from me. Sure, it was reused advice from Jillian, but it was my words, my memories.

I tug my laptop over, stretching my fingers above the keyboard. "Give me a second to think." My mind immediately latches on to a memory I had nearly forgotten about. "Four or five years ago, Jill and I were on the couch watching cartoons. It was a weekend morning, maybe Saturday? Anyway, Julie and this guy she was dating at the time—Mark, I think—walked into the kitchen. He straight up opened the fridge and chugged our bottle of orange juice. Like, drank it right out of the carton. I remember Julie had this look on her face, like shock mixed with disgust and complete embarrassment. Jill made a comment that we'd never see Mark again after that. When I asked why, she said Julie has gotten the ick."

"And the ick is irreversible," Suzy says, catching on.

I smile back. "Exactly."

Suzy watches over my shoulder as I type out the response. When I'm done, I read it over:

Sounds like you've caught a case of The Ick! The cure? Well, there isn't one! As your doctor, I'm prescribing you one final phone call with your boyfriend to pull the plug on this relationSHIT—Sorry, I had to! Remember that your feelings are valid, the ick is very much real, and millions of women before you have fallen victim to it. Future advice? Reinforce the rule to all new partners that the toilet must be flushed. You've got this!

"Relation*shit*?" Suzy reads out loud, laughing. "That's genius. It's perfect, but I'd lose some of the exclamation marks."

I feel oddly offended. "How come?"

"Don't you think it may come off too childish? I think you should try to sound more mature, right? If you're giving off the image that you have all this relationship experience, people would probably expect you to be older."

She makes a good point. I doubt most people would trust heartbreak advice that comes from a teenager. I replace all the exclamation marks with periods, and it reads way better, way more mature. I post it.

Suzy rests her chin on her hands, her eyes lit with excitement. "What if this blows up? By next week, maybe you'll have hundreds of messages. Even your sisters don't have enough advice to cover all that."

No, they don't. And even if they did, Jill is so busy with work and Julie with wedding plans that I doubt they're available to offer me advice when I need it. I may need to do this on my own. But as Suzy just pointed out, it seems like I can.

Plus, *iDiary* has always been mine. I never shared the account with my sisters. It's always been a safe space for me—somewhere I can be myself without anyone's judgment. I don't think I want to lose that.

"For now, let's keep this between us." I say it almost too easily. After all, it's just some silly messages on the blog. This won't amount to much, if anything.

Suzy nods, then sits upright. "Oh! Can this be included in the doc?"

"Suz, I literally just said this is going to be a secret."

"Okay, but aside from Monte's and going home . . . You don't really do much. Don't look at me like that! All I'm saying is, it would be nice to have a bit more material to work with."

"Very interesting way to tell me to get a life," I say, ignoring the sting of her words. I'm painfully aware that my life is a bit boring.

"What about this. I film it, but you have the final say whether I use it or not. That way, I can get this all on film just in case."

"Fine," I say, too tired to argue. I then watch in shock as Suzy reaches into her backpack and takes out her camera. "You brought your camera?"

"Duh," she says, pressing a few buttons on it before pointing it at my face. "Okay, now go ahead and open the next message. We're rolling."

The only things that are rolling are my eyes. Still, I scroll to the next message. Before I can give it a read, I'm distracted by a bell chiming as the door to Bee's swings open, blowing in a flash of hot air. I look up to glare at the culprit, expecting to see someone from high school or a customer I recognize from work. Instead, it's Wilson.

Wilson, who thinks I'm currently at home sick, nursing a cold.

I sink down in my chair until my eyes are level with the tabletop.

"What— What is happening right now?" Suzy is asking, her face semihidden behind the camera.

"Wilson just walked in," I say, panicking. Oh my gosh, he cannot see me. I am so fired.

Suzy spots Wilson at the counter, his back to us. She turns

the camera toward him. "You weren't kidding about the khakis," she says.

"I know. He's worse in person." And in approximately ten seconds he's going to turn around, spot me, and march over to terminate my employment in front of all these innocent bystanders.

"I can't believe this person you talk about all the time is actually real," she says. "It's like seeing Santa Claus in person. Or Bigfoot."

"Suzy." I say her name very sternly. "I called in sick today."

Now she looks confused. "I know that."

"I called in sick, and my boss is here, about to see me being very much *not sick*."

Her eyes double in size the second she understands. "Shit. *Shit*. What do we do? Okay, get under the table. Hide. Now."

I'm in the process of wiggling farther beneath the table when Wilson is handed his drink, turns around, and immediately locks eyes with me.

There is a solid three seconds where I think the world stops spinning, time freezes entirely, and the whole human civilization ceases to exist except for the two of us, in this café, locked in a death glare. Wilson looks like the top of his head is going to pop off and steam will shoot out of it. I think I probably look borderline ridiculous with eighty percent of my body shoved beneath the table.

Suzy is whipping the camera back and forth between the two of us, desperately soaking up every second of the most awkward encounter of my life.

Then I wait. I wait for Wilson to walk over, scold me, fire me, tell me to never step foot in Monte's again. But he doesn't do any of that. He takes his coffee and the brown paper dessert bag and leaves.

Stunned and speechless, I turn to Suzy and whack my head right into her camera.

"Sorry," she says. "The close-up got too close." Thankfully, she pops the lens cap back on and returns the camera to her bag. "That was strange."

"I really expected him to walk over here and yell at me," I say. I keep looking out the window, waiting for Wilson to change his mind and return.

"I can't believe I finally saw the infamous Wilson," Suzy says.

"Yeah," I say, not able to take my eyes off the window.

While chewing a bite of cookie, Suzy says, "You've been ranting about this guy for months, and you failed to mention how cute he is."

Now that catches my attention. "Excuse me?" My voice comes out in a squeak.

Suzy is back to typing on her laptop, as if the words she's speaking are not altering my world. "You made it seem like you were working with some maniac who was a total nerd."

"Suzy, I *am* working for a maniac who *is* a total nerd. Did you see the outfit? The khakis? He had a freaking walkie-talkie clipped to his belt."

"Sure, but I also saw the cheekbones, the full head of shiny hair, and the big brown eyes."

"His face looks hollow, his hair is too moisturized, and as someone who has brown eyes, consider me not impressed," I say.

And yeah, I cross my arms over my chest like a grumpy toddler.

"*Too* moisturized?" she says. "How can something be *too* moisturized?"

"I just know he wakes up and spends way too much time on his hair. Suzy, it's *weird*. And off-putting. Okay? Leave me alone." Maybe these excuses sound better in my head.

"You're off-putting," she says with a smile. "And your boss is cute."

It feels like my best friend has gone over to the dark side, completely abandoning me in my time of need. "I can't believe you're on Wilson's side."

She barks out a laugh. "I'm not choosing sides! All I'm saying is suffering through a job you hate doesn't sound as unbearable when your boss is kind of nice to look at."

The worst part is, now that she's spoken those words into the universe, they exist. And now I have to live in a world where my best friend thinks my mortal enemy is attractive.

CHAPTER 8

NOTHING COULD HAVE PREPARED me for walking into *The Rundown* on Tuesday morning. Maybe it's because of Jillian's all-over gloomy presence, but I half expected their office space to look like a cave. Perhaps a newly renovated dungeon. Definitely something with little lighting, lots of caffeine, and heavy rock music blasting through speakers. Maybe there'd be a graveyard next door.

Instead, *The Rundown* looks like what would happen if a unicorn and a fairy had a baby that was then adopted by a princess and raised on a life of glitter.

When we walk through the front doors of the office, there's an Ariana Grande song playing. There's a teeny-tiny waiting area, with a green velvet couch and a glass table stacked with memoirs written by various women entrepreneurs. Next to that is a bowl filled with candy and another overflowing with tampons.

"Holy cow," I say, peering farther into the office space.

"Don't bring Julie's cat into this," Jillian says.

The office is one open square. Every single inch of the walls is covered with something: Polaroid photos, motivational quotes, movie posters, framed newspaper articles, calendars, even a few group photos. Large desks covered in laptops, plants, half-empty lattes, and a few photo frames take up most of the space.

The room is also filled with a bunch of women who are staring right at me.

"Everyone, this is my sister Jackie. She is officially your go-to girl for all ridiculous coffee orders—Michelle, I'm talking to you," Jillian says.

A pretty Asian girl with bleached blond hair laughs. "Excuse me for liking my lattes with an absurd sugar-to-coffee ratio."

"Nice to have you, Jackie," says a stunning Muslim woman in a hijab. "I'm Fatima. I run our graphic design department. If you've seen any art on our website or socials, that's all me."

"Wait— even the animated wiener dog from a few weeks ago?" I ask.

Fatima smiles. "Yours truly."

"I run our fashion column," Michelle adds. "And for the record, my coffee order isn't ridiculous."

"It's a *little* ridiculous," Fatima says.

"I'm also a huge fan of anything loaded with sugar," I say, earning a smile from Michelle.

Then there's Maude, the social media coordinator, who runs their entire online presence. She's set up at the corner of the desk that has a pink iMac and an iPad propped up on a stand. I'm sort of mesmerized by the intricate braids running through her blond hair.

Next is another writer named Imani, who moved here from South Africa when she was seven and has the prettiest accent I've ever heard. Her desk space houses two plants and a Nintendo Switch that's currently charging.

I'm talking to Michelle about a piece she's writing on sustainable fashion when a door behind me opens and Camilla walks out. Camilla, with her waist-length black hair, big brown eyes, and bone structure that would put any supermodel to shame. She looks exactly the same as she did five years ago, which was when I last saw her. But now I know she's a cheater who broke my sister's heart, so she somehow also looks entirely different.

I guess because Camilla founded *The Rundown,* she gets her own office. "Jackie!" she says, walking across the room like she's about to hug me and— Ouf, there she is. Her arms wrap around my shoulders, and I have to remind myself that she's kind of my boss now, so maybe I shouldn't push her away.

"Hi, Camilla," I say as I'm slowly crushed to death from her embrace.

"We're so happy to have you. I think you're going to be the greatest addition to our team! Jill, did you give her the tour?"

Jillian is sitting at her desk, typing on her laptop. "She's gotten the rundown, yeah."

Everyone snickers. I wonder if that's a pun they use often.

"We've got a coffee machine, snack drawers, and an aux cord that's all yours whenever you feel like it," she says, gesturing at an empty desk right beside Jillian's. There's a cordless phone, a notepad, and an unopened pack of pens. "You can set yourself up with your laptop and whatever else you need. That phone is new for us, by the way. We actually just set up our office number last week, so we don't get *too* many calls. But you can answer it whenever it happens to ring. If you're unsure of any questions, put them on hold and ask one of us."

After Camilla disappears into her office, I dig into my backpack to get my desk set up. But when I reach in for my laptop, it's missing.

"Looking for this?" Jillian slides my laptop over to me.

"How'd you get that?" I ask, my heartbeat accelerating. I hope she didn't look at it. I'm still logged into *iDiary*.

"Took it this morning by accident. Again. Sorry."

I huff out a breath. "I really need to like, add a sticker to mine or something so we stop mixing them up."

I set myself up and obsess over how great this spot is. With Camilla's office directly behind me and Jill seated to my left, I have the perfect view of them both. No fleeting look or whispered conversation will go unnoticed. I'll go home every day with a ton of new information to report to Julie, so we can stay on top of what's going on with those two.

But before any spying can begin, everyone gets antsy an hour later. It turns out it's also my job to pick up lunch.

There's unanimous agreement on getting sandwiches from Patty's, a sub shop across the street. I place the order online—my first official task of the day—and pay with the company credit card Camilla lends me. There are two tuna melts, two turkey clubs on rye, one spicy veggie deluxe, and two BLTs. After adding a bunch of lemonades and bags of sea salt Kettle chips, I put on my sunglasses and head across the street.

I'm waiting for the pedestrian cross signal to change when I hear my name being called. Michelle is running over to me, now wearing a cute denim dad cap. "Hey," she says, a little out of breath. "I thought you could use a hand carrying all that food."

We get to Patty's a few minutes before the order is ready and end up taking a seat at a table. Michelle sips one of the lemonades, and I crack open a bag of chips.

"So," she says, "what do you think of our little woman cave so far?"

"It's nothing like what I was expecting and way better than I imagined," I say.

Michelle laughs. "Let me guess, you were expecting some boring office with a bunch of miserable writers stuffed behind desks, chugging black coffee, with massive bags under their eyes?"

"That is . . . exactly what I thought, yeah." I offer Michelle the bag of chips and she takes a handful.

"I've worked at places like that," she says. "Those offices give nine-to-fives a bad rep. There's a ton of cool places to work that don't suck the life out of you. And most of them are run by women," she adds with a wink.

That's the perfect intro for what I've been meaning to ask. "What's it like working for Camilla?"

"She's amazing." Michelle pauses to take a sip of her lemonade. "She's super easygoing and so understanding. I've never before had a boss that I wasn't, like, afraid to talk to like a friend, you know? Camilla just breaks down all those weird barriers and feels like one of us. You know her, right? I remember she and Jill go way back."

That's interesting—so the other girls aren't aware that Camilla and Jill are exes. If Jill doesn't want them to know, then it isn't my place to say. But still—it makes me wonder. "Yeah, they met in high school," I say.

"Supercool. Well, it's going to be so nice to have you around! I'm happy to tag along if you ever need a buddy when running these errands for us."

I smile at her genuinely. "I'd honestly love that."

"Sometimes the best way to deal with writer's block is to step away from your laptop and go back with fresh eyes. So I'm always down for a little walk or something to take my mind off writing for a sec. Do you write?"

"Uhm, not really," I say. I guess my blog is *kind of* writing, but again—top secret information. "I work at Monte's Magic Castle? It's like, ten minutes from here."

"Oh, no way! I went there all the time as a kid. Do you guys still do those shows every hour?"

"Unfortunately, yes," I say with a laugh, going back in for another chip. "I'm really just trying to save up some extra cash to drive my best friend to California at the end of summer."

"That sounds like fun."

"It will be, if it ever happens," I say.

"Well, you're one of us now. Maybe you can quit Monte's and find a permanent spot at *The Rundown*. I'm sure the pay is a lot better."

Michelle's words are like a new path unfolding in front of me. "I'm sure Jill would *love* that," I joke. I'm surprised she even agreed to let me into her space, when this job means so much to her.

Michelle leans across the table, lowering her voice. "Don't tell her I said this, but Jill talks about you all the time."

It's so absurd I have to laugh. "You're lying."

"I swear. The hardest people usually have the biggest soft spots."

When I try to picture Jillian sitting at her desk, chatting about me with her coworkers, it's like my imagination malfunctions. It's so unlike Jillian, I can't even envision that moment in my mind. But it must be true. Why else would Michelle say that? And what does Jill say about me?

The girl working at the counter calls my name. "Order for Jackie!" Michelle helps me with the paper bags, and we head back across the street. She fills the silence with chatter, explaining how she ended up at *The Rundown*: a combination of good luck, a degree in English literature, and an unstoppable love for fashion.

"How did you know you wanted to be a writer?" I ask while we cross the street.

"English was the class I hated the least in high school. When I had to decide what to study in university, that felt like a good enough place to start," she says. "What about you? Any post-high school plans?"

The question makes me tense up. "I'm still figuring it out."

We take a left on the main road, *The Rundown* now coming into a view a few units down.

As if she can sense the stress weighing me down, Michelle smiles warmly. "There's no deadline for figuring out your life," she offers. "If anything, I regret rushing into college. I'm twenty-seven now, and in hindsight, I'd go back and do everything differently."

Her words feel like a much-needed safety blanket. "Like what?"

"Like take a year or two off before university. Travel, relax, breathe. Just live for a second before rushing into another four years of stress."

This might be the first time in my life I've heard someone talk so positively about *not* going to college immediately after high school. Maybe I'm not making some huge mistake. Maybe I'm just taking a different path.

Michelle's words make me feel seen in ways I never have been.

As we approach the office, I hold the door open for her. "I can't even tell you how nice that is to hear," I say.

Michelle winks. "Hey, I'm happy to bestow my wisdom on someone who's young enough to take it."

Around five o'clock, I'm all but itching to check *iDiary* and my climb to online fame. I tap my foot the entire drive home, until Jill threatens to pull over and let me walk. After retreating to my bedroom and changing into comfy clothes, I pull back my bedroom curtains and look straight into Suzy's room. She's sitting cross-legged on her bed, her laptop propped up on her knees. It takes a few seconds before she glances over and spots me. I wave. She slides her blue light glasses onto her head and waves back. I settle in on the window bench, booting up my laptop, and take a bite of leftover pasta.

My phone rings.

"Hello, best friend," I greet, putting the call on speaker so my hands are free to type.

"How are you handling your new internet fame?" she asks.

"Horribly," I joke. "It's gotten to my head, and I think I'm better than everyone."

Suzy pauses. "You definitely already thought that before the fame."

I meet her eyes through the window and stick my tongue out.

"What does the blog look like?" she asks just as I'm pulling up *iDiary*.

"Checking now."

Turns out, my advice to @mirrorball03 and @livelaughloathe

worked like a charm. After their testimonies came and I posted them publicly, there were other messages seeking advice. Slowly, it seems like people are beginning to trust me. I'm getting fifteen to twenty messages a day. Which isn't too crazy, but still entirely unbelievable.

iDiary finishes loading. I'm slammed with notifications and six new messages, the most yet! A tiny bubble of excitement grows inside of me, floating closer to the surface. All these people waiting on me to help them. People who respect me, who desperately wait to hear what I have to say. It's like a high, and it keeps getting better.

"What's the damage?" she asks.

"Six new messages." Combined with the unanswered messages that have accumulated, there are now eleven waiting for me.

Suzy lets out a whistle. "That's a lot of people practically begging you to break their hearts."

"You make it sound so masochistic," I say. In a way, it is. But these are people looking for a fresh start. Looking for someone to give them the A-OK to start over and put themselves first. And if that person has to be me, I'm okay with that.

"Heartbreak awaits," she says.

We end the call, and I get to work.

It's past midnight when I emerge from the depths of the internet. I have answered all the questions, giving advice on everything from cheating to fights breaking out over dietary restrictions.

When I'm about to log off for the night, a new message comes in. It's from user @mkz123. They wrote:

My boyfriend and I had our futures planned out. We'd
finish college together, graduate, move to the city. Now
everything's different . . . He's taken a new job and
completely uprooted our lives. We're no longer on the same
page and this isn't what I signed up for. What do I do? I don't
want to hurt him, and I'm terrified of having this conversation
with him . . .

It takes me a moment to gather my thoughts. It's like I can feel
mkz123's pain through the screen. Her fear of a future changing,
the person she cares about leaving . . . It hits too close to home.

Before Suzy's face comes to mind, I remind myself to not take
this account personally. These are *other* people's lives. Not mine.

I focus back on @mkz123's situation. Gimmicks and dramatic
confrontations aren't necessary. I think it's all about face-to-face
dialogue and peacefully parting ways with someone you thought
would be in your life much longer. To answer her question, I write:

A cathartic conversation is what you need. Sometimes
people grow apart—plans change, futures change, hell, even
people change. What you needed last week could differ right
now. If your future together is not one you want anymore,
it's time to talk it out and let them go. Face-to-face can be
scary, but remember this is someone who loves you and will

want to know that you're struggling. Before going into the
conversation, try writing out what you plan to say in a letter.
That way, when the time comes, you'll be ready.

I post the message and try not to dwell too hard on it. I may
expect other people to take my advice, but that doesn't mean I
have to.

Moving my finger across the mouse pad, I click on the button
for Account Settings. Over the past week, my account has grown
in ways I never thought possible. @shitjackiesays was fun, but I
think it's time for a refresh. Plus, I'm running on full anonymity
right now. I don't want my name out there. Better to eliminate
even the smallest chance of someone tying this blog back to me.

What Suzy said earlier rings through my mind. *Six people
practically begging you to break their hearts.*

"Begging me to break their hearts," I repeat out loud, the
name coming to me.

I delete *shitjackiesays*, type in the new name, and hit Save.

Just like that, *pleasebreakmyheart* is born.

CHAPTER 9

JILL AND I WALK through the doors of *The Rundown* at nine the next morning. Imani brought in bagels that are still hot. I slather mine in cream cheese, grab a bottle of water, and take a seat at my desk. I'm expecting the same chatter as yesterday, but the women work in complete silence. Jillian had told me nine o'clock to noon is when everyone is their most productive.

I've eaten two bagels when Camilla steps out of her office around ten. She's wearing these vintage flared jeans and a tight button-up shirt that rests just above her belly button. "Time for our weekly rundown," she says, standing behind my desk. "Who wants to go first?"

"I will," says Maude. "I'm still working on my meet-the-writers campaign. Fatima is working on some of the graphics for it, and I'm planning on running it sometime next month. There's a huge trend for transparency on socials right now. Users who feel a connection with the people *behind* the brand are more likely to follow and engage with their content. I'm hoping that when this campaign launches, we'll see a spike in engagement and readership. If we do, I have a ton of ideas on how we can build this up even further in the future."

As Maude speaks, I open my notebook and jot down notes. Her ideas are so interesting. Before today, I had no idea that social media could even be considered a full-time job.

Beneath the table, Jill kicks my foot. "You don't need to write this down," she hisses.

I ignore her and keep at it.

"Maude, that sounds amazing," Camilla says. "Definitely keep me updated on dates for when that's going live. Fatima, run the artwork by me whenever you've got some rough drafts ready. Who's next?"

Everyone else takes turns sharing: Imani is working on a piece covering a new restaurant opening down the street, which I make a mental note to order takeout from one day for lunch, and Michelle is editing her article on sustainable fashion, which I already can't wait to read.

It's only day two, and it feels like the world of Ridgewood is slowly expanding. There are more people to get to know, family-owned shops to visit, new career paths to explore. I tap my foot excitedly.

When it's Jill's turn to share, she checks her watch before speaking. "I have someone coming in today for an interview in an hour. We'll be hanging out on the couch, if everyone could give us a bit of privacy."

I watch Camilla, who is looking around the room with something similar to pride on her face. "Thanks for the great works as always. Jackie, how do feel about reorganizing some files?"

Which is how I end up buried in boxes of paperwork dating back three years. There are bills, receipts, employee documents, and so many other papers I can't even decipher. Since the office is so small as it is, there's barely enough space for all of it. Luckily Jill has abandoned her desk, setting up on the couch for her interview. I take over her area for the meantime and begin sorting through these files.

I've barely dug into them when the front door opens and Jillian jumps off the couch like her legs are bouncy springs. I'm ready to ignore whoever she's interviewing so I can tackle the gigantic stack of papers, when I see a familiar figure standing in the doorway.

A figure that preoccupies the majority of my nightmares.

Wilson steps into *The Rundown* and crosses *so many* metaphorical lines. Monte's is mutual space where we can coexist, fine. The entire town of Ridgewood is also big enough for the two of us to live in. But you know what isn't? This teeny-tiny office, which is barely big enough to fit seven woman, let alone Wilson and his ego the size of Mars. The second his denim-clad legs step inside, these four walls have been tainted. Ruined. I watch in real time as this growing safe haven is invaded by rival forces.

It's beginning to feel like the only solution left is to move to another state, because this one is clearly too small.

Wilson has the audacity to make himself comfortable on the couch. Has he spotted me yet? Unknown. I'm too busy staring daggers into my traitorous sister's back—which is well deserved since she just stabbed me in mine.

Jillian waltzes back over to her desk. She may as well be whistling a show tune and skipping, she is so nonchalant. "Holy shit, Jackie. I've been gone for twenty minutes, and it looks like a tornado hit."

"Jillian," I say sternly. "How could you?"

She pauses, a sheet of paper dangling from her fingers. By the look on her face, she is genuinely confused. "What are you talking about?"

I cannot believe her. "You brought Wilson here!"

"And?"

"You know he's my enemy. You couldn't give me a heads-up?"

"Oh my God, Jackie." She sighs, shoveling more papers aside and grabbing her laptop buried beneath. "You're eighteen. You don't have an enemy."

I do, and she has now been added to the list. "What is he *doing* here?" I risk a glance at Wilson, who is thankfully looking down at his phone.

"I'm very obviously interviewing him," she says. "I'm writing a piece on Monte's and how Wilson's younger management style will shape the future of a Ridgewood landmark."

I think my sister has been abducted by aliens. "'Ridgewood

landmark'? Last week you referred to it as 'that dump Jackie works at.'"

"Can you"—she glances around, flashing me a look—"keep your voice down. I have to go interview him. We can discuss this later."

Before I can respond, she's walking back to the couch, her laptop tucked beneath her arm.

I get Jillian having to do the interview, I do. This is her job, and my emotions shouldn't get in the way of that. But I was venting to her about Wilson just a few nights ago. The least she could've done was give me a heads-up that he'd be here! Instead of him walking through the door and Jillian acting as if *I'm* the one being delusional.

Deciding I need to cool off, I go for a walk around the neighborhood—ignoring Wilson as I leave—and grab a croissant sandwich from a bakery nearby. When my break is over, I head back to the office and spot Wilson standing outside, like he's waiting for me. He's leaning against the window, his obscenely tall limbs causing him to obstruct a poster that reads Women: Half the Population, All the Brains.

"You're blocking a very important message," I say, nodding toward the window. Wilson glances behind him, takes an absurd amount of time to read seven words, then scootches over.

"Does that apply to all women but you?" he asks.

"Congratulations. That's the first decent comeback you've ever had."

Before I can shove my way inside, he asks, "When did you start working here?"

"Yesterday," I say casually, crossing my arms.

"Does that mean you're leaving Monte's?" He asks it with a little too much excitement.

"Luckily for you, I'm not. I'm working here mornings that I'm not scheduled at Monte's."

He crosses his long legs and leans back against the window, away from the poster this time. "Oh yeah? *Is* that lucky for me?"

"Yes," I say. "Good luck trying to find someone with low enough self-worth to wear a frog costume four times a week."

I don't know what Jillian said to put Wilson into a good mood, but he laughs at that. For a split second, I swear his eyes run over my blue dress before finding their way back to mine. "I'm sure I can find someone," he says. "And probably someone with a lot less attitude and a way better work ethic."

"Don't talk about Anita like that," I say. "Why are you, like, being weird?"

Wilson's eyebrows draw together. "How am I being weird?"

"You're smiling. Stop it, it's off-putting."

Wilson pushes off the wall. Standing up straight, he towers over me. "Your sister's really great is all," he says. "Hard to believe you two are related."

"Okay, *wow*. And you were just complaining about *my* attitude?" Because it looks like he's about to leave and I'm not done annoying him yet, I add, "How did the interview go? Should I expect your resignation once this tell-all is published? What skeletons are coming out of your closet?"

"You should," he says. "It'll be filled with lots of scandals, like how I gave our night cleaners a raise, or my idea to hire real chefs to create an entirely new menu that focuses on food that is actually, you know, edible and slightly nutritious."

I gasp. "You know we Americans hate nutrition." I mean, I did just eat a pastry for lunch that is half butter so, case in point.

But . . . It sounds kind of like a good idea. Back when I was waitressing, there were more than a few moments where customers asked for something green on the menu—to which I could only recommend the fried pickles. Still, I would rather melt into a puddle than admit that to Wilson's face.

"I know *you* hate nutrition," he says. "Don't think I'm not aware that you and Anita are responsible for our candy supply running out so quickly."

"Prove it."

"Jackie, we have cameras everywhere."

"Then I'll see you in court."

I'm sure he is about to sling some retort to one-up me, but a baby blue Mini Cooper pulls up on the street, with all the windows down and the radio blasting. Kenzie is in the driver's seat, waving out the window.

"Hi, Jackie!" she calls.

"Hi!" I wave back, then turn to Wilson and add, "Please just tell me how much you're paying her to date you."

"Whatever you're thinking, double it," he says.

I gasp the biggest gasp of all gasps. "I knew it!"

Wilson just shakes his head like a disappointed parent. "I'll see you at work tomorrow," he says. "Unless you're still too sick to come in for your shift."

Somehow, my gasp grows bigger. "I made a miraculous recovery."

Wilson purses his lips. "I can see that." Then he gets into the car with Kenzie, they kiss, and she tosses me another wave before her tires screech and the Mini flies down the road.

CHAPTER 10

BECAUSE WILSON IS ETERNALLY tasked with ruining my life, I don't get to go to *The Rundown* for work the next day. I'm scheduled for an opening shift at Monte's that I couldn't wiggle myself out of.

Now there's an hour to kill before my shift begins, and I've decided to spend it torturing myself—also known as straightening my hair. Luckily, this time I have a distraction: my newly budding status of *relationship expert*. I'm sitting cross-legged on the floor in my bedroom, directly in front of the mirror, with my laptop propped open to *iDiary*. As I feed a new curl through the iron, I read a message and start thinking of a response.

The current one has me stumped. User @allisonjones wrote in about a friends-with-benefits situation she's stuck in. The dilemma is simple: he caught feelings and she didn't. Now she's unsure how to let him down gently while still maintaining the "friend" part.

No matter how far back I think, I can't remember a specific moment where Jill or Julie went through something like this. Probably because friends-with-benefits wasn't something they were oversharing with their thirteen-year-old sister. Every solution I come up with just feels wrong. Like, leading him on obviously doesn't work, because that's cruel. But then ending things won't work either, because then @allisonjones loses the friend *and* the benefits.

When I've finished straightening my hair and have thought myself into a spiral, Julie opens my door, and I discreetly shut my laptop with my foot. She walks into my bedroom like she owns the place, looking very summery in a yellow sundress. "It smells like a campfire in here," she says, wrinkling her nose, then spotting the flat iron. "I really don't understand why you do that to yourself. Your curls are so pretty."

"*Your* curls are so pretty. Mine are frizzy and unmanageable," I say. Then I realize that since she's here, I may as well ask the expert. "Question for you. Before Massimo, did you ever have a friend-with-benefits?"

Her hand flies to her mouth. "Do you have a boyfriend? Oh my gosh . . . do you need relationship advice? Tell me everything!"

"I'm asking for a friend at work," I lie.

"Oh." Julie's face falls. "What's going on?"

"The other person caught feelings," I explain. "She doesn't know how to end things without losing a friend."

With a grimace, Julie makes herself comfortable on the edge

of my bed. "Her first mistake was thinking friends-with-benefits can work," she says. "It *never* ends well. Like, ever."

"So how does she fix it?"

"I don't think she can. Once you cross that physical line, it's so hard to go back to the way your friendship was before. I tried it out once when I was, like, twenty-one? Anyway, didn't end well. He was . . ." She trails off, staring down at her hands in a way that's very un-Julie-like.

"Everything okay?"

She manages a laugh, smiling down at me. "Yeah. Sorry. I didn't expect it to be this hard to talk about. Wow, it was a *long* time ago, and somehow, it still stings."

I turn my body to face her, tucking my legs up to my chest. "What happened?"

"He was one of my best friends," Julie says carefully. "And I lost him. We completely ruined our friendship. I still regret it to this day."

"What do you think went wrong?" I ask. I'm not sure if this is research for my blog anymore or genuine curiosity.

"We forgot how to be friends after that," she explains. "I'm sure there are people out there who can make friends-with-benefits work, but for most people it feels impossible. And it sounds like your friend is one of them."

"So what do I tell her?" I ask.

"Well, she immediately needs to stop sleeping with them. I'd probably give it some time to air out. Maybe a week or two. See how they're both feeling after that, and if a return to platonic friendship is possible. If not, she might lose the friend."

That's what I was afraid of. "Relationships are so complicated," I grumble. Running this blog has taught me that *so* many people are unhappy. Why does anyone bother to stick around in a partnership where you feel so unsatisfied?

"They are," Julie says, picking at a loose thread in my comforter. "Especially at your age, when you have a million things to figure out. My advice? Leave the serious commitment to your mid-twenties. It gets a lot easier to love someone else after you've spent some time getting to know yourself."

I rest my head on her knee. "You're going to make such a great mom someday."

Julie laughs. "Where did that come from?"

"I don't know. It's true, though."

She nudges my head. "You'll be a very cool aunt, but not too cool. Jill is going to be such a bad influence on my kids. My God, Jackie. Promise me you'll be a voice of reason and not encourage bad behavior?"

I can already picture Jillian sneaking them junk food when Julie isn't around. Or letting them stay up late watching R-rated movies. "Promise," I say.

"Speaking of— How's it going with Jillian?" Julie begins to whisper. "Any updates on the Camilla situation?"

"Jill isn't home. You don't have to whisper."

"I'm scared," she says. "I don't know how, but it feels like she's always listening." She peers around my room, actually shuddering, as if Jill is hiding in the closet, waiting to jump out and scream *Gotcha!*

"Anyway," she continues, "have you learned anything new?"

"No," I say honestly. "They spend a lot of time together. Like, they eat lunch together. Jill seems to have a different relationship with Cami. Like it's less formal than the other girls. But that could just be because of their history, and I'm reading too much into it."

"Less formal how?"

"No one goes into Camilla's office unless she asks them to or they knock first. Jill just walks right in."

Julie thinks on that. "That is weird. But you're right, it could just be because of their history . . . You're going to have to snoop around more."

"More? I don't want to jeopardize my job," I whine. I'm actually starting to really enjoy working there.

"Then be careful," she says with a wink. "And don't forget, we have that bridesmaid's dress appointment this weekend."

"I know," I say. I've been dreading it all week, simply because I'm not looking forward to trying on a bunch of pink dresses and having to look at my reflection from every single angle in a too-bright dressing room.

I give Julie a squeeze on her knee. "Thanks for the help. Wanna keep this streak going and give me a ride to work?" I ask.

Julie eyes the still-hot flat iron discarded on my bedroom floor. "Isn't it counterproductive to spend all that time straightening your hair just to shove your head into a frog costume?" Julie says, fluffing my hair out around my shoulders. It now hits right beneath my boobs, which means it's time for a haircut.

"Yes," I say. "But I'll continue to do it anyway." Simply because my natural hair makes me feel like I cannot step foot in public. When you spend your entire childhood *only* receiving compliments when your hair is straight, you begin to take a hint.

"Speaking of work . . ." I check the time and realize my shift begins in fifteen minutes. "We needed to leave like, ten minutes ago."

I tell Julie I'll meet her in the car and quickly type up a response to @allisonjones. There's a voice in my head that warns me not to—that part of Julie's life was hard enough for her to talk about. I'm not sure if she'd appreciate me repeating it elsewhere. But isn't it worth it if it stops someone from making the same mistake she did? If it saves someone else the heartbreak? If that's the case, I'm nearly certain Julie would be okay with it.

I post the answer to *iDiary* and head to work.

With three minutes to spare, Julie is dropping me at the front doors to Monte's Magic Castle. I head straight for the break room to don my costume and start my usual ritual of willing the tiny hands on the clock to move faster. But when I walk into the break room, the sight before me stops me dead in my tracks.

Our old, rickety white table is gone. The mismatched chairs thrown around it are gone, too. There is now a couch positioned against the back wall, two square tables with matching chairs, and a gigantic TV mounted on the wall that's playing a soccer game. Even our fridge has been replaced with a stainless steel one—and it has a built-in water dispenser! There are two Keurig machines on the counter and, oh my gosh, a tray of muffins.

"Am I dreaming?" I ask. A few of my coworkers are hanging out on the couch, but it's Justin who answers.

"I thought the same thing when I saw it yesterday." He lifts the lid off the tray and grabs a blueberry muffin. I can smell it from here.

"What happened?" I ask. I'm in complete disbelief. Justin holds the lid for me, and I grab a chocolate chunk one for myself. Yes, *chunk*. Not chip. There's a big difference.

Olivia, one of the entertainers seated on the couch, says, "Wilson happened."

I almost drop my muffin. "*Wilson* did this?"

Justin eats half his muffin in one bite. "I couldn't believe it either. I mean, the dude got us a TV. How is this the same guy who's tripping when we spend too much time in the bathroom?" He plops down on the couch, kicking his feet up on the coffee table. "He better not get on my case for watching the TV he put in here."

I . . . I don't know what to say. I was so mentally prepared for Wilson to screw up as our new manager that I never once thought to entertain the idea that he might—

That he might—

God, even the thought is unbearable.

That Wilson might actually do a good job.

Or maybe this is just his sneaky way of getting us to like him. Either way, my guard is up. No one owns that much beige without having a trick up their sleeve.

When my costume is on, I hit the floor. There are two parties tonight, which is pretty average for a Thursday. Every game in the arcade is in use, and my cheeks are starting to get sore from all the fake smiling. Time and time again, I am grateful to my parents for forcing me to get braces when I was thirteen. If I had known my face would live on forever in the iCloud accounts of a hundred moms, I probably would've gotten my teeth whitened, too.

When I finish posing for a photo, I feel a hand tap my shoulder. I'm expecting another eager parent. Thankfully, it's Kenzie. Only she doesn't look like herself. Her usual smile is gone, and her eyes seem a bit red and puffy.

"Hi, Jackie," she says.

"Hey," I say, slightly surprised when she pulls me into a hug. "Are you okay?"

She laughs it off, tugging at the strap of her purse. "All good, yeah. Just had a rough night. I was hoping you'd be here today, actually. Congrats on your fancy new job. What are you doing at *The Rundown*?"

"Working as an assistant," I explain, making note of her subject change. "My sister works there as a writer and got me the job. Plus, I don't have to dress up as a frog, so, you know, couldn't say no to better working conditions."

"I know Wilson gives you shit, but you're rocking that frog costume," she says, managing a small smile. This coming from the girl who is truly so gorgeous it's difficult to make eye contact with her? That compliment has done more for my ego than anything else that has happened in the last eighteen years of my existence.

"Thanks. I think the color green is growing on me." To turn the conversation back to her, I add, "So, what are you doing here? Wait—is there another party for Wilson's family? Please say no."

"No, thank God. But how's the week been with Wilson in charge?" Her voice sounds casual, but her eyes are alert, like my answer to this question is very, very important.

"It's been better than I expected," I say, taking a break from trash-talking Wilson around his girlfriend while she seems so upset. "He redid the break room, which is pretty cool."

"Do you love the TV?" she says. "That was all my idea."

At that, I get excited. "I knew it! No offense, but I *knew* Wilson would never put a TV in the break room."

Kenzie tucks a black braid behind her ear. "His first idea was to get floor-to-ceiling shelves and fill them with books."

"Yeah, that sounds more like him," I say.

"Speaking of . . ." Kenzie looks down at her hands. I notice she's gripping a white envelope. "Is he here right now?"

"I saw him leave a few minutes ago," I say. "Probably on his lunch break."

Kenzie looks like that's exactly what she didn't want to hear. "Damn it. I have to give him this, but I'm in a rush and can't stick around . . . Do you mind?"

"Do I mind what?"

She holds up the envelope. "Giving this to him when he's back?"

That does mean I'd have to speak with Wilson, and I've been purposely avoiding him for mortal-enemy reasons. But Kenzie looks a little bit stressed, like this would be a huge help. And as much as I dislike Wilson, I kind of like his girlfriend.

"Sure." I grab the envelope and tuck it safely into my pocket. "But you should know I'm very nosy and may read it."

"No, you can't!" She says it so loud, a few kids playing nearby stop to stare at us. "I just mean— It's private, okay? Please make sure he gets it."

"Sure, yeah." After an awkward second passes, I add, "I was only kidding about reading it."

"I know you were. And thank you for doing this," Kenzie says as her phone vibrates. "Shit—I have to go. Thanks again, Jackie. You're the best."

"No problem," I say, waving as she heads for the exit.

A few minutes later Wilson walks through the door. He's holding a brown paper bag, tailing it to his office in a flash of long legs and disheveled hair. My gosh, why is everyone in a frantic rush today? I run behind him, trying to catch up, but these stubby frog legs are betraying me. I settle into some embarrassing combination of a waddle-run and manage to wedge my leg in before his office door shuts.

The shriek Wilson lets out when he spots me standing in the doorway is marvelous. Where is Suzy and her camera when you need her?

"Jackie," he says, hand to his chest. "Holy—you scared the shit out of me."

"Hey, that's the first time you've actually called me by my name." Maybe we are moving past frog territory. Maybe now, as a manager, Wilson will embody some professionalism and begin referring to me as—

"First *and* last," he says. "What do you want, Froggy?" He takes a seat at his fancy boss desk, and I very much dislike this power dynamic we've got going on here. Wilson is pulling food out of the paper bag—a sandwich wrapped in parchment, a can of soda.

"You eat lunch in your office? Don't you have like, friends to eat with or something?"

He pops the can open. "All my friends are back in the city," he explains. "The friends I had in Ridgewood have moved away for college. If you must know."

Then he pulls out a bag of Cool Ranch Doritos.

"Cool Ranch?" I ask in disbelief.

Wilson unwraps the sandwich. "Yes. What now?"

"That's *my* favorite flavor," I say, incredibly offended.

110

"Okay," he says slowly. "Are you expecting me to offer you one? Because I'm not going to."

"No. I'm simply disgusted that we have something in common," I say.

I can't help but laugh when Wilson literally throws the bag of chips into the garbage can. "I hate that flavor," he says, "and we have nothing in common." He instead chomps down into what appears to be a turkey sandwich on herbs and cheese bread. I purposely don't mention that is also my go-to order.

Over a bite of food, he says, "Glad to see you're still feeling better." An unnecessary reference to my sick call the other day.

"My doctor said he's never seen antibodies like mine," I say.

"Very weird flex."

Maybe if I stare hard enough at the sandwich, he'll choke on it.

"How's the other job?" he adds, adding fuel to the fire. "Have you decided to quit yet?"

"You do realize you're my boss and could fire me whenever you want?"

Wilson stops chewing. "You're right. Jackie, you're fired."

"Ha ha ha, hilarious."

Wilson just smiles to himself, proud of his joke, before turning his attention to the stack of files he skims over while eating. His hair is falling into his eyes again, and I begin to hear Suzy's voice echo throughout my head: *You failed to mention how cute he is.*

111

I try to view Wilson through unbiased eyes. I guess he is really tall, which is probably good. His brown hair turns golden when it catches the light, and it curls behind his ears in little waves. A thick row of eyelashes frame his eyes, which make them pop on his face. Another girl—Kenzie, for example—would probably say his eyes are nice. And when he bites into his sandwich, his teeth are straight, pearly white, behind full lips that are so pink it's like he's wearing lipstick.

Wilson runs a hand through his hair, messing it up a bit. I swear I catch a whiff of some product he uses that smells really good, too. The top button on his dress shirt is undone, which is very unusual—

"What are you doing?"

I snap back to attention to find Wilson—the real, very annoying, and not attractive version of him—gawking at me.

"You have a piece of lettuce in your hair," I lie.

"Oh." He ridiculously starts patting his head. "Is it gone?"

"Still there. Maybe pat harder."

He keeps patting. When I'm finally unable to contain my laughter and it erupts out of me, Wilson catches on. It takes about half a second for his eyes to narrow into a rather impressive glare.

"Get *out*."

He continues to eat his sandwich. I hover in the doorway like a sleep paralysis demon.

"Is there a specific reason you refuse to leave?" he says curtly.

That's when I remember the letter. I toss it onto his desk. It lands smack on top of the document pile. "Kenzie gave me this," I say. "It's for you."

He stands up so quickly he nearly knocks his chair over. "Kenzie's here?" Wilson says.

"She *was* here," I clarify. "She handed me that letter, told me to give it to you, then left."

"Oh," Wilson says, sinking back into his chair. He studies the envelope, holding it up to the light as if it'll reveal a secret message. Then he's back to looking at me like I'm a monkey in a zoo. "Well? Do you mind?"

"What? *Oh.* Yeah. I'll, uh, just leave now."

The truth is, I'm so deeply invested in this situation that I *need* to know what it says. But I'm also not going to give Wilson the satisfaction of asking, so I launch my master plan: standing right outside his office door, trying to catch some vocal reaction that'll hint at what Kenzie wrote in the letter. When ten minutes have passed and Wilson has been as quiet as a mouse, I conclude that it must've been some boring, mushy love letter. I'm walking down the hallway when the office door abruptly slams open and Wilson steps outside.

I pretend to act innocent. "Oh! I was *just* about to go back to work and—"

But Wilson isn't listening. In fact, he's walking too quickly, rubbing at his eyes, and heading for the back door. "Jackie, not now," he says, his voice taking on a new edge.

I instantly follow behind him. "Where are you going?" When

he opens the exit door and pushes through it, I add, "You can't just leave!"

But that's exactly what he does. Wilson walks straight out the door. As I'm about to follow, Anita comes running down the hallway. "Where's Wilson? The kiosks are out of tickets, and there's a dozen teens up my ass about refilling them. They're so high on sugar I think they might kill me."

"Um." I stare desperately at the door Wilson vanished through. "Wilson left."

Panic flashes across Anita's face. "What do you mean he left?"

"I mean I just watched him run out of his office and leave through that door."

"But Wilson is the only one who knows how to refill the machines," she says. "And those kids are *feral*, Jackie."

I see my chance at leaving early disappear before my very eyes.

"Well, he's not the *only* one."

Anita pauses. "*You* know how to refill the ticket kiosks?"

I nod. "Monte Jr. taught me once months ago. I think I still remember how to do it." Anita looks at me like I've begun speaking a made-up language. "Don't be so surprised that I'm *somewhat* good at my job," I say.

"No offense, but I'm beyond surprised."

"I'll handle the tickets," I grumble, already annoyed at Wilson for ruining my night. "Go drink some water or something. Your face is like, six different shades of red."

It takes me about twenty minutes to get the kiosks up and

running. It would have been faster if I had spent less time cursing Wilson under my breath.

Honestly, his little date with Kenzie—or *whatever* he ran off to do—better be worth it. Because of him, I'm stuck doing manager-level duties while earning nonmanager pay. All while surrounded by a horde of kids on a sugar high and their equally annoying yet less-sugared-up parents.

When I see Wilson tomorrow, I just may kill him.

CHAPTER 11

"HOLY CRAP," I MUMBLE to myself.

I'm sitting alone in Julie's car, parked outside of Monte's. My shift begins in five minutes, and I'm most likely going to be late. An *iDiary* account with fifty-seven thousand followers called @makeupbreakup reshared ten of my posts last night with the hashtag "#breakup-advice." From that, my account has fully blown up. All my notifications are maxed out at one hundred, and I'm gaining so many followers that the count jumps by hundreds every time I refresh the page.

Right now I'm at 3,072.

I refresh, and boom—two hundred more have piled in.

Am I going viral?

Every message I've answered on my account has gained hundreds of likes. There are way too many comments to count. Even my unread message count won't stop growing. Right now, there's over one hundred. With every passing minute, the number rises.

I'm glad I skipped the coffee this morning, because this has given me enough energy to last the day. I feel like some sort of celebrity, basking in the glow of strangers' compliments. I've never been told so often that I'm *good* at something. It's like all the validation I've been craving for the past eighteen years has now been thrown my way.

For the first time, it feels like I'm effortlessly good at something—something I enjoy, too. Because I do enjoy this. Answering these questions, helping other people, it makes me feel happy. Like, I'm *really* good at something that is positively affecting other peoples' lives.

Even just getting out of the car is a struggle. I want to drive back home and spend the day answering questions. Sadly, I can't. I'm tucking my phone away when Suzy calls. I shoot her a quick text and promise to call her later.

As I walk toward Monte's front door, I notice something weird: Wilson's car isn't here. Which is very strange, considering that he doesn't ever miss a day of work, if we ignore his blowup last night. In fact, since he took over as manager, a few people swear he's been sleeping here. It's a rumor that's been fueled by people working the night shift who have spotted him in his office well after midnight.

When I step inside Monte's, Anita walks toward me like she's on a mission. And she's not in her squirrel costume.

"Jackie—"

I interrupt. "What's going on?"

"Everything," she says. "Wilson didn't show up today. And he never returned last night."

"What? Where is he?"

"No one knows. He just disappeared. And we can't call him, either. None of us have his number. I called Monte Jr. a few times, but he hasn't picked up."

"This is impossible. This is Wilson we're talking about, the most responsible person on the planet. He wouldn't just abandon his job."

"Seems like that's exactly what he did," Anita says.

The next question on my mind is whether or not he's safe. Anita seems to read my thoughts. "I think he's okay," she says. "He must have come by last night to lock up at some point, and then again this morning to open the doors—that's how we got in today. But he's leaving before anyone sees him. Weird, right?"

"So weird." I can barely focus on what Anita's saying. My mind spins with a never-ending list of questions. If Wilson isn't here, how do we run Monte's? And if he isn't here, where is he?

And wait— Why exactly do I care so much? For the first time, I look around Monte's and realize that there isn't a boss in sight.

"So you mean we're alone at work, no management, no customers . . . And we're basically getting paid to do *nothing*?" I'm beginning to think this might actually be the best-case scenario.

Anita shakes her head. "I thought the exact same thing. Until

I realized today is payday. Without Wilson here, no one's cashing a check."

Abort mission. This is very much *worst*-case scenario.

"Shit. I need my check." If this place goes down in flames, that's one less source of income, which means I can kiss my end-of-summer dreams goodbye.

I let out a loud sigh. Of course Wilson would leave me here to clean up his mess.

"Here's what we're going to do," I say. "You stay out here and make sure everything is okay. I'm going to check Wilson's office. Maybe there's a file somewhere with his contact info on it."

"Good idea." We high-five. "Let's do this."

I walk into Wilson's office like I own the place and take a seat in his chair. It smells alarmingly like the cologne he wears. It's like woodsy, peppery, but then a little sweet like fruit? I hate that it actually smells good.

Okay. I need to focus. *We're hunting for clues now, Jackie.* I don't know when I became Cupid *and* Nancy Drew, but I'm kind of loving these new titles.

First things first, I try to log into Wilson's computer. Of course it's password protected. I try different variations of Wilson's name, Kenzie's name, their names combined. I debate trying his birthday before realizing I have no idea when it is. Eventually, I give up. The computer is a bust.

Moving on, I search the drawers for some document with his

cell phone number on it—even an address would suffice—or for any spare keys lying around we can use to lock the doors. Each drawer is so meticulously organized it feels like an actual crime to be digging around inside it. One has boxes of pens, staples, sticky notes, gum packets, and Band-Aids. Another is filled with files overflowing with papers. I briefly skim through those, with no luck. Just old forms signed by Monte Jr. that date back nearly a decade.

The last drawer I open sticks. I jiggle it a bit, really using a lot of force, and manage to pop it open. There are two things inside: a white envelope and a black tie. The tie may as well not even be there. I'm locked in on the envelope.

Kenzie's envelope.

The one she gave to me to pass along to Wilson.

The letter he read before storming out of here and never coming back.

I become overwhelmed by morality for a split second. On the one hand, the contents of this letter may be extremely private. Even though I dislike Wilson, it still feels wrong to dig around in his personal life like that. Not to mention this is Kenzie's private business, too. Whatever she wrote in that letter was never meant to reach my eyes.

On the other hand, these are dire circumstances. Wilson can't be reached. Monte Jr. isn't picking up, either. And if this letter was given to Wilson the last day he was seen at Monte's, the contents of it may be vital for figuring out what is going on with him and saving this business. Wilson would want that, no? For us to find a way to keep Monte's running, no matter what?

With my mind made up, I open the envelope. Inside is a sheet of lined paper folded into a neat square. The paper is creased everywhere, like it's been read and reread a hundred times. I unfold the letter and see what must be Kenzie's handwriting. Looping cursive letters fill the page. Before I can stop myself, I begin to read.

Wilson,

I never meant to tell you this in a letter. I was told that writing it out might help process my emotions, and honestly, this just felt . . . better. Easier. It might make me a coward, but this feels like the best way to get this off my chest.

I loved our life together back in NY. We had the city, school, dreams that were so aligned and a future that felt so attainable. But then your uncle got sick and you decided to take a year off school to go home and run the business for him. And believe me, you did the right thing. If I were you, I'd do that, too. I wanted to support you—I came here to Ridgewood for the summer with you. I thought this would be enough. That you, me, us would be enough.

I don't think it is. This small-town life isn't what I want, Wilson. I want to be in the city, and I want you there with me, reaching for the same goal. I want to graduate from business school together and build a career. But your life has taken a different path, and I don't think I can follow you down it anymore.

It feels so selfish to say this to you. You are going through so much, so much more than I can even imagine. I'm sorry for adding to it. I'm sorry for turning into another burden, but I can't be with you anymore. This new direction was never a mutual decision, and I should've spoken up sooner.

I'm going to be flying back to NYC in two weeks. Maybe we can talk before I leave?

I'm sorry.

Kenz

I end up reading it twice. Then I fold the paper on its creases and place it back in the envelope. It feels fragile, like I'm holding this intimate part of both Kenzie and Wilson in my hands. I don't like this—I don't like knowing this and holding up a magnifying glass to their relationship.

The contents of the letter have affirmed that I shouldn't have read it, but I'm glad I did. At least now I understand what caused Wilson to leave. At least now I know why he hasn't been at work. Although I'm still very annoyed with him, I'm not sure I can blame him for leaving. I wouldn't be here either if the person I loved just ripped my heart out.

For the first time, I feel something for Wilson that isn't a deep hatred. It's more like . . . pity. Compassion, maybe. There isn't an urgent desire to check on him or be a shoulder for him to lean on. But . . . I hope he's okay.

Poor Kenzie, too. To sit back and watch the life they built together slowly slip away? Not to mention how guilty she feels, knowing this breakup is quite literally happening at the worst possible moment for Wilson.

Then I remember another detail Kenzie mentioned. *But then your uncle got sick and you decided to take a year off school to go home and run the business for him.* Monte Jr. is sick? But I saw him just last week. He looked okay. He looked *normal.* Sure, a little stressed-out and red-faced, but when is he not? If he's sick, why didn't he tell us? Is it so serious that he's keeping it a secret? Is that the real reason he stepped away?

I begin to feel lightheaded, but that's not even the half of it. Wilson *left* business school? I thought he was just here for the summer. That, I don't know, he was taking online classes while running Monte's. I had no idea he actually took *a year* off school to be here.

Holy. My brain short-circuits with information overload.

Anita opens the office door. "Hey," she says, leaning against the wall. "Any luck?"

"Close the door," I say.

She does. Then I tell her everything.

When I'm done, Anita's eyes fill with tears. "Monte Jr. is sick?"

I nod. Watching her cry is bringing tears to my eyes, too. "I had no idea."

"None of us did," she says, her voice a whisper. "We need to handle this without involving him. If whatever he's going through is serious enough for him to step down, we can't risk dragging him back here."

I nod, completely agreeing.

"What do we do now?" she asks.

"We need to find Wilson."

"Easier said than done," Anita says. "Wilson hasn't made a single friendship with anyone who works here. No one knows how to contact him."

I sigh, holding my head in my hands, my hair pooling on the top of the desk. "We don't get paid enough for this," I grumble.

"We don't," Anita agrees. "Actually—what are *you* doing here? You hate Wilson. You should be, like, celebrating that his life is falling apart."

"I'm not a heartless monster," I say, peeking out between my hands to glare at her.

Anita reaches across the desk. "Let me see the letter." I hand it to her. She kicks her feet up on the desk and begins to read. "Maybe you missed something," she says.

"Like what?"

"Like a secret code or invisible ink."

I snort. "Sure, because that sounds like something a nineteen-year-old girl would do."

I wince as Anita rips the envelope open and unfolds the paper. Well, delicacy be damned. "I once had an ex capitalize certain letters in the text she sent dumping me," she says while she reads.

"What did the message spell out?" I ask.

"'Fuck you'," she says.

I choke back a laugh. "Fair enough."

Anita reads the letter in record-breaking time, then tosses it onto the table. I quickly fold it back up and return it to the desk. For some reason, I feel this compelling urge to keep Wilson's office as tidy as I know he likes it.

"You're right," Anita says. "Nothing in there but heartbreak. Kudos to whoever told her to break up with Wilson in a letter. I don't know about you, but in-person breakups are *extremely* overrated. Like, just dump me over the phone so I don't have to look at your face ever again, geez."

I freeze mid-movement, zeroing in on what she said.

"Anita," I whisper.

"What? What just happened? Why do you look like that?"

"What do you mean by 'whoever told her to break up with Wilson in a letter'?" I ask.

"Uhm." Anita grabs the letter, opening it again. "Right here, Kenzie wrote, *I never meant to tell you this in a letter. I was told that writing it out might help process my emotions.* It sounds like someone gave her advice to break up with him like that—Jackie, what is it? You're scaring me."

It can't be possible.

There's no way that Kenzie wrote into *pleasebreakmyheart* and asked me how to break up with Wilson. I would've recognized her name, her photo, her situation. *Anything.*

"Hello?" Anita presses, waving the letter in my face.

"Hold on." I'm tapping through my phone, pulling up *iDiary* and scrolling through every message I've answered in the past weeks. There's nearly a hundred of them. I skim the messages and the usernames, but nothing seems remotely familiar. Nothing seems like Kenzie . . .

Until it does.

There it is: last Tuesday, user mkz123, who wrote about how the future she planned with her boyfriend was uprooted when he decided to take a new job and move back home. And my response? To try writing out her feelings in a letter before talking to him.

Even the username mkz123 must be short-form for McKenzie, Kenzie's full name.

But that's pretty standard advice. It doesn't necessarily mean . . .

Then I see it. An unread message waiting in my inbox from mkz123, thanking me for the suggestion to write out her feelings in a letter. *You were right*, the message reads. *It made the breakup a lot easier.*

I bang my head on the desk. This cannot be happening.

There's pressure on my shoulder. I realize it's Anita's hand. She's standing next to me. "Jackie," she says carefully, "you're scaring me."

I ruined their relationship. I practically drew Kenzie the blueprint on how to break Wilson's heart, and now Monte's and all my coworkers are feeling the brunt of it. And I can't even confide in Anita. She can't know about this blog, especially now. No one can know about what I've done.

Unfolding my limbs, I sit up in Wilson's chair, catching another whiff of his cologne. An unfortunate plan begins to form in my mind, like Tetris blocks falling into place.

I stand up. "I know what I have to do," I say, already exhausted just thinking about it.

"What?" Anita asks.

I say five words I never thought would leave my mouth. "I'm going to find Wilson."

CHAPTER 12

TURNS OUT IT'S SORT of difficult to track down the person you have spent the past few months ignoring, avoiding, and altogether denying their existence.

It's even more difficult when you're kind of, maybe just a teeny-tiny bit, hoping to *not* find them, so you have a great excuse to not get yourself mixed up in a situation that you single-handedly caused.

That is, until a very disheveled Wilson Monroe casually walks into *The Rundown* office at ten o'clock on Tuesday morning. I have the phone pressed to my ear, jotting down a message for Camilla, when the doorbell chimes. Not only is he not wearing his usual beige khakis, but he seems to have forgotten his morning hair-care routine. His waves flop around his head in fluffy tufts, somehow making him look about three years younger. The usual business-casual attire has been swapped out for jeans, sneakers, and a plain black T-shirt. For once, Wilson looks like a regular nineteen-year-old guy.

Most alarming, though, is the expression on his face. Usually sharp and focused, he now looks lifeless. Dark circles kiss the skin beneath his eyes, which is still the slightest bit swollen. It looks like he hasn't slept in days. Even the way he walks is off. His posture is normally ramrod straight, and he takes these annoyingly long, determined steps. Now he kind of slumps around, like a hunched-over version of himself.

I immediately turn to Jillian, who looks as confused as I am.

"What is he doing here?" she whispers as she stands up, nearly tripping over her chair in her rush to greet Wilson.

Curse them and their hushed voices. No matter how far I scoot my chair over, I can't hear a single word they say. I watch Wilson's mouth move. He keeps running a hand through his hair, which may explain how wild it looks.

There's a tiny part of my brain that struggles to comprehend that This Wilson and Manager Wilson are the same person. I feel like my mind is malfunctioning in real time. Put me through a CT scan, and my skull may come up empty.

Wilson sits on the couch, on the edge of the cushion, like he's prepared to make a run for it at any moment. Jill returns to her desk and immediately begins typing furiously on her computer.

"What's going on?" I hiss, watching her chipped black nails tap the keyboard too quickly for me to piece the letters together.

"Pulling up the transcript of our interview. There's something

Wilson said that he now wants off the record," she says, her eyes trained on the screen as if this is a national emergency.

Whatever this top secret information is, I'll decipher that later. Right now, I need to weasel my way into speaking with Wilson—a sentence I never thought would cross my brain, but here we are.

"I need to talk to him before he leaves," I tell Jillian.

Her head swivels to face me so quickly it's like a scene from a horror movie. "You want to talk to Wilson? Your *mortal enemy*?"

"First, thank you for finally acknowledging that he is in fact my enemy. Second, yes. Desperately. When you finish, don't let him leave."

Jillian prints the pages and returns to Wilson's side, moving so quickly she nearly trips. When she hands him a pen, he begins to presumably cross out the now "off the record" part of the interview.

And because Jillian is completely unreliable, I watch as Wilson stands and walks out of the office, his gaze planted on the floor like he is maneuvering himself over molten lava instead of hardwood.

Maybe the fastest I have ever moved in my existence, I bolt out of my chair and chase him, sparing a split second to stare daggers at Jillian before crashing outside. I immediately regret wearing these stupid sandals Julie coaxed me into. With every step, my foot all but slips right out of them. Despite a pebble nearly taking me down, I manage to make it to Wilson's car as he removes the keys from his pocket.

"Wait!" I call.

He spins around quickly, but I'm moving even quicker. I miscalculate how fast I'm going and, with a loud *thud*, I slam right into his chest.

The level of self-hatred I feel skyrockets when the first thing I notice is that the cologne scent from his office chair is here as well, tucked into the soft cotton of his T-shirt.

I may be taking another whiff—I also may be suffering from severe brain damage from events unknown to me—when Wilson literally pries me off him like I'm a dead mosquito being flicked off his skin.

"What are you doing?" he says, staring straight down at me.

For some godforsaken reason I am relieved to see that familiar look of disdain cross his face.

"Just, you know," I say between pulling in an embarrassing amount of air, "testing your reflexes." To make matters worse, I pat his chest. "Good job. You passed." I have to clasp my hands behind my back to physically stop myself from doing a thumbs-up.

"Are you done?" he asks. "Can I leave now?"

"Can you *leave* now?" I repeat, unable to hide the anger slipping into my tone. "And go where, Wilson? To Monte's? The place you've completely abandoned?"

His nostrils flare. He looks away so quickly I can't make out the next expression that crosses his face. "Yes, Jackie, to Monte's. I'm going there right now. Did you want an outline for the rest of my day? Perhaps the week? I can share my calendar with you, too."

I nod so quickly I might morph into a bobblehead. "Sure, yeah, that'd be great. Maybe then your employees can actually know when you plan on showing up, signing their paychecks, and doing your *job*. Gosh, Anita and I have been busting our asses to keep that place afloat while you're sulking around."

"Wait— What? *You've* been helping?"

The look of shock on his face is so evident I want to kick his shin. "Yes, I've been helping. Turns out that, lucky for you, I spring into action in the most dire of circumstances."

Wilson scratches at his head, tripping over his words. "Oh. Well— Uh, thanks for, you know, doing that?"

I glare at him. "I can't believe you abandoned us."

Wilson looks more run-down than our office. He runs a shaking hand through his hair as he sighs. "I don't expect you to underst—"

"That you got broken up with? Of course I understand. It's horrible, and I'm so sorry that happened to you. For what it's worth, I actually thought you and Kenzie were decently cute together. And you're allowed to sulk and be sad and sit in bed with the blinds closed for as long as you want, but you can't abandon everyone at Monte's. Not when we're relying on you." The words come out rushed, slung together like one giant run-on sentence. "Do you even know how hard I had to work while you were gone? I gave about ninety percent more effort than I usually do, Wilson. *Ninety percent.*"

The last expression I expect to see on his face is embarrassment. His cheeks are red, his eyes looking so intensely at the ground he may as well be talking to it. "How do you know about the breakup?" he asks.

It's the most vulnerable I've ever seen him. Suddenly, the rush of anger I was feeling fades. Now I just feel . . . Well, I feel kind of bad.

I may have had to spend some time working harder than usual and taking on more tasks than I'm used to at Monte's, but in the past few weeks Wilson's life seems to have entirely flipped upside down. He took a year off business school, moved cities, took on a new job, and now his girlfriend—the person he loves—has broken up with him. In comparison, it makes what I'm going through look, well, pretty insignificant.

I guess I was so used to Manager Wilson that I forgot that Regular Wilson is a real person, too. He may be a year older than me, but that doesn't mean he's immune to struggling with all the same stuff.

It takes me by surprise—the level of sympathy I feel toward him. After all these months working together and annoying one another, it sucks to see him like this: quiet, resigned, heartbroken. Like, who am I supposed to bully at work if not him?

I feel the weight of my phone in my pocket, feel the burden of the hundred-plus unread messages waiting for me on *iDiary*. And for the first time, I feel something like fear. If my advice hurt

Wilson this much, what could it do to the others?

"Jackie. How do you know about the breakup?" he asks again when it's clear that I've spaced out.

I blink up at him, take in the hurt coating his features like a fresh layer of paint. "I read the letter," I say. Right there in the middle of the street, as dozens of cars rush by and probably my entire team watches through the windows, I confess.

The part about me giving Kenzie the advice remains tucked away in the most private corners of my brain.

He immediately looks mortified. "No."

"Yes," I say.

"Why would you do that?"

"I didn't know what else to do," I say honestly. "I was looking through your office, trying to find a spare key or your cell phone number. Some way to reach you and figure out what was going on. And the letter was just . . . there."

Because it's the right thing to do, I add, "Look. I'm sorry. I know I shouldn't have. I regretted it the literal second I read it. But at the time it felt like the only way to figure out what happened with you. And"—I cough—"Anita was worried."

The most fleeting of smiles crosses his face. "Anita was worried?"

"Yes," I repeat. "Only Anita. *Stop looking at me like that.* I wasn't worried about you. Can you stop?"

I am now beginning to think this is a nervous tic of his, because Wilson rams his fingers through his hair yet again, this time sticking up his roots and making his hair appear to have seven cans of hair spray living inside of it.

"I really messed up," he says. "I told my uncle he could rely on me, and now—" He cuts himself off, as if that sentence was veering into territory I don't have access to.

"I just can't do this right now. This job, this town— All of it. I need a second. I'll run it by my uncle—"

"Your uncle is sick, Wilson. You can't bring him into this."

"How do you know—" He closes his eyes, sighing. "The letter. That you read. Right."

We stand in awkward silence for a moment. Wilson can barely look me in the eye, and I find it way easier to look anywhere but his face. The hurt etched across it is doing something strange to my heart. Something I would very much like to ignore.

"How do I fix this?" he asks. "My uncle trusted me with Monte's. I can't let him down." Then he quickly adds, "Sorry. I shouldn't even be dragging you into this. You already helped keep Monte's going while I was away. I caused this problem, and it's up to me to fix it."

Well . . . That's not *entirely* true. There's a teeny-tiny way that I caused this problem, too. Which probably means I'm semiresponsible for trying to help fix it.

Dammit.

While Wilson seems to search for answers in the sky, a plan pops into my head. One that just might be crazy enough to work. Once the idea is out there, there's no taking it back. I very well may immediately regret the next words I'm about to say. But as the person solely responsible for Wilson's broken heart, it only makes sense that I try to un-break it.

And, look, I'm not *totally* selfless. If all goes well, my promotion could be back on the table, which means more money for the road trip. I believe that's called a win-win.

"Look, here's what we're going to do," I say.

Wilson tries to cut me off, but I give him a warning look and carry on.

"You are going to come back to work. Your uncle is going to continue getting better, far away from the stress of Monte's. I'm going to get my promotion to waitress, and I'm going to help you win Kenzie back." I force the last sentence out.

A painful ten seconds pass, with Wilson staring blankly at me before he bursts into a fit of laughter. "You cannot be serious," he says.

I point to my face. "Does it look like I'm joking?"

"Why would you possibly want to help me win Kenzie back?"

For many reasons I won't be sharing with him. For right now, I'll settle on telling him what he *will* believe. "Because I want to be a waitress again, and the second you got hired, my promotion flew out the window. So when I help heal your broken heart, I get my old job back."

"But you hate Monte's," he points out. "And you hate *me*."

"Wilson, will you just shut up and accept my help?" Holy crap. I've never met a human being more difficult than this six-foot-something buffoon.

"No," he says, "I won't. Why do you want to help me? We hate each other, Jackie. Like, that's our entire thing."

"And this doesn't change that at all. Believe me, I still hate you. In fact, I don't think I've ever hated you more. But right now, we have a common interest, which is keeping Monte's afloat. So if fixing your fragile little heart is going to solve all our problems, then let's do it."

Wilson studies me like I'm a candidate for a job interview. "What makes you think you can help me win Kenzie back?"

Duh, because I'm the one who helped you lose her in the first place. Surprise!

I hold a finger up for each reason I list. "Because I'm a girl," I say. "Because I know what Kenzie probably wants from you. Because I have two older sisters who have basically taught me the ins and outs of relationships. Because—and I cannot stress this enough—I'm your only hope. And if you were a big enough goof to lose her the first time, I hardly doubt you can win Kenzie back on your own."

Wilson looks at me like I'm speaking a different language. "I don't like that you're making sense," he says.

"So do we have a deal?" I ask, ignoring his comment. "We maintain enemy status while I help you win Kenzie back, therefore saving your family business, and when all is said and done, I get repromoted to waitress."

A minute passes without a response.

"Well?" I ask.

"I'm thinking about it," he says.

"Wilson, your options are eternal sadness or let me save your ฉฉ."

"No," he says. "My options are eternal sadness *or* spend a significant amount of time with you. Like I said, I'm thinking about it."

This annoying, frustrating, irritating person stands there for another two minutes—I counted—chewing on his lip and alternating between looking at me, his car, and the sky.

"Wilson, you cannot be serio—"

"Fine," he says. "Let's do it."

He extends his hand. I shake it. His grip is firm, determined.

Well. I guess that's that.

CHAPTER 13

WILSON IS WAITING FOR me in his office the next day.

Well, not really.

Wilson is *in* his office working when I barge through the door and toss my backpack onto the floor. He looks up from the stack of papers he was thumbing through. "Good morning?" He says it like a question.

"Morning, business partner." I make myself comfy in the chair across from him.

"We're not business partners," Wilson says, returning his eyes to the papers. He is back with his usual composure—perfect hair, clean, buttoned-up shirt layered with that hideous green vest, probably ate a fiber-rich breakfast and took a shower before he arrived. Yawn.

I try again. "Acquaintances?"

"No."

"Batman and Robin?"

"No."

"You can be Batman," I offer.

He flips the paper over. "Still no. And what are you doing here? Your shift doesn't begin for another twenty minutes."

I clutch my chest. "You memorized my schedule? That's so sweet."

Finally, his eyes lift up from the paper and meet mine. "I *make* the schedule."

"And you always schedule us together. That *must* mean something," I say. At this point, I'm just having fun annoying him.

"Yeah," Wilson says. "It means I'm here open-to-close every single day and don't have a choice."

I sigh. "You're such a vibe killer. What are you reading?" I ask after a second of silence passes.

"Résumés," Wilson says. He runs his finger along the edge of the stack of papers. There's *a lot* of them. Like, that pile is an inch high. I'm shocked so many people want to work here.

"For what position?" I ask.

Wilson presses two fingers to his forehead and briefly closes his eyes. "I'm hiring more cleaners for the night shift, if you must know."

"That's not a terrible idea."

"Gee. Thanks."

"And you answering those questions proves we're business partners," I add. "I mean, that *is* the kind of information you pass along to a partner—just saying."

Wilson plants his elbows on the desk, resting his chin in his hands. "You know what? You're insufferable, but at least you're consistently insufferable."

I smile wide. "It's all about the consistency, baby. Feel free to pass over some of those résumés. I can help you choose who to hire. I'm good at separating the losers from the cool people. Like, for example, you're most definitely a—"

Wilson's face takes on a startled expression, as if I just suggested burning Monte's to the ground and running away to Mexico with the insurance money. "Don't finish that sentence," he says. "And that sounds like a terrible idea."

"All great ideas start out as bad ideas," I say, ripping off a quote I read somewhere in Suzy's bedroom. "So by that logic, we're getting somewhere."

A drawer to the desk creaks open and Wilson carefully places the papers inside. Perhaps he thought if he left them out a second longer, I'd infect them with my gaze.

He looks at me, his brown eyes tired but alert. "Why did you come in here?"

"So we can start planning how to win Kenzie back," I say. Honestly, the faster we bang this out, the better. I'm trying to shed the froggy costume as soon as humanly possible.

A little wrinkle forms between Wilson's eyebrows. "We're not discussing this at work."

"Why not?"

"Because someone may hear us," he hisses.

"Right. We don't want to scare off all the eligible women who are waiting to win your heart." I turn around to face the doorway, cupping my hands around my mouth. "Go home, ladies! He's off the market!"

"I have a question for you," Wilson asks, leaning across the desk.

"Fire away, boss."

"Do you store all this sarcasm in your body? Or is there some, like, external life source that you export it from?" he asks very seriously. There is the tiniest of smiles tugging up the corners of his lips—a smile he's actively trying to squash back down. And for the strangest of reasons, seeing it is the biggest relief.

"Great question, William. Uhm, for privacy reasons, I'm unable to disclose that information to you."

"Privacy reasons," he repeats. The smile is back, tugging away. It's very concerning.

"I don't expect you to understand," I say, kicking my feet up on the desk and putting them back down point-five seconds later after the glare Wilson gives me, like two bright-red lasers shooting from his eyeballs.

He slowly removes his arms from the desk. "Jackie, how many pairs of feet touched this desk while I was gone?" he asks. His eyes run over the wooden surface as if he has some superhuman vision that allows him to see traces of DNA and microscopic dirt.

"Can I just say, I love how you've been calling me by my real name."

"Jackie, how many pairs of—"

"I don't know! Like two?"

He begins to stutter like a robot malfunctioning. "T-T-*two?*"

I know for sure Anita's feet touched it, but I'm not about to throw her under the bus. I grimace. "Maybe one?"

"Maybe?"

For the next few minutes I watch Wilson take every item off his desk and proceed to run a Lysol wipe across it. After two more wipes have been tossed into the garbage bin and the poor wood has met his cleanliness standard, he meticulously places all the items in the exact same spot as before. Then he sits back down in his chair, breathes, and sips from his coffee cup. "Better," he says. "Remind me to put a lock on the door."

"Kind of dumb you don't have one to begin with," I say, sniffing the clean, lemony scent. My thought is this—if chemicals shouldn't be inhaled, why do they smell so good?

"What were we talking about?" Wilson asks, looking drastically more at ease.

"Winning Kenzie back," I say.

He slouches over in his chair, pain hidden in the curve of his shoulders. "Right," he says, an immeasurable amount of longing in that one syllable. "Like I said, I don't want to talk about this at work."

"Then where should we talk about it?" I ask, digging into my backpack and taking out a Twix bar.

Wilson eyes the candy. "After work?" It sounds like he is forcing the words out.

"Can't," I say. "I have to be home for dinner. My sister's fiancé is coming over. It's a whole thing." Julie has now sent twenty-two texts in our group chat, detailing the food we're ordering tonight, the movie we will be watching afterward, that the cake in the fridge is not to be touched, and that everyone must be on their best behavior.

Keep in mind, no one has responded to any of those twenty-plus texts. She is holding a one-way conversation.

Wilson presses his lips into a thin line, as if he is physically trying to stop himself from speaking. "I usually grab lunch around noon," he forces out, wincing. "You can come."

"What if," I say, "you ask nicely."

He huffs out of his nose like a fire-breathing dragon. "Starve, then," he says.

"Win Kenzie back on your own then," I counter.

I can see the internal debate in Wilson's head, two miniature versions of him battling between sucking up to me and simply self-combusting.

"Jackie," he finally says, brown eyes on mine, "will you please come to lunch with me?"

I smile sweetly. "Well, if you insist."

After talking himself down from lunging at me from across

the desk, he says, "I'll meet you outside at noon." Then he checks his watch, noting the time. "Your shift began three minutes ago."

"But we're having so much fun. What if I don't—"

"Hop to it."

Wilson sweeps me out of his office with a very rude look. For reasons unknown to me, I start counting the hours until my lunch break.

Wilson drives us to an undisclosed location in a shiny white Lexus. The car is immaculate—no garbage, dust, dirt. Not even a single blade of grass. It looks like it was just driven home from the dealership. It even has that indescribable new car smell to it.

Halfway through the ride, Wilson catches me looking around. "What?" he asks.

"Nothing. Your car is very clean," I say. Not even an empty water bottle in the cupholder.

"Sorry," he says quickly, almost like a reflex.

I half expect him to drive with his seat at a ninety-degree angle, two hands planted firmly on the wheel at ten and two, and to go exactly the speed limit. It seems like the obvious choice, given he's so uptight you can bounce a quarter off him. But as we drive through the side roads, it turns out I was completely wrong. He drives like a normal teenager, one hand on the wheel, the other on the armrest, that kind of relaxed ease that comes with doing the same thing hundreds of times. But he's Wilson, so of course he stops for three seconds at every stop sign and slows down for yellow lights instead of gunning it like Jillian does.

We drive in complete silence, the music from the radio interrupting my thoughts now and then. I glance out the window, curious as to where Wilson goes for lunch. I try to piece the roads together like a puzzle—if he makes a right, we could be going to the sushi place; a left and we're heading in the direction of Dad's favorite barbecue spot.

After ten minutes, he pulls into a parking lot I know all too well. Because Angelo's is here, a diner my family has been visiting since I was a kid. Back when my mom still worked full-time and my dad was a stay-at-home dad, he took me and my sisters here every single day because he's a terrible, awful cook who had us living off of spaghetti with cut-up hot dogs. Three years ago, they changed management, and the food kind of went downhill, so we stopped going.

"Have you been here before?" Wilson asks, cutting the engine.

"Been here? I practically lived here when I was a kid." I'm already halfway out the door, my stomach grumbling just thinking about greasy fries and inhumane amounts of ketchup.

For once, Wilson has to use his long legs to catch up with my short ones. I all but run through the parking lot, sidestepping a moving car and jumping onto the sidewalk. The diner looks the same as always—shabby roof, red-and-white-striped awnings, a neon sign in the window that says OPEN, and white-painted writing on the front window that reads FRESH QUALITY FOOD. HUGE PORTIONS. REASONABLE PRICES. It feels like a relic

146

that's been frozen in time. If Jill wants to write an article about a Ridgewood landmark, she should start here.

We head inside and ask for a table for two. A smiling older woman with a gap between her two front teeth leads us to the corner booth. The leather seats are torn, and TVs are hung around the walls, all showing the same news channel. Apparently we're getting rain tonight.

I breathe a sigh of relief. Just as I left it.

I open the large laminated menu, smiling when it feels sticky beneath my fingers. It's so nostalgic. So nice to know that sometimes, there are things that don't change.

"I didn't think this would be your kind of scene," I say to Wilson, my eyes scanning the menu, the one thing that *has* changed.

When I glance up, Wilson hasn't opened the menu. He sits with his hands folded on the table, watching me. "Why is that?"

"It's . . ." I begin, struggling for the right word. "Old and kind of shabby. I thought you'd eat somewhere where the menu isn't sticky."

One side of his mouth kicks up. "Notice how I'm not touching it," he says.

I hate that I did notice. "Good point."

A young girl about my age approaches our table, smiling brightly. Her blond hair is tugged into two cute pigtails, and she has the clearest sky-blue eyes. Her name tag says Tammy. "Hi guys. Oh! Hi, Wilson, welcome back. Can I start you with some water? Any soda? Juice?"

Wilson orders a water. I grab an iced tea. Tammy smiles and disappears behind the bar jutting out from the far wall.

"I take it you come here often," I say. After all, Tammy knew his name.

"It's a family spot," he says curtly. Then, as if deciding that sharing some detail about his life won't make him immediately nauseous, he adds, "My uncle came here a lot. It was our go-to spot after we closed up at Monte's."

With the mention of Monte Jr., a weight blankets the conversation. There's so much I want to ask, but I'm not sure how much I'm allowed to know.

"How is he?" is what I settle on.

Wilson's eyes meet the table. "He's doing okay. The doctors caught the tumor pretty early on."

Oh. I don't know what to say. "Can you tell him I say hi? That I'm thinking of him?"

Wilson looks at me. There's something in his gaze—something like gratitude. "I'll tell him," he says gently.

"And can you tell him our new boss sucks? And that he should come back to work whenever he's able to?"

Wilson snorts. "Not happening."

Worth a shot.

Tammy comes back with our drinks. I notice she sets a straw down with mine, but not Wilson's. "You two ready to order?" she asks, flipping open her notepad and clicking her pen.

I barely read the menu, but I'm craving my usual. "I'll do the

BLT, please. Can I get it with a fried egg added? And then fries on the side. Extra crispy."

Tammy begins to write down the order, then stops. She just stares at me, her eyebrows furrowed. Confused, I glance at Wilson, who is looking at me with the same expression.

"Yeah," Tammy says, blinking. "Of course. Uh— the usual for you, Wilson?"

"Yes," he says, sounding slightly dazed. "Thanks."

Tammy smiles, then walks over to the register. I watch her punch our order in. Every couple of seconds she glances back at me.

"Is it suddenly a crime to add an egg to a BLT?" I ask.

"No," Wilson says, drawing out the vowel.

I cross my feet beneath the table and lean back against the booth. "Then what's with the matching reactions?"

"You ordered my usual," he says casually, but his eyes are offset with this intensity that makes me shift.

So, Wilson and I happen to have the same taste when presented with a menu overflowing with artery-clogging food. Big whoop. A BLT is, like, an American staple. I doubt he's the only person who orders that.

I doubt it's a big deal.

In fact, I doubt it means anything.

"Your go-to order is a BLT with a fried egg?" I can't help but ask.

He sips from his glass. A bead of water drips down his chin. "With extra crispy fries on the side."

"And let me guess, you're going to smother them in ketchup like me?" I ask.

Wilson's face puckers like he's sucked on a lemon. "God, no. That's disgusting."

I breathe an audible sigh of relief. "Then we're not that similar after all," I say, deciding to conveniently ignore everything else. That we both visit this restaurant. We both prefer Cool Ranch Doritos *and* have the same sandwich order. But aside from those three extremely irrelevant things, we could not be more different. We are night and day. Salt and pepper. Oil and water. Any other analogy that dispels this unknown feeling snaking in right now.

"You drown your fries in ketchup?" Wilson asks.

I nod proudly.

"Let me guess—do you also like pickles?"

"Love pickles," I say. I am the proud friend who willingly eats everyone else's pickles at dinner. "Why are you looking at me like that?"

"Your taste buds are cursed," Wilson says.

I stab my straw on the table until the paper rips and the plastic pokes through. "Clearly not, since we order the same meal," I counter.

Wilson watches as I place the plastic straw in my iced tea and take a sip. The collision of sugar and a crisp, cold beverage does things to my body.

"I see you also have no regard for the environment," he points out, frowning at my straw. The straw Tammy didn't give to him.

Dammit. I can't be feeling that Wilson is, somehow, a better—rather, more environmentally conscious—human than I am.

"In my defense," I begin between slurps, "I'm a big plastic hater. Like, gigantic. *But,* I have this thing where I don't like my mouth touching cups that other people's mouths have also touched. So yes, I occasionally use a plastic straw. But I also shut the water off when I brush my teeth and walk instead of drive, so I'd like to think that makes up for it." I conveniently leave out that the reason I opt for walking over driving is because I'm too poor to afford a car.

"You do realize you eat off a fork that's been in about a thousand people's mouths," he cruelly points out.

If it's possible to get the ick over cutlery, I now have it. Wilson must see the grotesque look on my face, because he laughs.

"I really could have gone my whole life without knowing that," I say, fighting off a wave of nausea. Suddenly my appetite decreases about ten percent. "Actually, I'm surprised that's something *you* don't worry about, Mr. Clean."

Wilson leans against the booth seat. He rolls his shirtsleeves up to his elbows. "I do worry about it," he says. "Hence why I order finger foods."

"Don't say *hence* like some middle-aged man," I say for literally no reason other than to be annoying.

He dismisses me with an eye roll. "We came here to talk about Kenzie. Not my vocabulary."

I lean across the table, resting my chin on my palm. A sticky substance touches my elbow. "But now that we're on the topic, I have some suggestions. For one, you always—"

Tammy interrupts with two gigantic plates of food. And by gigantic, I mean they're at least three times the size of a regular plate. "Two BLTs with a fried egg, with extra crispy fries on the side," she says, placing a plate in front of each of us. "Enjoy, you two." With a wink that doesn't sit right with me, she walks off.

The next few minutes are spent inhaling. I realize I haven't eaten anything today, aside from a shabby blueberry muffin for breakfast, so I eat with the gusto of a starving man.

"I could write love poems about this brioche," I say through a mouthful of food.

Wilson, like the dignified human he is, swallows before speaking. "Please don't," he says, reaching for a fry.

When I have eaten half the sandwich and a fair share of fries, I wash it down with some iced tea and lean back, rubbing my tummy, which now looks about four months pregnant. "Death row last meal," I say. "Go."

To my surprise, Wilson doesn't even hesitate. "Filet mignon, mashed pota—"

"You did not just say filet mignon."

Wilson pauses mid-chew. "I did just say filet mignon. And I was about to say mashed potatoes with butter before you interrupted."

"Would you also like the guards at this hypothetical jail to serve you caviar? Perhaps an aged bottle of pinot grigio?"

He actually thinks about it. "Sure. I don't see why not."

"New question—how much did you weigh at birth? After the nurses removed the silver spoon."

I giggle at the joke. Wilson looks like a grumpy little man. "Hilarious. Let me guess your death row meal—chicken nuggets and fries?"

"Yes. Obviously, like any normal person," I say.

"What about vegetarians? Vegans?"

I wave him off. "I'm a simple gal, William. I need some chicken nuggets, a fat plate of fries, and like, a solid half bottle of ketchup. Maybe a crisp iced tea."

"Dessert?" he asks, going in for another fry.

"Ouf, that's a hard one." Julie is such a great baker that I've spent my entire eighteen years doped up on sugar, butter, and semisweet chocolate chips. "Chocolate fudge brownie. No— Wait, chocolate dip doughnut. Or maybe a chocolate lava cake. You know what? All of the above."

"I'm sensing a common theme of chocolate," he points out.

A wave of dread washes over me. "Wilson Monroe, please don't tell me you're a vanilla guy. *Please.*"

He sighs. "I'm a vanilla guy."

"Judas!"

Wilson actually bursts out laughing. I'm wondering if maybe getting him out of Monte's is the key to unlocking his personality.

I feel like I'm looking through a window and the curtains are finally open.

"Chocolate is too sweet," he says like a crazy person.

"That explains so much. Like, so much. The vanilla, the khakis, the gelled-back hair. It all makes sense now."

Wilson tilts his head, amused. "You can't possibly think that makes any sense."

"It does! Like, okay. You probably track how much protein you eat during the day, text with caps on *and* proper grammar, and wear slippers in your house. Am I right?"

Something like embarrassment takes over his demeanor. "It pains me to admit that yes, you are."

I sigh happily, leaning against the cushion. "I can read you like an open book, Willy."

"Don't call me that," he says.

"Now, here's the real question," I say. It's probably time we direct this conversation back to what's important. "Can you read Kenzie like an open book?"

He doesn't hesitate. "Yes."

"Then why didn't you see the breakup coming?"

At that, he goes silent. "I had been . . . working a lot," he says after a moment. "Maybe I wasn't around as often as I should have been."

If we're going to kick off this plan to win her back, I need to learn more about Kenzie. About what she likes and dislikes, how she spends her time. I have to figure her out, right down to the bones. That way, we can start building this back up again.

"Tell me about her," I say, grabbing my iced tea and sipping as Wilson goes on.

"She's a business major like me," he begins. "She wants to move to New York City one day. She gets her nails painted every three weeks and doesn't drink caffeine, only decaf tea. She's allergic to hazelnuts, and her longest run was seventeen miles. She somehow doesn't like the taste of water and always puts flavor packets in it. She's a Leo and she constantly reminds me of that, even though I don't really know what it means. She's . . ."

He continues, but I'm too stunned to speak. I guess I sort of assumed that Wilson was a shitty boyfriend if he got dumped so easily. Or at least checked out. But maybe he wasn't.

No, he definitely wasn't. You don't remember all those things about a person you never loved.

Now I can see the heartbreak take over his face like a cloud blocking out the sun. It's more than nostalgia. It's longing, pain.

"Jackie?" he says, calling me back to life.

"Hi, yes—was not expecting you to hit me in my feels. Geez. Uhm, okay. What kind of things would Kenzie do for you?"

I see him begin to close himself off. "Why?"

"Because people usually love others in their own love language. So the way Kenzie showed you love is probably how she wants you to show her love, too." I mentally thank Julie for teaching me this last summer when she cried over a basket of chocolate-dipped fruit that Massimo had sent to the house.

Oh—I need to save this for the blog! *Mental note: love languages.*

I wince when I remember the hundreds of messages that have been piling up, messages that I've sort of been avoiding. Wilson has been serving as a disturbingly real reminder that the words I post actually have an impact on someone's life. That somewhere out there, there's a person on the receiving end of my advice who is mere inches from potentially having their heart broken. Witnessing Wilson sulk around for days seems to have put a very inconvenient soft spot on my heart.

Although there are people waiting for me on *iDiary* who need my help, there's also a person sitting across from me who needs it, too. And yet Wilson seems more pressing.

Tammy arrives at our table to quickly fill up our water. Wilson waits for her to leave before he says, "Uhm, she was always giving me things? Like cookies she baked, or a notebook she saw and thought I'd like. Or if I mentioned I needed a new T-shirt, she'd pick one up without me asking her to."

I nod, the plan clicking into place. "Gift giving. That's my sister's love language, too. Okay, perfect. So we need to plan some extravagant gift for her—"

"No," Wilson says, cutting me off. "Nothing extravagant. She doesn't like that. She's sentimental. All she ever wanted for her birthday was a card, and she'd always remind me to write a long message in it. She even had this box in her closet where she'd save all our things. Like, the coffee sleeve from a café, stuff like that."

Wilson talking about Kenzie is entirely different from Wilson not talking about Kenzie. One is smiling, happy, with this faraway look in his eyes. The other is sad, slouched, like a flower taken away from sunlight for too long.

"Okay, so we stick to the same plan of buying her a gift, but nothing too fancy. Instead, something that shows her how you remember all her little details. What about a gift basket? You can make it yourself, fill it with all her favorite things, then deliver it to her house."

"That sounds great, actually," Wilson says.

"Then why do you look disgusted?"

His nose is all scrunched up.

He crosses him arms defiantly. "I'm not used to you having good ideas."

"Okay, rude. I suggested two months ago that we get a vending machine for the break room that dispenses candy for free. That was a *great* idea."

"Jackie, that's terrible. At this rate, you'll lose all your teeth by thirty."

I shrug. "Then start giving us full-timers benefits so we can actually afford to go to the dentist."

"It's not in our budget," he says like a true boss.

"How convenient."

Tammy appears again, smiling wide. "Can I grab some to-go boxes?"

"Sure," I say as Wilson says, "No thank you."

In less than ten seconds, she's back with a Styrofoam box. We both groan.

"Don't give me that face. I have no choice," I say to Wilson as I shove the rest of my food into this nonbiodegradable hell. We both pay for our bills—is it weird that I expected Wilson to pay for mine?—and leave. We stand outside Wilson's car, sweating our asses off in the heat.

"So, a gift basket," he says. "You think it'll work?"

I hug the box of food to my chest. "It's a starting point."

Wilson nods. He grabs his sunglasses out of his pocket and puts them on. "Let's get back to work. Your lunch break ended eight minutes ago. Don't worry—I'll deduct it from your pay."

And just like that, we're back.

CHAPTER 14

JULIE'S CAT—WHO I HAVE now named Mr. Chunks—and I have built the kind of bond that most people can't understand. We keep each other company without disturbing either one's peace. We both understand the desire for as little human connection as possible, and that's why he is my new favorite family member—sorry, Julie. You've been booted out.

I sit on the couch with my laptop while he sleeps beneath the couch, his soft snores filling the late-night silence. Mr. Chunks still hasn't braved the unknown and traveled out from his hideaway. He remains nestled against the wall the entire day, coming out to eat only at night when everyone is asleep. How do we know this? Well, Julie claims that his food bowl is empty in the morning. So he must be sneaking out to eat when no one is around. Maybe he's self-conscious, poor guy.

After spending the day with Wilson—what the hell kind of

sentence was that?—I felt the need to distract myself with as many forms of technology as humanly possible in order to stop replaying our conversation over and over in my head.

Or I stop thinking about the look in his eyes when he talks about Kenzie.

Or that he knows she gets her nails done every three weeks and doesn't drink caffeine.

A world where Wilson Monroe is a good boyfriend is not a world I can happily inhabit. And somehow, here I am, alive on this planet and working with this person I thought I had entirely figured out. Just when I'm getting smug, he comes in with an entirely new personality that catches me off guard. Up until this point I assumed that Wilson's chest was filled with rocks, ribs, and maybe, like, a very large piece of coal. Turns out he in fact has a heart. It may be about five sizes too small, but it still beats faintly inside of him. And when it does, it clearly beats for Kenzie.

Yeah, I need to adjust the volume on my music. I shove my headphones deeper into my ears and crank it up. The TV is on too, even though I can't hear it. I need the visual distraction though, just in case I begin veering off course.

Another thing: How do we have the same order? Down to the extra crispy fries? The same restaurant? Why do so many of my favorites intertwine with his when he is my *least* favorite thing?

I fan myself with my hand, beginning to feel warm. Did Julie shut the air-conditioning off again?

Okay, focus. *iDiary*. Gosh, I wish someone had warned me that having two jobs and running a somewhat popular blog would be difficult. I open the app and am once again bombarded with an insane amount of notifications. My follower count has now grown to nineteen thousand, and my inbox is so full it's a flood risk.

I'm still hyperaware that my advice could hurt someone, but it feels almost *more* cruel to leave all these people stranded without answers. I at least owe it to them to provide the service they signed up for. Maybe I simply need to go about it more cautiously now.

I click on the first unread message from @sarah.shining. They wrote:

Lately it's been feeling like my partner is drifting away from me. They're dodging my calls and are never free to hang out. I can't tell if she's hiding something from me or is on the verge of breaking up with me, which is the last thing I want. How do you confront someone who is avoiding you?

For the first time, I try to analyze this message from the perspective of the partner. If they are pulling back from the relationship, there might be a good reason. Maybe they are going through a big life change, something too scary to talk about. Or maybe this is a moment that can be used to bring them back together, not pull them apart.

Normally, I'd write up some sassy response advising @sarah.shining to dump their partner for their dodgy behavior. Now I think I'm going to say the opposite.

I write back:

It's always scary when you feel your partner pulling away from you. When your first instinct is to assume something is wrong in the relationship, try to remember that maybe it's not about you. Maybe they're struggling and need to feel their partner reaching out. Perhaps this is a moment where you need to step up—let them know you're there to talk, to confide in. Use this as an opportunity to bring you closer together. At least that way, you did all you could to help them.

After I post the response, the doorbell rings. It's past eleven p.m., which means it can only be one person. The door swings and open, and yup, it's Suzy. She has a scowl on her face, camera slung around her neck, and a pint of ice cream in one hand.

"Well, well, well. If it isn't my best friend, Jackie Myers," she says, holding the ice cream hostage against her chest.

I try to recall if I've done something lately to upset her, and I can't remember. With a sinking feeling, I worry that this might be the problem in itself.

"Hello," I say slowly, hesitantly. "Did you want to come in?"

"No. I'm standing here with my camera and a container of ice cream because I want to sit on your driveway."

I open the door all the way. "Come in, meanie."

It isn't until we are on the couch, spoons in hand, digging into the ice cream when Suzy finally eases up on the hostility. "You never called me back last week," she says, digging a piece of cookie dough out of the carton—which is, quite honestly, her most toxic trait. She never leaves any for the rest of us.

And then it dawns on me—Suzy texting me before work, asking me to call her urgently, and me forgetting to do all of that.

I sigh. "I'm the worst friend ever. I'm sorry."

"Not the worst friend *ever*. But you have been a bit distant lately. What's going on?"

"I've been so busy, Suz. With working two jobs, helping Wilson win back Kenzie, and running this blog. It's like I barely have—"

"I'm sorry. You're helping Wilson with *what*?"

I wince, totally realizing I forgot to fill her in. By the time I do, we have finished the entire ice-cream carton, and Suzy sighs, understanding just how hectic my life has become.

"I get it," she says, "and I think helping Wilson is the right thing to do. But this is also our last summer together, Jackie. Can we not spend it totally apart?"

I nod, agreeing. "Yes, definitely. You're right. I'll free up some time for us to hang out."

She smiles. "Now get off your laptop before internet fame changes you," she teases.

"Pretty sure I'm still a loser, but now I'm a loser who's about to break twenty k followers," I inform her.

At that, her eyes grow wide. "No kidding."

I hand her my laptop and she scrolls through the account, the word *wow* momentarily taking over her vocabulary.

She hands it back to me. "You know, I was doing some research, which is actually what I wanted to tell you about last week when you never called." She pauses dramatically to pin me with a laser-shooting glare. "Basically, when you hit twenty thousand followers, you can monetize your account."

I blink. "What?"

"Yeah," she continues casually. "It's some program you sign up for, and they add a shit-ton of ads to your page. The larger the number of people who view them, the more money you earn. I don't think it's anything crazy—maybe like a hundred bucks or so a month. But still, it's something."

I immediately begin researching this and find an article under the *iDiary* Help section. It's titled "Join Our Creators Program!" and it says that you can earn around two to five dollars for every thousand account views.

I do some quick mental math, remember that I can barely count, and pull up the calculator app. "One hundred thirteen," I say. "That's how many more followers I need to join the program."

Suzy scoots closer to me on the couch, peering at the laptop screen. "How long is that going to take?"

I refresh the page. "Now I need eighty-six."

"Oh, damn. So not long at all."

By the time we finish the pint and I get brain freeze twice, I refresh the screen and see those glorious four zeros. "Twenty k!" Suzy whisper yells. A banner instantly pops up on the top of the page, prompting me to join the creators program.

"Wait," Suzy says as I'm about to click the button. "It's going to make your account really ugly. Like, there will be ads *everywhere*, Jackie. Might that deter some people from looking at your page?"

"Maybe," I say, "but once I save enough money to afford my car, I'll leave the program and disable the ads. Easy-peasy."

"You're sure?" Suzy asks, discarding the empty ice-cream container on the coffee table.

"I'm certain." I click the button and enter my contact information and mailing address. It explains that revenue will be mailed out in monthly checks, as long as the amount is over ten dollars. After signing up, ads can take up to forty-eight hours to appear. I skim through the rest of the terms and conditions, then hit Submit. When I look up, I'm grinning. Suzy has her camera out, recording me.

I can see myself watching her documentary months from now. Maybe at that point I'll be watching it from California, or when I'm a writer at *The Rundown*, or when I've been repromoted to waitress at Monte's. Maybe then I'll have a hundred thousand followers and I'll have been interviewed for one of those morning talk shows. Maybe I'll know exactly what I want. Exactly who I am.

For maybe the first time ever, looking ahead doesn't feel so dull. Or scary. Or limiting. Now, looking ahead feels exciting. It feels like new paths have been rolled out before me, like I can go this way or that if I please.

"I can see it, Jacks," Suzy says, spinning the camera around so we're both in the shot. "In a month from now, we're going to be cruising down the Pacific Coast Highway."

When I close my eyes, I can see it, too.

CHAPTER 15

"PRETTY SURE THIS CLASSIFIES as unsafe working conditions," Jill yells, aiming the words at Camilla's closed door. The air-conditioning broke last night, and the office is teetering on one billion degrees.

I'm slouched over in my desk chair, sweat dripping from my eyebrows while I type out summaries of all the businesses that have called in this week looking to be featured. Once that's finished and all websites have been linked, I'll email the list to Camilla. We typically get a couple of calls like that per week, some local business for free press coverage. As Camilla puts it, "We lend a voice to people who are overlooked."

While I jot down the contact info for a new candy store in the neighborhood, I'm surprised by my own good mood. Normally, I'd be trying to find an excuse to leave early and head home to the air-conditioning. But I'm actually enjoying this. I *like* doing this, in the same way I like running *pleasebreakmyheart,* the same way I used to like being a waitress.

I just can't put my finger on the thread that connects them all. Why don't these jobs make me itch out of my skin, like all my previous attempts at finding something to love?

It dawns on me then. I think the commonality between all of them is taking care of people. I spent my entire life around two older sisters who took care of me in more ways than I can count. I remember how safe it made me feel, how protected, how supported. Now I get to turn the tables. *I* get to be the one helping others. And maybe that's why it feels so rewarding, to be paying that sentiment forward.

Which is why I don't complain when I spend the next hour calling every HVACR company in town to find someone to come fix the air-conditioning. When I have someone booked in, I email it over to Camilla.

Seconds later, the door to her office opens. Her thick brown hair is clipped up, and a slight sheen of sweat glistens on her forehead. "Jackie found someone to come tomorrow to repair—"

"*Tomorrow?*" they all groan. I slide down in my chair, hiding from view.

Camilla leans against the doorframe, dabbing a yellow polka-dot cloth on her face. "It's the soonest they can make it. Jackie, can you open the front door? Try to get some sort of breeze in here?"

"Sure," I say, grateful for an excuse to step away from my

laptop. I grab a heavy vase off the coffee table and use it as a door-stop. Even with the door entirely open, it barely helps. It's stagnant and humid outside, without so much as a trace of a breeze.

My phone buzzes with a text from Wilson, who has clearly violated some sort of employee-confidentiality agreement to get my number. He sent a photo of a brown wicker basket with two handles on the side and a white fabric basket that looks like the one Julie has in her bedroom. With the photo, he wrote *Which one?*

Of course he texts with uppercase letters.

I'm assuming he's choosing a basket for Kenzie's gift. *shouldn't you be at work?* I write back in all lowercase like a normal person.

Air-conditioning broke so we closed early. It will be fixed by tomorrow in time for your shift. Don't worry.

oh thank god. i was SO terrified i'd have the night off.

It's beginning to feel like the universe is playing some kind of joke on me, throwing in yet another similarity between me and Wilson. It's not enough that I spend the day sweating through my clothes. Now I need to know that he's doing the same thing a few miles away? Ridiculous.

The bubble to indicate he's typing pops up, then goes away like he's changed his mind. Then pops up again. *Which basket is better?*

are you asking because you value my opinion?

No.

I perch myself on the couch, fingers flying across the keyboard. *then ask someone else,* I write back.

He responds with: *Jackie.* I can so clearly hear his voice saying my name, stressing the *k* sound too harshly, that familiar mix of impatience and intolerance.

He sends another text. *Fine. I value it a very small bit. Which basket??*

the one on the left.

You couldn't have said that from the beginning and spared me this conversation?

"Who are you texting with that big smile on your face?"

I jump, looking up to find Maude standing in front of me with a knowing smirk on her face.

"What? I'm not—" But I realize that she's right. I *am* smiling. At my phone. While texting Wilson.

The heat has officially driven me insane.

"Fine, fine, keep it a secret. But I hope it works out." Maude winks, grabbing a candy from the bowl before returning to her desk.

I shrug off her comment, suck in one final breath of fresh air, and head back to my desk. Camilla is standing next to it, chatting with Jill. The sight of them together reminds me that I've completely dropped the ball on figuring out what the hell is going on with them. This looks like the perfect time to jump back in.

Camilla steps to the side when I sit in my chair. I expect them to immediately stop talking as per usual, but they continue the conversation like I'm not even there.

"Have you figured out how to contact her?" Camilla asks, leaning against the back of Jillian's chair and staring at her computer screen.

"I can't find an email anywhere. Her account is like a freaking crypt. No name, contact info, nothing. She's completely anonymous," Jill says, ending with a sigh.

Despite the heat, I feel a cool tingle down my spine.

"Maybe we need to bite the bullet and contact her like everyone else does," Camilla says.

Jill spins around in her chair until they're face-to-face. "Send her a message? Isn't that too . . . informal?"

171

I try to sneak a peek at Jill's computer screen, but it's angled too far away. There's no way they can be talking about what I think they're talking about.

"I'd normally say you, but it seems like the only way to get a hold of her. If we want to nail this story, I'm thinking we have to get creative. Send her a message, let her know the story we're trying to run, and include your email address. The second she responds, let me know."

"Yeah. Will do," Jill says. By her tone alone, I can pick up on the stress she's feeling.

I watch as Camilla gently lays her hand on Jill's shoulder. "And great work." Then she heads back into her office, keeping the door open this time.

Jill spins her chair back around, facing her computer. She catches me staring. Her eyes narrow. "What do you want?"

I nod at the computer. "What was that about?"

She blows out a long breath and looks around the room quickly. Michelle, who sits closest to us, has her headphones on, and everyone else is too distracted to notice. Still, Jill leans in and lowers her voice when she says, "There's a promotion up for grabs."

"No way. What's the position?"

"Senior writer," she says quietly. "It comes with a big pay increase, too. Like, huge."

I smile widely. "That's amazing. Have you spoken to Camilla about it?"

"I have, but she's considering a couple other people in the office, too. Which is why I need to nail this interview, to show her that I'm the best journalist we have."

"You are," I say. It's true. I've subscribed to *The Rundown* for over a year now, ever since Jill first started. I've read so many articles written by her coworkers, and, don't get me wrong, they're all great. Every single one of them has such a unique voice and style that creates this literary montage. But Jill's pieces have an intimacy to them, as if she totally immerses herself in these peoples' lives to write articles that perfectly capture *them* in a vulnerable, flattering light.

Jill is like me—we both see Ridgewood as a stop along the way. It's not where we're meant to end up. Julie is different. Julie has a career here; she's building a family. She wants the white picket fence and the husband who comes home from work at five. For her, Ridgewood is enough. It's home in a way that it will never be for the two of us.

I know what this promotion means to Jill. A better job, a better résumé, a better chance to move to a different newspaper in a city far, far away. It's the same reason I work two jobs and fight to afford a car. It's a means of escape. A way to go see Suzy, sure. But it's more than that. It's the comfort that comes with knowing that at any moment, at any chance I have, I can get in, drive, and never look back.

Sometimes reality is easier to face when it feels like you have an escape route.

Even with the stress and the heat I can see the sparkle of excitement shining in her eyes. "This is *the* story, Jackie. If I can make this happen, the job is mine."

A bead of sweat drips from my brow. "What story is it?" I ask, dreading the answer.

Jill clams up. "I don't want to say too much and jinx it," she says, superstitious as ever. "I need to send off this message and hope for the best."

I gulp. "You got this."

My mind is racing with every worst-case scenario. I try to gaslight myself into believing I'm fine, that nothing is going on, that I'm reading too much into nothing, but I can't shake the feeling that the person my sister is desperately trying to interview is *me*.

To quiet my mind, I begin my next task: transcribing old interviews. But I'm too distracted to make it through a single sentence. My gaze keeps wandering back to Jillian, who has been typing and deleting the same sentence a dozen times now.

"Pssst . . . Jackie," Michelle calls from her desk, her headphones now resting on her neck. "You okay? Your face is beet red."

I touch the back of my hand to my forehead and feel how hot it is. "Fine, yeah. Just hot."

Michelle heads over to the mini fridge, then tosses a can of Diet Coke at me. By some miracle, I catch it. "Drink that, and water, too. You need something to eat? I have a protein bar in here somewhere . . ." She begins digging around in her purse.

I press the cold can to my neck. "This is great. Thanks," I say. I *do* feel like I'm about to pass out, but the heat has nothing to do with it.

"You do look terrible," Jill chimes in, fingers hovering above her keyboard. "Do you want to go home?"

"No," I say quickly. I need to stay here and monitor this potential situation.

Jill only shakes her head. "Whatever you say," she says, returning her attention to the computer screen.

The next five minutes tick by in slow agony. I've retyped the same sentence into a half-blank Word document about thirty-seven times. I've chugged the entire can of Diet Coke, and now the caffeine is making me feel jittery. My foot is tapping on the floor. I'm unsure when I even began doing that, but I can't seem to stop.

Then Jill pushes away from the desk, her chair wheeling a few feet back. "Done," she declares, standing up and stretching her neck. My gaze followers her to the mini fridge, watching as she pulls out a water bottle. Then she starts talking with Fatima, buying me a few seconds.

I can't help but look at my phone. I have to check. I have to *know*.

After dimming the screen brightness, I pull up my *iDiary* inbox and wait for it to load. As soon as I see the text, I sink into my chair.

Hey pleasebreakmyheart. I'm Jillian, a journalist from the women-owned and -operated online magazine called The Rundown. We're fascinated by the community you've built here and would love to learn more about you, the account, and what inspired it. Send me an email over at jill@ therundown.com so we can schedule a time to talk.

I read it again, hoping the text will begin to rearrange itself into an entirely new message and I'm actually just illiterate. But nope, the letters remain exactly where they are.

So Jillian's promotion relies on her securing an interview with me, where she will no doubt figure out who I am and blow the entire anonymous presence I've now spent weeks building. Where she'll realize I've been recycling bits and pieces from *her* life, reusing and rewording them to fit into new molds. I had convinced myself she'd be proud of me, but after seeing how this blog affected Wilson, I'm not so sure anymore. What if Jill feels betrayed? Taken advantage of? *Exposed*?

What if I have to go back to pre-*pleasebreakmyheart* Jackie? The version of me that wasn't good at *anything*?

I can't lose this blog. Not yet.

But I can't let Jill lose this promotion after hearing how badly she wants it.

As the rest of the day flies by, I desperately try to come up with a solution. Then it's five o'clock, and Michelle is offering me a ride home. As usual, Jillian is staying late. If I had a feeling

176

that she and Camilla were secretly back together, this full-on confirmed it. Everyone knows "staying late" is the universal way to say "sleeping with my boss." I just need to poke around a bit more and find concrete evidence to confirm these suspicions.

By the time Michelle and I settle into her car, I realize that I forgot my backpack in the office.

"I'll be right back," I say, already annoyed at having to abandon the air-conditioning blasting at my face.

I run back up the street. As I'm waiting for the light to turn red so I can cross, I see the front office door open. Jill walks outside, then Camilla behind her. Camilla locks the door, and the two of them walk to Jill's car, which is parallel parked right outside.

I'm so hung up on the fact that the door is now locked, with my backpack inside, it barely hits me that they are getting into the car *together*. When it does, I come to a full stop.

Jill's car windows are barely tinted, and I watch as they sit down inside, talking and grinning the entire time. And then the worst possible thing happens.

They kiss.

CHAPTER 16

THE ENTIRE CAR RIDE home with Michelle, I don't say a word. I'm completely lost in my own head.

Jillian and Camilla kissed. There's no doubt that they're back together.

The realization flings me back through time to the heartbreak Jill went through. To the crying, the angry stomping, the way talking to her felt like trying to run your hand along jagged glass. She was this explosive version of herself for months all because of Camilla.

Then I think about Julie, who is president of the We Hate Camilla fan club and is going to absolutely lose her mind when she finds out about this. Even if Jill could forgive Camilla so easily, she's going to have a hard time convincing the rest of my family to do the same.

Maybe there's more to the story. I know Jillian—she will

gladly take a grudge to her grave. For her to forgive Camilla means there must be something she isn't telling us. Some other crucial information that led to their breakup that she's kept close to her heart.

When Michelle pulls up in front of my house, I'm feeling sick to my stomach. I thank her for the ride and head inside, pausing at the front door. I really can't spend tonight sitting across from Jill at the dining table, pretending I didn't just watch her make out with Camilla.

I need to get as far away from this house as possible, which is how I end up at Suzy's for dinner.

We sit outside with her parents on their deck, eating barbecued beef short ribs, loaded baked potatoes, and a gigantic salad. Suzy's dad is Korean, and her mom is an American who loves to cook, which results in dinners that are heavy on classics while Ms. Cho tries to tie in some of the food her husband ate growing up, too. Tonight, the beef falls right off the bone and has this tangy flavor that's both sweet and spicy.

After dinner, we retreat to Suzy's bedroom, which looks more like a movie theater. She has a projector on the ceiling, a drop-down screen on the wall, and a bunch of beanbag chairs over a fuzzy polka-dot carpet. We have a lifelong history of spending Friday nights here, loaded up on popcorn and watching whatever movie Suzy deems a must-watch. At the end of the night, I usually scroll through my phone while she writes up her Letterboxd review.

While Suzy sets up the projector, I reluctantly answer a few messages on *pleasebreakmyheart*. I still can't bring myself to abandon the blog entirely. Leaving all these people hanging just feels wrong. Plus, it's gotten to the point now where I can barely keep up with the demand. I'd need to employ an entire team of people to make it through the hundreds of unread messages.

"Romance or drama?" Suzy asks.

"Drama," I say instantly. While reading through these heartbreak horrors, the last thing I want to watch is two people in their picture-perfect relationship.

I fire off responses for the three most recent messages, making sure to leave the advice more open-ended and less do-this-or-else. It seems to be the only way I can continue running this blog with a clear conscience, knowing that at the end of the day, the person asking for advice—not me—is in charge of their own fate.

The fourth message I read stumps me. It's from @katiecat99:

What do you do when you're the problem, not them? I have a life's worth of trust issues that are stopping me from letting my boyfriend in. I don't want to let him go, but it feels nearly impossible to open up to him. What do I do?

My heart instantly hurts for Katie. In a way, it seems like this question is less about their relationship and more about *her*. It reminds me of something Julie said once: right person, wrong

180

time. Who she said it about, I can't remember. But the sentiment rings true.

I write back:

First, you are the furthest thing from a problem. Sounds to me like there's trauma you are sorting through, and you're allowed to take time and space to navigate that. I think here you need to prioritize communication. Talk with your boyfriend and let him know your struggles. This is a time for him to be patient and understanding. If he can't offer you that, perhaps you need to focus on yourself and healing from your past before letting someone else in. I wish you the best!

I post the message, smiling to myself.

"What are you grinning about?" Suzy asks, collapsing back in her beanbag chair.

"I think I just gave some pretty great advice."

"Yeah? How's the blog going?"

"Good," I say. "I've taken a bit of a new approach, and I think it's working out well."

"Why is that?" she asks. On the screen, the opening credits for *The Social Network* begin to play.

"The situation with Wilson made me realize that there are real people on the receiving end of my advice. I guess I'm trying to be more careful with what I put out there."

Suzy smiles. "That's a great idea." Then the screen takes up all her attention. "There's this one scene with Andrew Garfield that's *amazing*, Jack. You'll see."

I pay attention for the first half of the movie. Then my mind decides to fixate on the Camilla and Jillian situation. Do I confront Jill? Do I tell Julie? I can't seem to figure out what lines I do and do not cross, or if it's even my place to cross them at all.

Then there's Jillian's interview, which I completely forgot about until right now. That's a whole other trap I need to somehow get myself out of. It feels like I'm jumping through loop after loop, and at some point I'm bound to trip up, fall, and land flat on my face.

When my phone rings, the sound startles me so bad I scream. Suzy pauses the movie. I look at the screen and find an incoming call from—

"Wilson?" I say, shocked. It's half past nine. What could he need at this time?

Suzy practically climbs into my beanbag chair with me. "Oh my gosh. Put it on speaker."

But I already have the phone pressed firmly to my ear, Wilson's breathing pulling through from the other end. "Hello?" I say.

"Jackie. Hi."

The sound of his voice lightens the tension that's been building in my chest.

I can hear the surprise in his two words, too. But is it surprise that he called, or surprise that I picked up? "Are you free?" he continues.

"I'm at my friend's house," I say slowly. Suzy is mouthing for me to put the phone on speaker. Reluctantly, I do.

Wilson sighs, the frustration clear in the ragged breath. "Do you think you could—" He stops himself. I hear footsteps, like he's pacing back and forth. "You know what? Never mind. I shouldn't have—"

"Wilson, spit it out."

He does. When he speaks, it sounds as if he's forcing the words out through clenched teeth. "I need some help. I'm struggling with this gift basket."

"You just place the items inside, Willy," I say. Wilson asking me for help fills me with so much righteous air I may as well be a balloon.

"I—" Another sigh. "I can't make it look nice."

I have this clear vision of him pinching the bridge of his nose, absolutely despising himself for having to turn to me.

"Nothing fits right," he continues. "And I can't figure out how to make everything stay *up*." As soon as he says that, there's a crashing noise in the background as if, on cue, an item fell out of the basket. Wilson swears beneath his breath. "See?"

I hold back a laugh. Beside me, Suzy is snickering into a pillow. "Have you tried watching a tutorial?"

"Of course I have, Jackie," he deadpans. "That's the first

thing I did. Clearly, they are quite difficult to follow."

I have this sudden image in my head of Wilson intensely studying a computer with flushed cheeks, inserting each item into the basket this way and that, losing his patience when nothing seems to be working just right.

"Which basket did you choose?" I ask, remembering the text he sent earlier.

"The one you suggested."

I grin. "Good."

"So—is that a yes?"

"I don't believe you asked me a question," I say. If Wilson was a remote, consider all of his buttons pressed.

The line goes silent for so long I think he may have disconnected. Then his voice returns, laced with the classic annoyance. "Will you come by and help me assemble this godforsaken basket?"

I turn to Suzy for approval. She rolls her eyes like she's annoyed, but nods anyway.

"Sure, I can come. Where are you?"

"Monte's."

I groan. "I don't step foot in there unless I'm getting paid."

"You can leave an hour early tomorrow," he says with no hesitation. If it wasn't clear before, it is now—Wilson has officially hit rock bottom. Luckily, I'm ready to take advantage of it.

"Deal," I say. "Be there in fifteen." I hang up the phone for no reason other than to annoy him just a tiny bit more. Suzy is already up, pulling a gray hoodie over her T-shirt. "This should be quick," I say to her. "If you give me a ride, we can be back in under an hour and finish the movie."

Suzy thinks on it. "Fine. But I get to bring my camera and record whatever I want."

"Not *whatever* you want—"

"Take it or leave it," she cuts in stubbornly.

It's late. It's dark. The best footage she'll get is me walking to and from the door to Monte's, which isn't very damaging. "I'll take it."

In five minutes, we're in her dad's car, driving through an eerily quiet neighborhood.

"Don't you think this is a bit weird?" Suzy asks after a few moments of silence.

"I don't know," I say, looking at the McDonald's sign as we drive past. The yellow neon *M* is tipping over, making it look more like a *W*. "The sign's been broken for so long. I doubt anyone will ever fix it."

Suzy snorts. "Not the sign, dummy. I mean Wilson calling you and asking you to help him."

"It's a little weird, sure. But this is what we agreed on." Even as I say it, I'm not entirely certain I believe it myself.

"You really think you can win back his ex?"

The million-dollar question. "We better," I say, "because that's the only way I'm getting my old job back and we're affording a road trip."

Suzy pulls into the parking lot. The second she shifts into park, her camera is in her hands and trained on my face. "I shouldn't be more than fifteen, twenty minutes," I promise, jumping out of the car and running to the front door. I can feel the camera following my every move, searching for a story that may or may not already be there.

All I know is that before Suzy agreed to hit Pause on movie night, a big glaring *yes* had already formed in my head. That no matter what her answer was, I would have ended up here at Monte's somehow. And I tell myself I'm doing this to honor our deal: Wilson wins Kenzie back and I get to ditch the frog costume for my old waitress job. But as I walk up the sidewalk to the front door, I realize that there has been a pivotal shift I hadn't thought about. Or maybe I did, but I chose to ignore it.

Because when I raise my hand to knock on the glass, I'm filled with a very specific feeling. Only this time, it isn't annoyance.

This time, it feels suspiciously like excitement.

CHAPTER 17

WILSON'S OFFICE LOOKS LIKE a war zone. There is a basket on his desk and three thrown in the corner. Crinkled-up tissue paper is littered all over the floor, and there are so many *things* covering his desk that the wood is barely visible.

Wilson matches the dishevelment, too. The top two buttons on his shirt are undone, and his hair sticks up at fifteen different angles. His eyes are red, and the skin beneath them puffs out, like he's rubbed that spot one too many times. Seeing him look so off in the space where he's normally the most put together feels strange. I catch myself doing a double, triple take.

"Four baskets?" I ask, picking up a white one that looks like it once belonged to the Easter Bunny.

"I couldn't decide which was best, so I bought them all," he says, sinking into the desk chair like a defeated man. "*Why* are there so many different types of basket? What do people do with these?"

It's so ridiculously innocent, I can't help but laugh. "Use them for decor," I say. "Fill them with blankets, pillows, pet toys, anything."

"Well, they need to be banned," he says very quickly, like this is a conclusion he arrived at hours ago.

"If you say so." I grab one of the discarded baskets from the floor and sit in the chair opposite his. "First, let's declutter your desk. Which of these aren't going in the basket?"

Wilson picks up some things—candy packets, a tube of lip gloss, some sort of stuffed-animal key chain—and I shove them all into the basket. I grab a candle that seems to have dropped on the floor and broken, probably what I heard when we were on the phone.

"What about this?"

He glares at it, as if this candle personally offended him. "No."

Without asking further questions, I add it to the pile of items that didn't make the cut. A familiar gold hue catches my eye. I lift up the Twix bar, which was half buried beneath a pink bow. "What about this?"

Wilson dismisses it. "Oh, I got that for you."

I freeze, my eyes flicking up to his. "You what?"

"I got that for you," he says again, casually. "You eat like, one a day, Jackie. I'm very aware how quickly our Twix stock runs out—and the reasons behind it."

"I . . ." I trail off, unable to form a single thought. My brain is stuck on Wilson's not only knowing what my favorite chocolate bar is, but getting me one and having it on hand.

He plows ahead before I can catch up. He turns the computer screen toward me. I snap out of my daze and see a YouTube video pulled up, with a smiling elderly woman and a beautifully wrapped gift basket as the thumbnail. It's titled *Assembling the Perfect Gift Basket: A How-To Guide.*

"That's the woman you were cursing? Look at her sweet smile, Wilson. She only wants to *help* you," I tease.

He quickly shuts down the computer. "She's done enough damage. Now—what do we do?"

The brown basket Wilson chose sits atop his desk. A bunch of miscellaneous items are thrown in haphazardly, a few of them standing upright, lending me to believe that maybe, at one point, they all were. But there's a big step Wilson missed and, if we were to watch the video, I can almost guarantee it would be step number one.

"You need to stuff the basket so everything inside of it is elevated. That way, you can actually see what's in the basket without having to dig inside," I explain.

Wilson sits up straight and begins to empty the basket. "What do I stuff it with?" he says slowly, like he's beginning to catch on to his error.

"I don't know. Maybe the five hundred sheets of tissue paper on the floor?"

For the next few minutes we gather all the crumpled-up paper. The thought of Wilson entering into a battle with paper and somehow losing makes me laugh the entire time.

"Stop that," he warns, shooting me a look. We're both crouched on the floor, paper in hand.

I reach for a piece that's white with rainbow sparkles. "I didn't say anything."

"I can practically hear you making fun of me in your head."

"If you don't want to feel left out," I say, standing upright, "I can make fun of you out loud."

"That's actually worse, but thanks," he says sarcastically.

When we have gathered up all the discarded paper, I ask Wilson to sit, so he is out of my way, and I get to work. It really isn't that difficult—I stuff the paper in the basket until it nearly hits the rim; it'll boost up all the items and provide a sturdy base for them to rest on, so nothing is falling over.

"Ta-*da*," I say, presenting the basket to Wilson.

He has this shocked look on his face, like I just solved some impossible riddle that has stumped humanity for centuries. "Thanks," he says, gently holding it with both hands. I see something like relief flash across his face. "What now?"

"Now just . . . add whatever you want on top."

Wilson nods slowly, his eyes raking over the items left on the desk. When he reaches for a tiny Starbucks gift card, I swat his hand away.

"Big items first," I advise. "Big items at the back, and smaller items go in the front so they don't get blocked." I resist the urge to tack on a *duh* at the end of that sentence.

"Oh," he says with something like embarrassment.

I take a seat, cracking open the Twix bar as he places a baby pink teddy bear in the basket. The chocolate is a tiny bit melted—probably from being at the bottom of that pile for hours—but it doesn't stop me from happily munching away.

Munching away on the chocolate bar. That Wilson bought for me. As a surprise. Because he somehow remembered a tiny detail about me that I guarantee my family doesn't know.

"For the record," I say between bites, "I don't eat *that* many of these."

Wilson doesn't look at me when he speaks, his eyes trained on his hands like he's performing brain surgery. "I've seen you eat one a day for weeks."

Well I didn't realize you were watching me so closely. "Fine," I say. "Then let's turn the mirror and talk about *you*. For starters, your obsession with that shirt."

He blinks. In a split second, his eyes are heavy on mine. "What?"

"You wear a white button-up shirt to work every single day. Why is that?" I dig into the wrapper, searching for the second bar, which is why I'm too distracted to see the way his face changes. When I finally glance up, the concentration is gone. Wilson leans back against the chair, his eyes far away.

"My dad always wore one to work," he says.

Perhaps it's because I'm terrible at picking up on social cues, or possibly because I don't know Wilson well enough to pick up on his, but I ask anyway. "Where did he work?"

I realize far too late, it's a ridiculous question.

"Here," answers Wilson. "He was the manager before Monte Jr. started."

I grab a bag of assorted sour gummies and place them in the back of the basket beside the teddy bear. "Why'd he quit?" I ask, genuinely curious. I'm not too well-versed in the history of Monte's.

"He died," Wilson says quietly.

The gummies fall from my hand, knocking the teddy bear right over and taking the entire basket down with it. "Shit. Sorry." I bend over, picking everything off the floor and placing them back on the desk with the coordination of a one-handed baby.

"Here." Wilson takes over, fixing the basket and continuing to load it with all the items he picked out.

I sit there dumbfounded, having had no idea that his father passed away.

Unsure what to say, I opt for silence.

But it stretches on too long, so I desperately search for a way to fill it.

"When he worked here," I begin carefully, like I'm treading water, "he wore that shirt every day?"

The smallest of smiles lights up his typically stoic face. "Not this exact one. That'd be weird. But yeah, wearing a nicer shirt to Monte's was this thing my dad always did. He used to say you should always present yourself at your best, no matter the situation."

I'm hit with something that feels deeply like shame. I spent months mocking Wilson's shirts, his khakis, the way he always came into work looking a little too polished. Now, learning the reasoning behind it, I've never felt like a bigger jerk.

Wilson continues. "When I started working here, I decided I wanted to honor him. It's a small thing, but— I don't know. It felt right."

Within seconds, the puzzle of Wilson's life begins to click into place. Him always taking this job a bit more seriously than the rest of us. The way he left school to be here for his uncle. How, without hesitation, he stepped into the exact role his father used to fill. All the sharp, jagged edges of Wilson begin to come into focus, like I've rubbed my eyes and can see clearly through the fog.

Wilson rolls his eyes. "Please don't look at me like that."

I nearly choke on my own saliva. "Like what?"

"With the dead-dad pity. There's a reason I don't tell anyone." The basket is nearly full. He props the Starbucks gift card against the teddy bear's leg.

"It's not pity," I say honestly.

His eyes pin mine. "Then what is it?"

"I . . ." Maybe it's understanding? Sadness? Guilt? The regret that I should have acted differently? "I don't know" is what I settle on.

"Why are you telling me all this?" I ask a second later. "We aren't exactly known for having deep chats."

"I'm telling you because you asked," he says easily, "and a lot of people don't. Most think the subject is forbidden. But it's sort of the opposite. I want to talk about him. Actually, I wish people asked about him more."

"Does Kenzie ask?" The question is out there before I'm entirely sure of my reasoning behind it.

At that, he pauses. "No. She doesn't." The tone draws a clear line in the sand. This, on the other hand, *is* off topic.

"So Monte Jr.'s illness brought you here?" I ask, having a feeling that I know the answer already.

"It did. But I would have made my way back here eventually. The plan was to graduate from business school, *then* take over Monte's, figure out a way to grow it, expand. Put a Monte's Magic Castle in every state. But when my uncle got sick, I had to cut some corners. I ended up back home a lot quicker than I expected."

He put his life on hold, uprooted his relationship, to show up for his family. To sink his feet into the footsteps that were right here waiting for him.

"Wow," I breathe.

The finished basket sits untouched between us.

"Does anyone here know about your dad?" I ask. I'm assuming they don't, or we'd have acted a lot differently.

Wilson shrugs. "It's not a secret. There's a paper in the break room that outlines all the old managers at Monte's. I don't think anyone cares enough to read it." *Or to ask,* is what he doesn't say.

"Maybe you should tell them," I say, picking at a thread in my leggings.

At that, he chuckles. "I don't need to guilt people into liking me, Jackie."

It still catches me by surprise every time Wilson calls me by my real name.

"The people here . . . like you," I lie. I can't even say it with a straight face. Before the sentence is out, I'm laughing.

I look up to find Wilson smiling, too.

"You do realize my office shares a wall with the break room," he says, informing me for the first time of that very important fact. He must see the look of embarrassment on my face, because he adds, "Yeah. I hear everything that's said about me."

"We all really loved the TV in the break room," I offer.

"Kenzie's idea," he says, his expression turning solemn at the mention of her. "Look. I know everyone thinks I'm uptight. Or a tyrant, or whatever it is you all want to say. But—but I'm carrying a generations-long legacy on my shoulders. So if I'm a little too strict, it's because I'm . . ." He takes a moment to let out a breath. "Well, I guess it's because I'm afraid of letting everyone down."

It's quite jarring, the sudden urge I have to hold Wilson's hand and tell him everything will be okay.

"You're doing a good job," I say, surprised to find I genuinely mean it.

Wilson gives me this incredulous face. "I missed a few days of work and left my family business in *your* hands."

"Hey, these are great hands," I say, holding up my palms. "And you had a good reason for it."

"I could be doing a better job," says Wilson.

"Sure, you can ease up and not lose your shit if we go two minutes over our break—"

"It's more like fifteen minutes," he cuts in.

I glare, as if to say, *See? This is what I mean.* "But this place is still open. And I can say confidently that if it was up to anyone else to run Monte's, this place would be shut down the very first day. So cut yourself some slack. You're doing a *decent* job at least."

Under the table, Wilson's foot knocks into mine. "Thanks, Froggy."

For some reason, when Wilson says it this time, I don't mind it as much.

"Shall we finish up this 'godforsaken basket'? I believe that's what you called it?"

"Please," he says.

We get to work. I place a giant piece of translucent silver wrapping paper on the desk, and we fold up all the corners and wrap the basket. I tie a pretty decent bow around it, and Wilson sticks on a little tag that says To: Kenz. From: Wilson.

When all is said and done, we did a pretty good job.

We stand side by side, admiring our work propped up on the desk.

"It looks better than Mildred's basket," he says.

"Who?"

Wilson clarifies with a laugh. "The woman in the YouTube video."

"Of course her name is Mildred."

When we finish, I make no move to help Wilson clean up our mess—after all, I can only show him so much kindness at once—and we walk out of Monte's together. When I spot Suzy's car still waiting in the parking lot, I breathe a sigh of relief.

"When are you giving Kenzie the basket?" I ask as Wilson locks the door.

He frowns at his watch. "I was planning on stopping by her house tonight, but it's too late now. Probably tomorrow."

"If you need some emotional support, I don't mind tagging along." The words have left my mouth before I've fully decided to say them.

Wilson blinks down at me, like they've surprised him, too. "Yeah. Maybe. Thanks."

"And hey—when you give her the basket, don't be a weirdo about it."

Wilson looks amused. "What does that mean?"

"Like, don't hand her the basket, then drop to your knees, begging for forgiveness. This is supposed to be a nice gesture, something that lets her know you miss her and are thinking of her. Got it? Don't scare her away before we've fully gotten started."

The words burn going out. I try not to think about why.

"Got it. I won't be a weirdo." He says *weirdo* like it's our own private joke.

We stand in the parking lot together, both looking everywhere but at each other's eyes. It feels different now. Like the dynamic between us has shifted. I'm not entirely certain just yet what that means, but I don't exactly hate this new feeling in my chest.

"Well, I'll see you tomorrow," he says, kicking at the ground.

"See you," I say, waving before heading off to Suzy's car. I dare to risk a glance back. When I do, I find Wilson halfway to his car, staring back at me. I look away shyly, tugging open the passenger door and hopping inside.

In the silence, I let out a shaky breath.

"Well." Suzy's voice startles me so badly I shriek. I turn to her and find the camera still in her hand. It dawns on me that she got that entire moment on video.

"Well, what?" I ask, pretending to be casual. If you looked under my shirt, you'd see the faint outline of my heart beating through my chest.

Suzy pops the lens cap on the camera, setting it on her lap. "Well, I finally figured out what your documentary is missing."

I look out the window. I can see Wilson sitting in his car, the soft glow from the dashboard illuminating him.

"And what's that?" I ask, keeping my eyes on his face.

"A little romance."

CHAPTER 18

"YOU'RE UP, KIDDO," JILLIAN says, punching my shoulder on the way back to her desk.

Since learning of their secret relationship, I've found that the easiest thing to do is simply avoid speaking to and looking directly at Jillian and Camilla. I have developed an irrational fear that they will take one look at my guilt-ridden face and instantly realize I know everything.

Well, maybe not everything. But I do know that they're back together, and carrying around the weight of *that* secret is already giving me back pain.

I head over to the green couch that Maude sits on, waiting. She is kicking off her meet-the-writers campaign—only it has turned into a meet-the-staff campaign—and has slowly begun interviews. Michelle went first, then Jill, now me. There's also a Polaroid camera on the table that Maude's been using to take our photos. She said that Fatima's working on some cute creative pieces to launch the segment on our social channels, and something about it embodying an "early two thousands scrapbook vibe" that I completely love.

"Jackie! Hi, get comfy. Just give me one second to finish this off." She is typing on her laptop, her brown tortoiseshell glasses perched so far on the end of her nose I think they may fall off. I settle into the cushion, then wonder what to do with my hands. I grab a candy from the bowl and unwrap it. I realize too late that it's grape flavored. I'm about to spit it back into the wrapper when Maude's blue eyes flicker back up to mine. She pushes her glasses up her nose and says, "Okay. You ready to start?"

I smile through the grape-flavored pain. "Yeah."

"Awesome! So for a little overview, this campaign is meant to introduce you to our readers. It's not so much about the office or your role here, but rather the person *behind* the role. Does that make sense?"

My palms begin to sweat. It's like when someone asks what you do for fun, and suddenly you can't think of a single hobby of yours, so you end up sounding like the most boring human being alive.

"I think so," I say, knowing the only interesting thing about me is an anonymous blog that I can't speak about.

"Perfect. Let's begin with something easy. Favorite chocolate?" Maude asks.

I find myself smiling when I say, "Twix." It brings me back

to last night in Wilson's office. An unfamiliar warmth spreads through me, enough to fight off the air-conditioning that is—once again—blasting through the office.

"Jackie?"

It's just something about the fact that he remembered. Maybe being the youngest daughter has gotten me so accustomed to a very specific type of invisibility. Like how chocolate-caramel ice-cream cake is my favorite for my birthday, but my parents constantly get me vanilla Funfetti every year, a flavor I know to be Julie's favorite. Or when I was thirteen and my parents didn't want to buy me new clothing, I created a sense of style that was a mash-up of my sisters. Being the youngest has always felt like taking scraps from everyone else's life and gluing them together to make this secondhand version of mine.

So when Wilson put the stupid Twix bar in front of me and casually admitted to remembering this tiny, unimportant detail, it felt like someone was holding a magnifying glass, looking through it, and seeing me clearly for the very first time . . .

"Jackie? Everything okay?" Maude's voice cuts through the memory.

"Sorry," I say. Heat floods my cheeks, as if she can read my mind and see who it was stuck on. Or rather, who it seems to be stuck on more often than not lately.

"What was the question?" I ask.

Maude smiles kindly, ignoring the rabbit hole I fell into. "First concert you ever went to?"

"Oh, that's easy—Shania Twain," I say, calling up the memory. "I saw her as a kid with my mom and sisters."

Maude smiles down at her laptop. "Jillian said the same thing."

I risk a glance in her direction. Jill's sitting at her desk with her headphones on, nodding along to whatever song she's playing too loudly. Staring at her is the most uncanny feeling—like staring into a fun-house mirror, the kind where your reflection still looks faintly like you, but distorted in enough ways that you are unrecognizable.

For a short moment I wonder when our one-way path diverged in the forest, when we reached this impasse where we both decided to head in different directions. Jillian, with her relationship. Me, with my blog. When did sharing secrets turn into keeping them?

As the interview is wrapping up, I realize that Maude has left the heavy hitter for last. "Five years from now—where are you?"

I pause, waiting for that familiar heart-crushing feeling, like my bones are shrinking. And it's still there, but it's a lot fainter than I'm used to. For the first time, a question about my future doesn't send me over the edge. Instead, I take a second to look around me—at this office, the women sitting in it, my desk, where I've sat and learned too many new skills to count. I still don't have all the answers regarding my future, but it feels like I've found a safe place to explore a new side of myself.

"I don't know just yet," I say, "but I think I'm closer to figuring it out."

The look on Maude's face is an answer in itself. "I love that," she says kindly. "And for what it's worth, I know you will."

After she snaps my photo, Maude dismisses me and calls to Fatima. Back at my desk, I pause my music the second Camilla drags a chair over and sits next to Jill.

"So, where do we stand?" Camilla asks, her brown hair skimming Jillian's desk. I notice how closely they sit; how their bodies have this natural call-and-response. It's so completely obvious now that they're together.

Jillian closes her laptop with a huff, swiveling her chair to face Camilla. "Still no response. With all the messages pouring in, I wouldn't be surprised if they never received mine in the first place."

"Resend it," Camilla says without hesitating.

"I will. But I don't have a good feeling about this one, Cami."

I stare straight ahead at my laptop screen, pretending to be reading. Still, I haven't been able to decide on how to handle this situation. With the planning for Kenzie, running the account, and working two jobs, it feels like I've barely had enough time to even process this whole interview fiasco.

"We have to get this, Jill. This person and their account is only going to get bigger. Now is the time to get in and be the first person to get the scoop. Imagine how big a deal that would be? If *The Rundown* was the first online mag to report on this?"

Jillian grins, captivated by the vision she's spinning. "That'd be unreal."

I find myself thinking that maybe I can find a way to make this work. Maybe I can make a fake email to use to contact Jillian. I can set boundaries for the interview and make it very clear that any personal information is off-limits. That I'll only agree to do it on the condition that my anonymity be respected.

And then Camilla comes in with a sledgehammer, shattering that dream to pieces.

"What I want," she begins, "is this to be exclusive to *The Rundown*. No one gets to interview the person behind the blog except for us. With this first article we build a relationship, ask easy questions that are relatively harmless. Then, when we've gained their trust, it'll be easier to dig into the *real* story. Who are they? Why did they begin this blog? Where does this advice come from? I want to know every last detail."

I can physically see the moment when Camilla places the world on Jillian's shoulder, and Jill just sits there, trying not to get crushed by the weight of it. "I'm on it," she says, her voice wavering the slightest bit.

When Camilla leaves to talk to Michelle, I sneak a glance at my sister. "Everything okay?" I ask, feigning ignorance.

"Great," she grits out, fingers flying across the keyboard, eyes locked on the screen. "The owner of this social account won't reply to my messages. Shit. I *need* this to work out."

I see an opening and take it. "If it feels useless, maybe change direction? I'm sure there's tons of other emerging internet personalities you can interview. The other day, I saw this account

205

blowing up that's just a girl reviewing every type of Oreos and ranking them best to worst."

Jill manages a tight-lipped smile. "Thanks, but no thanks. It has to be this account, Jackie. You see how desperately Cami wants this. It's the only way I'll snag the promotion. I'll just keep reaching out."

I know that when I open *iDiary*, I'm going to have another message waiting for me.

This time, I know what to do.

Everyone slowly trickles out at five o'clock. As usual, Jill remains at her desk and Camilla in her office. I hang behind on the couch, waiting for Wilson to arrive. He sent an SOS text during my lunch break, shamefully admitting that he requires assistance to bring the gift basket to Kenzie's house.

> What if I slam the brakes
> and it flies off the seat?
> What if it breaks?

maybe try not to drive like a crazy person? is what I wrote back.

He's such a damsel in distress.

Still, I lost the battle—potentially on purpose—and got roped into being the gift basket's bodyguard. Though I suppose this *is* the job I signed up for.

When Wilson's car pulls up outside, I wave goodbye to Jillian, who barely looks up from her laptop, and head out to meet the person who is slowly feeling less and less like my enemy.

"Hello, partner in crime," I say, sliding into the passenger seat. I'm met with instant satisfaction when I realize that Wilson has the seat cooler running. For once, the leather doesn't scorch my thighs.

"Hey," he says, looking very polished in his usual getup. I can't exactly pinpoint what it is, but something about him seems different today. Brighter. Happier, maybe. "And I'm not acknowledging that nickname," he adds.

"Where's the precious cargo I've been tasked to protect?"

He snorts out a laugh. "Behind you. Be *careful*, Jackie."

I reach behind and ever so gently grab the gift basket from the back seat, placing it firmly on my lap. It looks as perfect as it did when we assembled it last night. "What if we scrap Kenzie and I keep this bad boy instead?"

Wilson actually pauses for one, two, three seconds. "No," he says sternly, driving with one hand on the wheel, and we start the drive to Kenzie's house.

"But you thought about it," I say.

"I did not."

I grip the basket when he goes over a speed bump. Wilson cuts me a glare. "*Be careful*," he says.

"You do realize you're the one driving?" I say. "And let the record show that you did pause."

"Did not."

I opt for a subject change. "How are you managing to leave Monte's so often? Shouldn't the boss actually, you know, *be there*?"

Wilson throws his arm around the back of my seat, checking his blind spot before switching lanes. "Your coworkers are a lot more capable than you think," he says, making a right at the traffic light.

He leaves his arm there, inches away from me.

I swear I can feel his fingers graze the back of my head.

I swallow. "You're dying to get back there and make sure the place hasn't burned down, aren't you?"

"Very much so, yes."

We pull into a residential area, and the car slows. The streets are lined with newly built homes, with towering arches and gray brick. A woman in a bright pink workout set is running along the sidewalk, her fluffy golden retriever following behind.

Wilson hasn't pulled his arm away yet.

"Who is she staying with again?" I ask, trying and failing to recall the conversation we had about Kenzie weeks ago.

"Her aunt and uncle." Something like nerves have crept their way into Wilson's usually steady voice. "Her family lives in New York City," he explains, "so she's staying here for, well—I don't know how long anymore."

I watch the way his brows form a knot between his eyes. It must be such a weird feeling, to go from knowing everything about someone to knowing nothing.

We pull up in front of a house where Kenzie's baby blue Mini Cooper is parked in the driveway. When I look over at Wilson, it looks like he's trying to steady his breath.

"Nervous?" I ask.

His smile is different from the few I've seen before. It's timid, shy. Like he's trying to tuck it away into the corners of his face before I can notice it. But he's too slow. Or maybe I'm too quick, because I seem to have gotten really good at recognizing Wilson's smiles and the way they seem to brighten his face like the sun after a storm.

"A little," he whispers.

His hand is still on the back of my seat.

I feel the smallest sensation, like someone twirling a strand of my hair, and attribute it to the wind.

When I sneak a glance, all the car windows are closed.

"It's Kenzie," I say, scrounging up some shred of certainty. "The person you love. The person you've spent months of your life with. She isn't a stranger you need to impress, right?"

His pink lips press into a straight line. "No. I guess she isn't."

I hand Wilson the basket, only because it seems I can't stand to be touching it anymore. "Go knock on that door and hand her this. That's all you have to do."

"What do I say?"

I pause for a split second, taking in a moment so brief that I doubt he even notices. It's the way Wilson sits there uncertainly, the way his fingers toy with the pink ribbon on the basket. The nerves ripple off his body in tsunami-like waves, but I can't begin to fathom why. This is Wilson—the guy who notices, who pays attention. Who knows Kenzie's allergies, the way she takes her tea, the color she paints her nails. I bet if I sat here and asked, there are a hundred more facts he could spit out about her, all while that faraway, blissful contentment paints his features with a lovestruck hue. It dawns on me that he's nervous for no reason. There is absolutely no way Kenzie won't take him back. How could she not? How could she lose this twice?

Sure, he's a pain in my ass. And yes, he may take his job a bit too seriously, if not for good reason. But Wilson has good intentions. He isn't impulsive or irrational. Every move, every word, is meticulously thought out—and Kenzie happens to be the lucky one who occupies most of his thoughts. He has put so much effort into getting her back that it actually stings my heart when I think about it too much.

Wilson is staring at me, his brown eyes peeking out shyly beneath a layer of thick black lashes.

"Say you miss her," I answer, my voice heavy with an emotion I still struggle to place. "And that you're thinking of her. That—that if she's up for it, you should find a time to talk."

Wilson nods, like he's committing this to memory. "Okay. Okay, yeah. I think I can do that."

He gets out of the car. When the door closes, my eyes meet the floor. I don't know if I can do it. Watch him walk up the driveway, watch his hand knock on the door—

There's a tap on my window. I glance up into Wilson's eyes, this goofy grin on his face.

I roll the window down. "Wish me luck, Froggy," he says.

I realize this is the pivotal moment. That speak now moment— where I'm sitting in the church pews watching their wedding procession, and I have one final chance to get up, say something, stop the future from unfolding the only way it can.

I swallow every word that hovers on the tip of my tongue and match Wilson's smile. "Good luck, Willy," I say.

He begins his trek up to the porch.

Even though I don't want to, I can't seem to look away. Not as he knocks. Or when the door is tugged open. Especially not when Kenzie stands there, her jaw wide-open. She takes the basket. She hugs him.

My phone buzzes with a notification from *iDiary*. I have new messages waiting. Finally fed up with putting off the inevitable, I open the app and dig through until I find the second message from Jillian. It just came in minutes ago. It says:

Hey! Jillian again from The Rundown. Checking back in to see if you're interested in talking with us. Would love to learn more about this fantastic account. I'm sure your followers would love to know, too. Send me an email jillian@ therundown.com. Thanks!

Hey Jillian, I write. *Thanks for reaching out. Unfortunately,*

I'm not interested in doing any interviews whatsoever. Take care.
I answer the message privately, for only her to see.

I can imagine her right now, hunched over her desk, desperately refreshing her browser, waiting for a response to come through. I can feel the excitement pulse through her chest when it does, then the way it dwindles down like a dying flame when she reads the response.

It could've worked out. We both could have won. But she had to pair herself with Camilla, the person who wanted to take a hammer and smash right through everything I've built for myself. I can't let that happen.

I look back at Wilson, who is still hugging Kenzie.

Now, more than ever, I can't lose my blog, too.

He walks back down the driveway toward me. I make eye contact with Kenzie and wave. Only she doesn't wave back. Her eyebrows furrow together.

The door opens, and the car shifts beneath Wilson's weight.

"How'd it go?" I ask. Now I'm the one who's nervous.

"Great," Wilson says. He leans back against the seat, lets out a breath. "She loved it. She agreed to meet up next week to talk before she goes back to the city."

My voice shakes when I respond. "That's amazing."

He turns to me, bright with excitement. "Ready to plan the perfect date?"

It's truly the last thing I want to do.

"You bet."

CHAPTER 19

I CURRENTLY LOOK ABOUT seven months pregnant. My belly is swollen, and I've eaten enough food to last me until the new year. Yet when the waiter places directly in front of me a plate stacked with medium-rare steak, rosemary garnished potatoes, roasted carrots, and a lobster tail, I don't even hesitate.

"This is the kind of wedding planning I can get behind," I say between chews. The meat is so tender it melts on my tongue. "Oh my *God*, Julie. This is so freaking good."

When Julie bites into her pistachio-crusted salmon, her eyes flutter closed. "Holy shit." When Julie swears, you know it's good. "Hun, what do you think?"

Massimo bites into the steak. "*Molto bene*," he says. An Italian's approval, too? This meal needs to win an award.

The three of us are seated in the dining room at Eagle High Country Club. It's an hour's drive out of Ridgewood and the venue Julie and Massimo booked last week for their wedding. Everything here screams expensive—the floor-to-ceiling windows, valet car service, velvet armchairs, and mysterious lounge that is members only.

We're in the middle of the food tasting, trying to decide how to narrow down the menu. Julie and Massimo were allowed to bring two people with them. It was supposed to be me and Jill, but she grumbled out some half-assed excuse that was obviously a lie and opted to stay home. I didn't complain, since I get to eat her portion, too.

When the meal is finished, Angelika, the general manager, guides me and Julie to the bridal suite while Massimo is shown to the room reserved for the groomsmen. The bridal suite is in various shades of cream. A soft-as-cotton white carpet covers the floor, and a beautiful curved couch sits in the center, large enough to easily sit a dozen people. There are white velvet ottomans, gold-rimmed mirrors leaning against the walls, makeup counters, and a wall lined with white silk robes. It's like entering a whole different world of luxury.

After Angelika leaves to give us a moment alone, we take a seat on the couch. We were advised to leave our shoes at the door, so we tuck our sock-clad feet beneath our legs, both of us naturally sitting in the exact same position. There are moments when our mannerisms mirror each other's so starkly, it makes me pause.

"So . . ." Julie begins. "What do you think?" Everything about her—her facial expression, the permanent smile, the awe in her voice—tells me that this is the wedding she has envisioned since she was ten.

"I think it'll be nearly impossible for any wedding to ever top yours."

"It's not a competition." Julie pauses, a sneaky smile playing on her face. "But you're totally right. No one can top this." After a moment she adds, "I guess if Jill were here, that would top *this*."

Just the mention of Jill makes me clam up. Somewhere over the past twenty-four hours I reached the decision that I'm going to confide in Julie about the whole Camilla-Jill situation. It's way too much for me to handle on my own. Like one misstep will bring everything crashing down.

I think I'm doing a good job hiding how awkward I feel, until Julie points it out.

"What are you hiding?" she asks.

"Nothing," I say too quickly.

Julie leans in, seeing right through me with that laser stare. "Spit it out right now, Jackie. You're going to cave eventually, so you may as well save us the time."

"I don't think now is the right time—"

"Tell me," she says. "Please."

I sigh. "I found out something about Jillian."

At that, Julie's entire demeanor shifts, her posture stiffening. "Did something happen at work?"

Fine. Part of the reason I want to tell her is selfish, too. Because I am sick of carrying this information around alone. Tired of feeling like I'm walking on eggshells. There are moments when you just need a big sister, and right now I need Julie's guidance more than I ever have. This problem has grown too big for me. I need an extra pair of hands—hands that are far more gentle than mine.

"Yes, something happened at work," I say, wincing as I remember Jillian and Camilla's kiss in the car.

"Well? What is it?"

"I think they're dating."

Julie's voice drops frighteningly low. "Who is dating?"

"Jillian and Camilla," I clarify. "I think they're back together."

"What do you mean you *think* they're back together?" I know Julie is back there, too. Back experiencing those months when we watched Jillian suffer silently while she kept everyone at arm's length.

I describe that day at *The Rundown*. "I saw them kiss," I say. "I don't know how to explain it, but after seeing them together, it all seemed so obvious. The way they act around each other at work, how Jill always stays late . . ."

Julie's fingers are pressed to her temples, like she's fighting off a raging headache. "This cannot be happening." She groans. "When was this?"

"Last week."

Her eyes narrow. "It took you a *week* to tell me?"

I shrink back into the couch. "I didn't know what to do," I say honestly. "I didn't know if I should get involved or—"

"We get involved, Jackie. Of course we get involved! After what happened the last time Jillian dated Camilla, my biggest regret to this day is that I didn't get involved sooner." Julie stands, then changes her mind and sits back down. "We need to talk to her."

"That's a terrible idea."

"What else can we do?"

"You know how Jill is with confrontation, or when anyone tries to tell her what to do. She shuts down, walks away, and it, like, fuels her to *keep* doing it," I say. I remember the day Jill drove me home from Monte's and I asked her to slow down—she was going fifteen over the speed limit. What did she do? She went thirty over the entire drive. She's like a child: if you tell her not to do something, it makes her want it even more.

"I can't sit back and— And wait, Jackie. Just *wait* for her to go through that heartbreak again," Julie says, choking back tears.

"But how do we know it's going to be the same as last time?" I ask, a thought I only just had. "Maybe it'll be different. Maybe Camilla has changed." When I see them at work, they seem pretty happy—like they make a good team.

"Cheaters don't change. Ever. Take it from the girl who's given them one too many chances."

"Give her some time," I beg. Jill only just found out that I turned down her interview, too. That may have already cost her the promotion. And if it did, this on top of it might be her breaking point. "Don't confront Jill right away. Wait a week or two? Maybe she'll confide in you."

Julie snorts. "The only person Jillian confides in is herself. She won't tell me anything, Jackie. Ever."

"If you confront her, it's going to cause a huge fight." That's the last thing I want. I hate when there's tension in the house, especially between my sisters.

"I know that."

"I don't want it getting back to Camilla and costing me my job," I say. That one is a bit of a lie. But I'm trying to find a good enough reason to convince Julie not to go home and storm into Jill's room.

"You think it would?"

I nod. "I doubt Camilla will want me in the office if it seems like I've been snooping around, digging up dirt on their relationship."

Julie's sigh fans across my face. "You might be right. God, I hate this. So we're supposed to, what? Sit back while Jill lets this girl ruin her life for a second time?"

I don't want that. Not again. "No. But for now, let's see what happens. I mean, I did *only* see them kiss. They might not even be too serious." Even as I say it, I don't believe myself.

Julie scoffs. "I doubt it that, but fine. For now we can lie low. But Jackie, the *second* I get the sense that something is off—if I so much as see them together or see Jillian hurt—I'm stepping in."

"I won't stop you if that happens," I say.

Angelika knocks on the door. A second later, her head peeks through. "Hi, ladies. How's it going in here?"

"Great! We're ready to continue with the rest of the tour," Julie says, transitioning back into composed bride mode so quickly it nearly gives me whiplash.

When dessert is ready, we return to the dining room. They've prepared a sampler plate, lined with all five dessert options for us to taste. There's everything from pistachio cheesecake to strawberry shortcake to a *mille-feuille*—thin, crispy layers of puff pastry filled with cream. They were all mouthwatering, but Julie opted for the pistachio cheesecake. From the second we sat down, I knew she'd pick it.

As Massimo drives us home, Julie gushes on about the wedding. The flower arrangements, the late-night food stations, the debate between a live band or a DJ. It feels like our conversation about Jillian never happened. The weight on my chest begins to lighten. I'm thinking that maybe this will end up all right. Maybe Julie will let this go and Camilla really has changed. Maybe this new relationship will finally bring Jillian the happiness she so desperately searched for in their last one.

But then Massimo turns the car onto our street, and I hear Julie's gasp even before I see the familiar Jeep Wrangler pulling out of our driveway. I look up fast enough to spot Camilla in the driver's seat. The look on her face very much screams *oh shit*.

Before Massimo has stopped the car, Julie flings open the door. "Stay in the car, Massimo," she says. Then she is up the driveway and barging through the front door and I am hurrying behind, struggling to catch up, going as fast as I possibly can and tripping over my own two feet in the process.

"Jillian!" She stands in the hallway, screaming her name.

I catch up, grab her shoulder, spin her around. "Julie—*please*. You just promised you wouldn't do this."

Her eyes burn with red-hot anger, a completely unfamiliar look on her face. "I promised I'd hold off until we saw them together, Jackie. She just left our freaking *house*."

Jillian walks down the stairs, looking like she just woke up from a nap. Or she just finished—

Oh.

Oh, no.

Julie must realize it, too, because her anger multiplies by about ten thousand.

She lets out the most sarcastic, cruel laugh I've ever heard. "Well, at least now I know the real reason why you couldn't make the tasting today, Jillian. Nice to know where my *wedding* sits on your list of priorities."

Jillian pauses midway in her descent down the stairs. "What are you talking about?" In a flash, I see her defenses go up, like a fighter entering a cage.

I step farther into the house, placing myself between them.

"How long have you and Camilla been back together?" Julie asks.

The color drains out of Jillian's face. "Excuse me?"

"We saw her pull out of the driveway," I explain, my voice weak. It's only a matter of time before I get brought into this.

I should've kept my mouth firmly shut.

"She gave me a ride home from work," Jillian says.

Julie scoffs. "On a *Sunday*?"

My heart is beating so fast I can feel it in my ears.

Julie is so angry her face has turned red. "Oh my God," she screams. "Can you be honest for once? Jackie saw you two kiss after work! We know you're back together, Jillian! The question is why in the world you would go back to her?"

I shrink when Jillian's gaze narrows in on me. "You *saw* us kiss?"

I want the floor to collapse beneath me. "After work one day," I say meekly. "You were in her car."

Jillian looks so betrayed. "And your first instinct was to run and tell Julie instead of asking me about it?"

Julie speaks up. "Don't try to pin this on Jackie. She didn't do anything wrong here. And if she had talked to you, what would you have done? Lied to her? Denied it? 'Cause we all know how much you *love* talking about what's going on in your life."

That strikes a nerve. "So that's what you two did today during the tasting, huh?" Jillian says, laughing. "You spent your time talking about me and my relationship, and how"—her voice goes high pitch, clearly mocking Julie—"Jillian is so closed off. Jillian doesn't tell us anything. Jillian this, Jillian that." She rolls her eyes. "Have you ever thought that *this* is the reason I don't tell you shit, Julie? Because you butt your nose into everyone's business and make it yours? You're *not* our mom. Stop trying to parent us for two seconds."

Julie's eyes well up with tears.

"Guys," I say, begging. "Please—"

"Well, I'm sorry that I care about you!" Julie retaliates. "Would you rather I be more like you? Stomping around the house, always in a bad mood? Refusing to talk to *anyone*? Refusing to share any detail of your life with your family?"

Jillian's lip quivers. But if there's one thing about Jill, she will never, ever let anyone see her cry.

"I'm sorry you think so negatively of me," she says, completely monotone. Like she's dug deep inside herself and flicked off the switch that controls her emotions.

I never know what to do when this happens. When they fight like this. I don't know how to console one of them without it looking like I'm picking sides.

"That's not true, Jill," I say, pleading with her. "You're just different. We don't hold that against you—"

"Clearly," she scoffs, turning back to Julie. "Keep going, Jules. Any other flaws of mine you'd like to shed some light on?"

"You always do that," Julie says.

"Do what?"

"Turn yourself into the victim," Julie says. "This isn't about picking you apart. This is about you going back to Camilla, the girl who cheated and broke your heart. Do you even remember how that broke you? And you're making me seem like a bad person for caring? For not wanting that to happen again?"

"My relationship is none of your business," Jillian grits out.

222

"We're concerned," I say, trying to explain. "We don't want you going through that again, Jill."

She snaps her attention over to me. "You're concerned? Is that why you took the job at *The Rundown*, Jackie? To what—spy on me? Report back to Julie? God, what other shit have you told her? What I eat for lunch? How long my breaks are?"

Julie slaps her hands against her thighs. "You're doing it again! Changing the subject and making it seem like we're being evil! We're concerned about you, Jill. Camilla is a cheater. She—"

"Don't talk about her like that." Jillian's tone brings the conversation to a halt. If there was even one final shred of doubt left, it's long gone. In those six words, it's never been more obvious that Jill is back with Camilla. Not only that, but she loves her again, too.

I step closer to Jill, who sits down on the step. She buries her head in her hands.

"We love you, Jill," I say. "After what Camilla did to you years ago—"

Her voice is muffled by her hands. "Camilla didn't do anything to me. Please stop this. Just leave it alone."

"She cheated on you," Julie adds. "She broke your heart."

"Please stop," Jill says, curling her knees to her chest.

But Julie keeps going. "You sulked around for months. You were depressed, you were never here. We worried sick about you every single day, Jill. I went into your room every morning and saw an empty bed. I wondered if you were even *alive*." Julie pauses, her voice thick with emotion. "I can't let you go through that again. I can't let Camilla ruin you again."

"Camilla didn't ruin me," Jillian whispers.

"Stop defending her! She's a terrible person that—"

Jillian stands up suddenly and begins to yell. "Camilla never cheated on me! I cheated on *her*! She never broke my heart. I broke hers."

I look to Julie, who looks to me. We are both shocked, our mouths hanging open.

"But you told us—"

"I lied," Jillian says. "I told you she cheated because I couldn't bear to have anyone else hate me."

I don't know how much time passes as the three of us stand there in silence, the weight of Jillian's words settling into our skin like fresh ink. It's the last thing I ever expected her to say.

"Jillian." Julie walks to her with her arms outstretched, like she's ready to hug her so tight the wounds will heal.

When Jillian looks at Julie, there is a coldness in her face that I've never seen before. "You want to know why I was at work today, Julie? Why I missed your tasting? Because I was up for a promotion, and Camilla wanted to tell me in person that I didn't get it."

My heart drops. I'm certain that if I look down, it'll be right there, resting on the floor.

"I had no idea," Julie whispers.

"Of course you didn't," Jillian says. "I'm too closed off,

remember? I never tell you anything." She doesn't even pause to say goodbye before she grabs her car keys, heads out the front door, and just . . . leaves.

Julie begins to cry. "I had no idea," she says over and over again. "Did you know she lost a promotion?"

"No," I say, feeling like I'm in a daze. Only I did know. Or rather, I assumed she had. And it's all my fault.

We stand there long enough that my parents walk through the door. "What happened?" they both ask.

I don't even know what to say.

I sit on the floor and pull my knees to my chest.

CHAPTER 20

JILLIAN DOESN'T COME HOME.

No one knows for sure where she went. Her phone is off—none of our texts or calls are going through. Or maybe she finally reached her threshold, blocked our numbers, and left. My parents, Julie, and Massimo sit at the dining room table, speaking in this awkward, hushed way. Like no one knows what to say or what to do. Julie is certain she went to stay at Camilla's. She's probably right. But everything feels off without her here.

Julie keeps saying "I had no idea." Whether she's talking about the promotion or Jillian's cheating, I don't know.

After taking a shower, I sit on the floor in the living room, my wet hair dampening the back of my tank top. My fingers comb through Mr. Chunks's thick fur, which is suspiciously soft. He still hides under the couch all day, but he's slowly begun inching forward. Now, he lies as close as he possibly can without actually coming out from beneath the couch. He purrs as I pet him, too, his vibrations buzzing through the floor.

"Still nothing," my dad says from the dining room, dropping his phone to the table after another failed call.

I watch my mom place her hand on his. "She's safe, honey. Julie was right—she probably went to Camilla's." But it doesn't make the situation hurt any less. She's supposed to be here with us, and we drove her away.

In my lap, my phone vibrates. For a hopeful moment I think it's Jillian. But it's only Suzy, asking to hang out tonight. *can't leave the house tonight, suz. long story, will explain later* I text back.

That's when I see *iDiary*, with that familiar red 100+ notifications badge on it. I open the app, searching for the familiar validation, the feeling of accomplishment that comes with using it. But I close the app before it even has a second to load. It just feels wrong now, like it's been tainted after what happened with Jillian. I can barely stand to look at it.

I turn to Mr. Chunks, sinking my fingers deeper into his fur, remembering the look of defeat on Jillian's face when she announced that she lost the promotion. The promotion that I willingly cost her. I remind myself it was the only way. How was I supposed to risk compromising my anonymity? I heard what Camilla said—she wanted my identity plastered all over the magazine's front page. But even as I think it, the justifications feel empty. I'd rather lose the blog than lose Jillian.

A couple minutes later Julie sits on the floor next to me. "You were right," she says, scratching the ultrasoft spot behind Mr. Chunks's ear.

I don't think being right is supposed to feel like this. "About what?"

"I shouldn't have said anything. I should have left Jill alone like you warned."

"You couldn't have possibly known any of this would happen," I say.

"I know," she whispers. "But I could've handled it differently. I didn't have to yell, I just— I don't know what happened. You know me, Jackie. I don't get angry like that. Ever."

I place my hand over hers. "This isn't your fault. She said horrible things, too. And honestly, if anyone is to blame for this mess, it's me."

I'm not sure if she's genuinely surprised or is only trying to protect me once again. "Why would you be to blame?"

"I shouldn't have said anything," I say. "Jill was right—I should've gone right to her when I saw them kiss. I made everything worse by telling you. And now she thinks we whisper about her behind her back." But we were only coming from a place of good. We wanted to help. That's it.

Julie squeezes my hand, her eyes searching mine for an answer I don't think I have. "I can't believe she cheated" is all she says.

I sigh. "Me either."

That's the part that's shaken me the most. That Jillian was

the cheater, and that she let our family go on for years thinking Camilla was to blame for their relationship ending.

"I wonder if she knows," I say, continuing my thoughts out loud.

Mr. Chunks is purring so loud it nearly drowns out my voice. "What?" Julie says.

"I wonder if Camilla knows that Jillian lied and told us she cheated," I repeat, suddenly feeling an enormous amount of guilt press into me. All the times I averted Camilla's gaze, ignored her attempts at small talk, treated her with anger for a crime she didn't commit. Not to mention that she gave me a freaking job—and a good one at that. One that now, when it's on the line, I realize how badly I don't want to lose.

"I hope she knows," Julie says. Mr. Chunks is swiping his paws out from beneath the couch, his nail snagging on her shirt-sleeve. I watch her gently pry him off. "Either way, that's their business. I'm not butting my head into their relationship ever again."

"Agreed," I say.

There's a collective intake of breath when a phone rings. I feel the vibrations against my leg. It's mine. My parents stand up at the table, looking at us from over the couch. "Is it her?" Dad asks.

My heart is racing in my chest, but it's only Wilson's name that flashes on the screen.

Oddly enough, the racing doesn't stop.

"Not her," I say.

Julie peeks at the screen. "Wilson? I thought he was pretty high up on your list of enemies. Why is he calling you?"

"Let's just say some changes have been made to that list in the past few weeks," I say.

"Oh yeah? And who's on it now?" Julie prods.

"Currently it's just Mr. Chunks."

She gasps. "Mr. Chunks? Why is my *cat* on your list of enemies?"

"I sat on the couch yesterday and he swiped at my ankle," I explain. "He drew blood, Julie."

"He must have felt threatened," she says, quick to defend him.

"By my *foot*?"

"Leave him alone. And stop calling him Mr. Chunks."

"It's catching on," I say. "Even Dad's been saying it."

I stand, brushing cat fur off my clothing. "I'll be back," I say, trying to exit the room in such haste that I stub my toe on the leg of the coffee table. I double over in pain, swearing under my breath as my toe throbs.

Julie doesn't say a word. She only watches me with the most amused look on her face—like she's caught on to something I myself have yet to realize.

By the time I make it outside and sit on the bench, the call has gone to voicemail. My heart sinks somewhere beneath the porch. I quickly call Wilson back, this intense feeling filling my chest. Like what if I'm too late? What if the moment is up, and he doesn't—

230

"Froggy . . . you're alive." His gruff voice floods me with warmth. I sink into the cushion.

"Unfortunately," I say. My eyebrows scrunch up as I try to pinpoint the exact moment I stopped hating that nickname.

"Hey, save that dread for Monte's." There's a soft rumbling noise on his end, the sound of him driving. "Wait. Everything all right?"

Before I can decide if the best course of action is brutal honesty or a downright lie, I find myself saying, "Not really. There's a bit of a Myers blowup happening at my house."

"Yikes," he says. I close my eyes and let his voice press into me. "What did you do this time?"

It makes me laugh. "Probably best if we *don't* talk about that."

"If you say so." Wilson fumbles over his next words. "I actually called to ask if you're free right now? I'm driving home from work and have to run some errands for the store. Thought my partner in crime could come along and help plan that date for Kenz."

The reminder of the date is like a bucket of cold water dumped over my head.

"So you admit we're partners in crime?"

Wilson clears his throat. "I never said that."

"You literally just did, Willy."

If his voice sounded great over the phone, his laugh is in a whole other league. "Are you free or what?"

231

"Uhm." I look back into the house. My parents are seated at the table, Massimo and Julie now on the couch. I can see the stress etched into their faces. I can join them and spend the night sitting in silence or help Wilson like I promised and secure that promotion. Suddenly the choice is nonexistent. Right now, I'd rather be anywhere but here.

"I'm free," I say, chewing on the inside of my cheek.

"Great, because I'm pulling onto your street."

I hear it then, a car coming around the corner. A pair of too-bright headlights illuminates the sidewalks and mailboxes. In a few seconds, Wilson's car stops at the bottom of my driveway.

"What were you planning on doing if I said no?" I ask, staring at him through the car window as he pulls up.

He stares right back. "Firing you?"

I laugh. "Pretty sure that counts as wrongful termination." I'm halfway down the driveway when I realize I'm wearing a pair of hand-me-down sweatpants that hang off my body and an old tank top that has been worn and washed so many times the fabric has worn thin.

The worst hits me when I'm too close to Wilson's car to turn back. My hair is wet, curly, and about to enter that untamable phase where the frizz takes over my head.

I'm about to tell him to give me a minute so I can run inside, get changed, and do something about this hair. But then the car window rolls down and I notice the way he's looking at me, and it's no different from the way he usually does. There's comfort in that, in the familiarity.

"What's the holdup?" he calls from inside the car.

"I'm wearing pajamas," I say.

One side of his mouth kicks up. "We can stop by Monte's and pick up your costume, if that makes you more comfortable."

It's dark out, but I trust he catches my eye roll. "Very soon that costume will be retired, and you'll regret ever making fun of me."

"Doubt it."

I run around to the other side of the car and step in. Again, it's like stumbling headfirst into a little Wilson-scented bubble. His cologne hits my nose and I resist taking a deep breath to commit it to memory.

We sit side by side in the darkness, our faces illuminated in different shades of red and yellow from the dashboard.

"You look different," he comments.

I'm very aware of his observant gaze flickering over my body. Goose bumps rise on the spots of bare skin his eyes take in.

"In a bad way?" I ask cautiously.

"No." Wilson speaks slowly, deliberately, like he's carefully choosing his words. "Not a bad different. Just, you know, different."

He's wearing his signature outfit: crisp shirt, pressed pants, everything so neat, except his windblown hair. These tiny details have grown so familiar to me, they barely register.

"Sounds like you're giving me a compliment," I say.

"Sounds like you're delusional."

We drive through the streets. It's cool enough to shut the air-conditioning off and open the windows.

"It's my hair," I say, fidgeting with the wet strands. "It's curly. I usually straighten it. So yeah. That's probably why I look different."

Wilson's gaze lingers on my face two seconds too long. "You should stop straightening it." He says it so causally, so easily. Like it's a passing thought that can be released into the air without the words catching somewhere in my heart.

"So where exactly are we heading?" I ask to change the subject.

"I have to pick up some stuff for Monte's."

"I know that, but don't we get deliveries once a week?"

"Yes, every Wednesday morning," he says. "But we're running low on some supplies that I can't wait around for—cleaning products, toilet paper, printer ink, certain chocolate bars." He pauses, cutting me a glare. I stick my tongue out. "And I thought we could pick up some stuff for the date with Kenzie."

By the sound of it, Wilson already has the date finalized. "What did you have planned?" I ask.

"The heat wave is breaking this week," Wilson says. I check the weather app on my phone, and he's right—it is. "And I vaguely remember Kenz saying something once about a romantic picnic.

Thought I could take her to Ridgewood Park."

"I mean it's no Central Park, but it'll do."

Talking about their relationship gives me this sinking feeling in my stomach. The thought of Wilson and Kenzie getting back together no longer fills me with relief, knowing I get my old job back, knowing my summer dream is on track. Now it just kind of feels . . . off. Shitty. Like I've lost something I didn't expect to.

"Will you help me pick out some blankets and stuff?" he asks.

"Sure," I say. At this point, I may as well officiate at their freaking wedding.

Ten minutes later we pull into parking lot of SmartMart—Ridgewood's one and only supermarket, and the only place you can simultaneously purchase a bag of Flamin' Hot Cheetos and windshield wiper fluid. I follow Wilson around like a child, and we take turns pushing the cart. First we head straight toward the outdoor section. Wilson picks out a boring white blanket, and I replace it with a cute yellow one with hearts on it. We find this adorable wicker basket to store everything in—to which Wilson groans and says, "*Another* basket?" I pick out some paper plates, cups and cutlery, a citronella candle to deal with the mosquitoes, and a pack of pastel colored napkins.

"I think that's good," I say, running through a checklist in my head. Wilson had already decided on getting takeout tomorrow afternoon before their date, so I think this is all we can prep as of right now.

When the date is handled, we continue into the food aisles.

Wilson throws all the boring stuff into the cart, like whole wheat crackers and boxes of tea. I keep trying to sneak in different items without him noticing—sour gummy worms, chocolate-covered raisins, an absurdly soft blanket, a pack of bubble gum. Each time he gives me a disapproving look that teeters on amusement, then places the item back on the shelf in its exact spot.

I manage to sneak a bag of popcorn into the cart, which lasts for six minutes before his gaze narrows in on it like a police dog hunting out drugs. "What's with you and junk food?" he asks, again returning it to the shelf.

"It's the superior food group," I say. He pushes the cart down the toiletry aisle and I hop on the back of it, grinning at him.

Wilson's eyes scan the wall of hand soaps. "Your body is probably dying for a vegetable."

"On the contrary," I say. "A vegetable just might kill me. That reminds me— What's going on with that new Monte's menu you had planned?" I'll mourn the day when our giant mozzarella sticks get replaced with sautéed veggies.

Wilson places an industrial-size container of soap in the cart. The lean muscles in his arm flex beneath the weight. "Still working on it."

I draw my eyes back up to his. "What does that mean?"

"It means there are about two hundred things that are important. Once those are dealt with, I can move on to the menu."

"What else is more important?"

"Upgrading our security features," he says, adding another

jug of soap to the cart. "Hiring more cleaning staff. Replacing those disgusting carpets with new flooring."

I gasp. "No way! I've developed a deep emotional attachment to the stains on our carpet."

He rolls his eyes. "My point exactly."

Wilson pushes the cart—and me—down the aisle. Now we've made it into the pharmacy area. There are shelves stocked with protein bars, shakes, cookies, and powders that capture his attention for a few minutes. He grabs a few packs and throws them into the cart.

"So you get snacks, but I don't?" I whine.

He's reading the nutrition label on the back of one of the protein bar packs. "If you're paying for your own snacks, go crazy."

Well, that changes things. "I thought this was on the company card."

Wilson laughs so hard he drops the box on the floor. "Company card? You mean *my* credit card?" He picks up the box, tosses it into the cart.

"Oh. Well, you should probably get one of those," I offer.

Wilson snorts. "Thanks for the financial advice."

"You know," I say, "if you actually listened, I might have some good ideas on how to improve Monte's."

Wilson pushes us down the next aisle. "Is that so?"

"Yes," I say, still hanging from the back of the cart like a child, even though I'm trying to be taken seriously.

"Let's hear it." He reaches for a pack of Advil.

"We need snacks," I say.

"Jackie, you're not changing my mind on the free vending machine idea."

"This is a new idea!" I say, laughing at the same time. "Look—you gave us this new fancy break room. Right? It's great and all, but it's missing food. Stuff to actually *eat* on our break."

Wilson veers the cart to the left of the store, heading toward the cashiers. "We have snacks. I pick up those muffins every morning."

That makes me pause. I knew the muffins were *somehow* getting into Monte's every morning, but I didn't once think about *how* they were getting there.

"And we are very grateful for the muffins," I say, "but by the end of the day, they're a bit stale. Most times, there's none even left for the closing team. Justin eats like, three a day."

The cart comes to an abrupt halt. I stagger off of it, catching my balance on an endcap.

"*Three* a day?"

"Okay, *ouch*." I pick up a few deodorants I knocked over. "Wait. Don't tell him I told you that. My point is we need more. Some nonperishable stuff. Granola bars, chips, cookies. Oh! Maybe some of those mini ice-cream sandwiches to put in the freezer?"

Wilson is fighting so hard to suppress the smile taking over his face. I watch his brown eyes light up like a flame. "Is this the next step in your master plan to get more junk food into Monte's?"

Obviously, yes.

"No," I lie.

Wilson sees right through me. "Hop on," he says, nodding toward the end of the cart. I do as he asks. He pushes me through the store, returning to the snack aisle. I'm bursting with excitement, ready to be let loose. "Pick a few things. Jackie—*a few*."

I don't know if it's the possibility of a future sugar high or the happiness in Wilson's eyes, but I've never been so thrilled to wander down the aisle of a grocery store.

I opt for one of those chip snack packs that comes with four different flavors, chocolate chunk cookies, a pack of apple juice, and individual packs of trail mix. I think that's healthy enough to please Wilson. I show him my haul. "What do you think?"

He surveys the cart, then gives me a thumbs-up. "Could've been worse."

It's the only stamp of approval I need.

On our way back to the cashiers I throw a bag of sweet-and-salty kettle corn into the cart, just because. If Wilson notices, he thankfully doesn't protest.

"Those new ideas you mentioned earlier for Monte's, were these yours or your uncle's?"

"All mine," he says. "My uncle wouldn't have made any changes."

"Why's that?"

"He's too emotionally attached to the way the store is now," Wilson says. "I don't think he ever would have changed a thing."

"But you're not attached that way?"

"Well." He pauses. "I guess I am, yeah. But the only way a business will stay relevant long-term is if it changes with the times."

"And that's why you're doing it?"

"I'm not changing too much," he clarifies. "Monte's will always be Monte's. But it could be a bit cleaner, have better food options. Stuff that doesn't come out of a freezer and go straight into the deep fryer."

"That sounds terrible. Maybe you should relinquish control of Monte's to me," I say. He takes a corner turn too sharply and I knock into another display. This time it's Oreos. "Hey! Watch it."

He grins, as if it was on purpose. "One second you threaten to quit, the next you're coming for my job. I can't decide if you hate Monte's or secretly love it."

"Hate it," I say quickly. "Deeply, deeply hate it."

Wilson doesn't look like he buys it. I'm not entirely sure I do, either. If I really hated Monte's, I wouldn't be spending my Sunday night running errands for the store or brainstorming new ideas to better it. But the more I consider it, I don't think it's Monte's that's beginning to grow on me.

No. The answer is much, much scarier.

"What?" At the cashier, Wilson pauses with the soap jug mid-air. He's watching me, a funny look on his face. Or maybe I was watching him first.

"Nothing," I say, quickly looking away.

We fall into a rhythm of stacking items on the conveyor belt. Of course he's brought his own reusable bags. I bag the items and place them in the cart while he pays, and we head back outside. Wilson presses a button on his car keys, and the trunk pops open. We stack all the bags inside. I'm assuming we're going to leave now, but he takes a seat on the edge of the trunk and pats the spot beside him. I follow his lead and jump up. My feet dangle off the ground. His reach it.

"I'm going to take a guess here and say you're *not* a fan of people eating in your car?"

Wilson rolls his eyes at me, nonetheless turns around to dig through the bags and pull out the popcorn I thought I snuck in. He tears it open and hands it over to me. "Not a single crumb, Jackie."

"Aye, aye, Captain."

I happily munch away, offering the bag to him. To my surprise, he digs in, and we sit there in silence, covered in semidarkness, eating popcorn in the trunk of his car.

"You have good ideas," I say after the silence has settled for a little too long.

He sighs. "I don't know how many of them are actually good."

"What does that mean?"

"I want Monte's to change. But I don't want to change it too much. I want it to always be and feel like the place my dad loved." He kicks at the ground with the toe of his shoe over and over again.

I nudge my shoulder into his. "Changing the menu and replacing the flooring won't erase him from it."

Then the most unexpected thing happens. Wilson leans his shoulder into mine, and he just   leaves it there.

"I know," he says softly. "It's an irrational fear, but it's still a fear."

I hand him the popcorn. He takes another handful.

"So start slowly," I say. "Don't make too many changes at once. Start with the security system and see how that feels. Then keep moving your way up."

"You're just full of good ideas tonight, huh?" he asks, his eyes piercing mine through the darkness. It doesn't sound sarcastic either. It almost sounds like a compliment. And it's dangerous, how badly I want it to be.

"I'm full of *great* ideas every night," I say. I yank the bag of popcorn back, smiling to myself. Wilson's shoulder is still touching mine, spreading this toe-curling warmth throughout me.

"You know . . ." I begin, staring down at my shoes. "It's really cool that you have Monte's. I mean, don't get me wrong, I still think that place is totally lame, but just having somewhere to be, somewhere where you have a role and responsibilities, with people counting on you—it's really cool."

"You think so?" he says, sounding taken aback.

"I do," I say. "I guess I've been struggling with that lately. Like, finding my purpose. Finding what I'm good at. I haven't even applied to college."

"I know tons of people who haven't applied to college," he says.

"Okay, Mr. Popular," I tease, smiling up at him. "Thanks for saying that. I just . . . it's really scary to be staring down at the rest of your life, especially when everyone expects you to somehow know exactly what you want to do with it. It's cool that you *do* know. I wish I had that."

Wilson nods. He looks at me like he gets it, gets *me*. Like he would sit here patiently, forever, while I lay my heart bare.

"I get it, really," he says after a moment of silence. "It was different for me. I have Monte's. I was basically born into the business, into this life that has already been mapped out. Don't get me wrong—that isn't a bad thing. I'm grateful, and it really helped take a lot of pressure off of me. But . . . Well, I guess I thought I'd have more time, too."

"More time?"

"I always knew that someday I'd take over the family business. When my uncle got sick, it felt like someone hit fast-forward on my future. All of a sudden *someday* become *today*. I left school not really sure when I'd be back, I moved back here, wrecked my relationship, and it was all expected of me. I guess I thought I'd have more time before my life got taken over by Monte's."

"But you love Monte's," I say, confused. "You're *good* at running Monte's."

Wilson laughs. "I'm glad it comes off that way. Most of the time, I have no clue what I'm doing."

If I were walking, that sentence alone would stop me in my tracks. "You're not serious."

"Completely serious," he says with an easy smile. "But it's good to know I pull it off so well."

"But you're Wilson. You're Wilson with the ironed shirts. You wear the same pants every day. You carry around a clipboard, for goodness' sake. You're telling me you're like, *confused*? Like the rest of us?"

"Kind of concerned that you hyperfocus on my wardrobe, but yeah, Jackie. I'm confused. I'm a nineteen-year-old running a freaking business. How could I not be?"

It feels like I'm looking at him in an entirely different light. "I had no idea. You hide it so well. You always seem so put together, so . . ." I trail off, my brain still struggling to catch up with the realization that Wilson isn't some business mogul. He's just . . . like the rest of us, trying to find his way.

"I'm scared about fifty percent of the time," he says.

"And the other fifty percent?" I ask.

"I have you in my office, busting my ass, making me feel somewhat normal."

A smile pulls across my face. It must be contagious because Wilson is smiling, too.

"So what I'm hearing is that me annoying you is actually a good thing," I tease. "Dare I say it's good for your health? Should I do it *more*?"

At that, he laughs.

It feels like a win.

"You do it just the right amount."

We stare at each other long enough that I have to look away. I'm scared that if I look at him for too long— Well, I'm not entirely sure what might happen.

"How long exactly are you stuck here running Monte's? How long until you can return to school? To your life?"

He shrugs. "No idea. Just until my uncle is healthy enough to take his old job back, or they find another Monroe to run it permanently. Probably half a year, at least."

"Then you have options," I say. "At least you managed to escape Ridgewood for a short time."

His eyebrows knot together. "You want to leave Ridgewood?"

"I do."

"And go where?" he asks.

I shrug. How could you possibly choose when the option is *anywhere*? "I don't really know. I'm still figuring out the whole college situation, so that may be a deciding factor. Maybe California? My best friend, Suzy, is moving there. Or New York City seems cool, too. I know they have a lot of great schools. But you live there, so yuck."

I laugh when Wilson sticks his tongue out. "It's a big city," he says. "You'd never have to see me if you didn't want to."

"But what if I want to? There has to be someone in that city ready and willing to annoy you at all times."

Leave it up to me to ruin all sentiment with a stupid comment.

But the realization still lingers: we both might end up with futures that take us out of this town.

"Hey." Wilson knocks his knee into mine. "About what you said before, with your future and college . . . You'll figure it out. I know you will. You're the most determined person I know."

That surprises me. "I am?"

"Well, most determined to hate your job, but yeah, it still counts."

I smack him very gently.

"And if you don't, or if it takes a bit longer than you planned," he says, "Monte's is always here for you."

I pretend to shudder. "That's exactly what I'm afraid of."

"Oh—here. Take this before I forget." He reaches into his pocket and pulls out a Twix bar, stuffing it into my palm.

I don't know how long I sit there staring at it, but when I look up, Wilson's eyes are waiting for mine. And they're different this time, too. His eyelids are heavy, shadowed by the dark brush of his eyelashes. In a moment so brief it almost escapes me, I swear his gaze drops down to my lips.

"You got me another one," I say, swallowing a lump in my throat. I don't remember him grabbing it off a shelf, or even paying for it.

He shrugs it off. "It's your favorite."

"Yeah. It is."

Maybe his eyes never looked down at my lips. But right now, I can't stop my gaze from dropping straight down to his mouth.

Those sarcastic, tilted lips that hand out smiles like they're a rare currency. I'm so overwhelmed with the urge to move closer, be closer, *stay* closer to him that I can't even think straight. I'm so aware of Wilson and the space he takes up beside me that I can't recognize anything beyond the two of us, anything more than this car and the way our feet dangle off the back of it—his on the floor, mine midair.

The Twix wrapper crinkles in my hand.

He remembered.

Not once, but twice. He remembered twice.

His voice is as soft as satin when he speaks. "You said earlier there was a fight at your house?"

The mention of the fight shakes me out of the moment. I reluctantly pull away from him.

Right. Jillian leaving. It's the first time I've thought of her since he picked me up. I've never met anyone who makes the bad moments fade, not the way Wilson does.

"There was, yeah," I say. "We don't have to talk about it."

"We can," he says. "If you want to, that is."

I don't know what to say. I don't know if I want to talk about Jillian and what happened earlier, or if I want to make a home out of this serene bubble we've created around us.

But suddenly I realize: I want to share the details with him. Maybe it's the cover of darkness acting like a safety blanket, or maybe it's the way we have somehow become friends these past few weeks. Somehow we've moved far away from the two kids who mocked each other at Monte's. Now we're walking a very thin tightrope, and I'm unsure what waits for me on the other end—or what waits for me beneath if I decide to fall.

"Jillian and my other sister, Julie, got into this big fight," I explain. "And I was kind of in the middle of it."

"What were they fighting about?" He asks it in a way that makes it very clear I can answer or choose not to.

I explain the situation—Camilla, the cheating, the years of lies, finding out that Jillian was the real cheater after all. Wilson sits there and listens. He never interrupts, never passes judgment. He only holds the popcorn for me as I speak, the Twix bar still in my hand.

"They have this almost passive-aggressive sibling rivalry," I explain, a detail I've never shared with anyone. Or ever said aloud, for that matter. "Like, Julie is the perfect daughter, and Jillian is the secluded, moody one who can never be like her. Does that make sense? No one has ever said that. And believe me—none of us actually think it. But sometimes it seems like Jillian really believes it. She believes she's the lesser twin. Like Julie is the better half."

Wilson is nodding, as if the information is slowly sinking in. "After what happened tonight, are you worried she'll believe that even more?"

"Yeah," I say, somewhat surprised that he pulled the thought directly out of my head. "That's exactly what worries me."

"Have you called her?"

"Her phone is off," I say. *Or she blocked my number and wants nothing to do with me.*

"Hey." Wilson places his hand over mine. For a split second, I don't even dare to breathe. "I met Jillian twice," he says, "and she seemed like someone who doesn't need anyone's help."

I smile. "She comes off like that. But I think it's all an act. I think she does need someone—maybe she's always needed someone, and we never saw it."

"As an only child, I'm probably the worst person to look to for sibling advice. But if I were Jillian, I'd probably want to cool off and have everyone leave me alone."

"You think that's all it is?" I ask.

I feel the slightest pressure from his fingers. "I do."

At this point I'd be surprised if the Twix bar hasn't melted completely in my hand. "Well, she should be at work tomorrow, so we'll see what happens then."

Wilson cocks his head to the side. "You're scheduled to open at Monte's tomorrow."

Oh shit. "Uhm," I say, pausing. "So, it looks like I need tomorrow off, boss."

Old Wilson is back, rolling his eyes and looking completely irritated by me. "I'll figure it out." The time on his phone reads 10:15 p.m. Wilson stands and stretches his arms above his head. "We should probably head back."

At that, the exhaustion from the day creeps in. "Please."

I must be more tired than I thought. When I go to jump out of the trunk, I misplace my footing and begin to topple over. The ground is rising very, very quickly and I'm anticipating how many scratches are going to cover me tomorrow morning, but the impact never comes. Right before I can face-plant into the ground, I collide with a very solid chest, one that belongs to a very solid guy whose very solid arms are wrapped around my waist.

A tiny "Oh" escapes my lips.

This time, when I look up at Wilson's face, I know exactly what he's staring at—my lips.

And his face is so close I can count the freckles fanning across his nose.

"Thanks," I say, my voice completely breathless.

"Careful, Froggy," he whispers.

I may have forgotten what my actual name is.

The moment multiplies around us. The darkness, the gentle summer breeze, the sound of cicadas flying overhead, the beating of my heart pressing too urgently into my rib cage.

Forget the popcorn and the snacks and all the other items I piled into the cart. What I really want is something I haven't even dared to think about. And from the way Wilson's face is inching closer, I'm filled with the blinding anticipation that maybe, just maybe, he wants it, too. Maybe our—

A phone rings. We both yell, jumping apart like we've been caught committing a crime.

In a flash, Wilson's phone is in his hand and Kenzie's face pops onto the screen. It's like a bucket of freezing cold water has been dumped on both of us.

I notice the exact second reality crashes back in, the exact moment he shuts down whatever it was between us that didn't get a chance to happen.

"Answer it," I say. What I want is for him to throw his phone across the parking lot.

Wilson silences the call. "She's probably calling about the picnic. I'll text her later."

He doesn't even look at me, just shuts the trunk and walks straight to the driver's seat.

It feels like I'm in some sort of trance. My feet pull me forward to the car. My hand clips in my seat belt. My brain is still somewhere in the parking lot, trying to imagine a future where Wilson kisses me, trying to understand these feelings swarming inside me.

"You think she'll like the picnic?" Wilson asks once we are driving down the street.

"Uhm." It takes me a moment to catch my footing, to ground myself in the harsh reality of what's going on here: Wilson is trying to get back with Kenzie, the person he loves. And I am the fool who offered to help.

"I don't see how she couldn't," I say, my voice sounding far away. "It's a good start for you two to sit down and talk. See if getting back together is on the table." Even as I say it, I desperately hope the answer is a big fat no.

Somewhere between making that deal with Wilson and this very moment, I've come to the complicated realization that I don't really want Wilson dating Kenzie. In fact, I don't think I want him with anyone that isn't—

Well, anyone that isn't me.

I want the sarcastic comments and the stupid, trivial arguments. I want what we've always had. But now, I think I want it in a new way.

"Let me know if you need help setting up." As soon as the words are out, I instantly regret offering. Do I really want to hang around and help Wilson create the perfect date for another girl? And I'm supposed to, what? Make a quick run for it before she arrives? Hide in the trees? Walk home in shame?

"Will do," he says.

The entire way home, we don't speak. Wilson doesn't bring up the almost-kiss, and neither do I. It's probably for the best. He's trying to win back the girl he loves. And I'm just the girl trying to mend his broken heart, even if it means breaking my own in the process.

CHAPTER 21

THE NEXT DAY, JULIE picks me up from *The Rundown* in the afternoon. For the entire drive over to Ridgewood Park, where I'm meeting Wilson to set up the picnic, she keeps hitting me with these weird glances. When I can't take it anymore, I say, "What is it?"

At a red light, she reaches over and gently tugs on my hair. "Your hair is curly," she says. "You never wear it curly."

I shrug, playing it off. "I wanted to try a new look today," I say casually. No other reason. Not because any specific person may have mentioned that they like my hair curly. Not because I'm currently driving over to meet said person.

Julie nods her approval, smiling like she knows there's more to it. "Well, I love it. You look adorable. I'm glad you finally took my advice. So . . . What happened at the office today?"

Today was my first day back at *The Rundown* since the blowout with Jillian. I barely slept last night. Instead, my mind played out every possible situation that might happen: Camilla firing me on the spot, Jillian ignoring me for the full eight hours, the two of them mutually hating my guts. What I didn't account for was Jillian not showing up for work and Camilla smiling at me the second she walked through the door.

I explain that all to Julie, who says, "Jill's probably working from home—Well, Camilla's home. I guess she's staying with her. Is it totally inappropriate for you to ask Camilla how Jill is?"

"Are you crazy? I'm not doing that!"

"It was just a suggestion!"

Not to mention that I have no idea how much information Jillian even shared with Camilla. The last thing I need is to accidentally tell Camilla some secret detail that Jillian never shared to begin with. No, Julie was right on Sunday: no more getting caught in their relationship. Whether it ends in marriage or a fiery explosion is no longer my problem.

"The good news," Julie continues, "is that my texts to her have started going through again. Which means she either had her phone off for two days or she finally unblocked my number."

I grimace. "Jillian is trigger-happy with the block button."

"Don't I know it." We're both thinking of the same thing. When Jill went to parties in high school, she blocked our entire family from her social media accounts so we couldn't see whatever craziness she was up to. It all started when I was thirteen and I showed Julie a photo Jillian had gotten tagged in on Instagram. I asked, "Why is Jill smoking?" and soon found out it wasn't a cigarette at all—aka leading to a three-hour say-no-to-drugs conversation with *Julie*, not even my parents. That was when Jillian first fell in love with the block button.

"I'm guessing she hasn't responded to any of your texts?" I ask.

"No. And every call goes right to voicemail."

When I study my sister's face, I can see how much this fight has affected her and how badly she's trying to hold it together for my sake.

"Looks like I'll have to reschedule our appointment this weekend for your bridesmaids dresses," she says, gripping the wheel so tightly her knuckles go white.

"Oh nooooo."

Julie snorts. "Yeah, I'm sure you're devastated, Jackie."

We drive in silence for a few minutes. Julie might have her thoughts stuck on her twin, but mine keep drifting over to Wilson, to that almost-kiss in the parking lot last night. The worst part is how it keeps replaying over and over in my head, like a broken record stuck on an infinite loop. And not in a bad way, either—in a *good* way. The memory makes something ignite in my chest, like the first spark from an ember before it bursts into flame. I still can't really wrap my head around what happened, but what I know for certain is that Wilson and I crossed some sort of line. Maybe it was a line we unknowingly drew in the sand, but it was there. Now we stand firmly on the other side of it. And no matter how badly we might want to, I don't think there's a way to go back to the moment before we almost kissed.

The strangest part is, I don't think I want to. Instead, I keep trying to jump ahead into the *after*. Playing out in my mind what could have happened if his phone didn't ring. If he had kept inching closer to me. If there wasn't all this baggage built up between us.

"Remind me again why you're going to Ridgewood Park?" Julie puts down the sun visor. I do the same. Wilson may have been right about the heat wave breaking, but the sun is still blinding.

"To help Wilson. It's a long story."

I see the exact moment Julie makes the connection. "Wilson, your boss, who called you the other night?"

"No," I lie. "Another Wilson." I turn the air-conditioning on. Suddenly it's a bit hot in here.

"And is this a date?"

"Julie, *please*. This is like, the furthest thing from a date." I'm not offering any more of an explanation, as it would be way too embarrassing. *Oh yeah, I'm going to help the guy I maybe have developed feelings for get back together with his ex-girlfriend. Couldn't be happier!*

She turns her signal on and makes a left at the light. We turn into the newly built residential area near the park. "I'm not going to pry," she says. "I've learned my lesson. But—I am here if you want to talk. Even though I know you won't."

"You're right. I won't, but thank you."

She reaches over and squeezes my arm. "Jill and I might be twins, but you two are way more alike."

It's not that I'm surprised we are alike—I already knew that. I'm surprised that Julie thinks so, too. "How so?"

Julie drives into the parking lot. A few people are hanging around, pulling blankets and foldable chairs out of their cars. Behind them, the park sprawls out. It's all flat land that ends in a soccer field before the ground hikes up into a hill that's dangerously unclimbable. On the field, boys in neon orange and lime green jerseys run around, kicking a ball back and forth.

"You two are more reclusive," Julie says, pulling the car over to the sidewalk to drop me off. "Before you get offended, I don't mean that in a bad way. It's just how both of you are. More private, more equipped to deal with things on your own. Maybe *independent* is a better word."

I've always known that Jill and I share the same itching desire to get out of Ridgewood. And it's pretty obvious we're not the oversharing type, like the rest of our family. But I never once thought that was a good thing. I thought our quietness, the mutual tendency to revert back into ourselves, was almost destructive. Like, we were the two black sheep in the family. But when Julie says it like that, she somehow sheds some much-needed positivity on it.

"I never thought of it that way," I say.

"Jillian used to be more open when she was a teenager. Do you remember?"

Do I remember? I built my entire blog off of Jillian's and Julie's tendency to overshare every detail of their life when they were younger.

"I do." I'm lost in thought, taken back to midnights spent bundled up on the couch. The fireplace roaring. Our parents already in bed. The three of us huddled together, sharing snacks and secrets. Back when boundaries didn't exist and we flowed in and out of each other's lives like a river running downhill.

"I guess I can't fault her for changing when she got older," Julie says. It seems like she's speaking more to herself than me. "I miss her so much, Jackie. I hope she shows up soon."

"She will," I promise. She has to.

"Do you need a ride home?" Julie asks, her voice heavy again.

"Uhm, maybe. I'll let you know."

When Julie hugs me goodbye, I hug her back even tighter. I know this is what she needs right now. Then I'm walking through the grass, sidestepping the dozens of other people set up on blankets. Looks like Wilson wasn't the only one with this great idea.

My phone vibrates in my pocket. My heart in my throat, I look at the screen and will it to show Jillian's name. Instead I see a text from Suzy. *What are you doing tonight? We need to watch the new J-Law rom-com ASAP. Come by?*

I text back, *too busy tonight. long story. sorry.* I tack on a sad-face emoji to lessen the blow. Then I spot Wilson farther down on the left, in a spot beneath a large tree. Strewn across the grass is a bouquet of flowers, the wicker picnic basket, the reusable bags I recognize from SmartMart, and paper bags that must be filled with whatever takeout Wilson chose. I watch him fan the blanket out—the yellow one with hearts on it that I chose—over the grass, but the wind keeps blowing it back against his body. I stifle a laugh. I know his patience is wearing thin.

To save the day as per usual, I run over and grab the corners of the blanket just as Wilson fans it out again. He doesn't even startle at my presence. He actually looks relieved.

"You're late," he says gruffly. And here I was, wondering if things would be different between us. Clearly, we are back on track.

"And you're losing a sad battle to the wind," I say as I take a few steps back and stretch the blanket out. "This picnic looks depressing."

"Please add blankets to the list of items I hate," Wilson says.

"Blankets and baskets, got it. Maybe also a hatred for the letter *B*?"

"It's too early to rule anything out."

Each holding a corner, we show the wind who's boss and set the blanket flat over the grass. Wilson immediately places a bag on either side to hold it in place. It makes me wonder how long he's been here struggling.

"For the record, you told me to be here at five thirty and it's"—I check my phone—"five twenty-eight. That makes me early."

He sits on the blanket as he begins to unpack the bags. "Guess there's a first for everything."

I take a seat beside him. "Is there a specific reason why you're in a terrible mood? Or just your usual personality?"

For the smallest second, I see that familiar tug of a smile on his lips. "I'm embarrassed to say that blanket kicked my ass."

"How long exactly were you struggling with it?"

Wilson takes his eyes off the bouquet to glare at me. "A very reasonable amount of time."

"So more than ten minutes. Got it."

He tosses the empty picnic basket at me, then hands me the paper bags filled with food. It smells so yummy, my stomach growls. "Less talking, more unpacking."

"I'm great at multitasking. Watch me do both." As Wilson unpacks the SmartMart bags and lights the citronella candle, I begin moving all the food into the basket. "What time is Kenzie coming?"

"Six," he says. Am I imagining the voice shake?

"Yikes. We better get to work." The paper bags are filled with food packaged in small cardboard boxes. I peek into a container filled with french fries, but I leave the rest closed. I don't want to risk letting the heat out and everything getting cold.

"How was work today with Jillian?" Wilson asks out of nowhere. I don't know why it still catches me off guard when he remembers these details, or why his remembering makes my heart flutter.

"She never showed up," I say. Wilson hands me the cutlery and napkins—I add those to the top of the pile.

"Shit. I'm sorry."

I shrug it off. "It's all right. I know we'll get through it eventually, but our fights don't usually last this long."

Wilson relights the candle when the wind blows it out. "I'd offer you a Twix, but I may have forgot to bring one."

It's like a knife straight to the heart. "You really think I'm a big baby who can be bribed with chocolate, huh?"

"That's exactly what I think," he says.

"Good, because I most definitely am."

I look up and find him smiling at me—it's the same smile from that night in the parking lot. Then I realize how different Wilson looks today. Long gone is his usual work outfit. Now he wears worn-in jeans, Converse, and a black graphic tee. His hair is different, too.

"What?" he says. "Quit staring at me."

"Did you get a haircut?"

Almost self-consciously, he runs a hand through his hair. "I did. You're looking at me like it looks bad, Jackie. What's the problem?"

The problem is that it's the opposite of bad. Wilson's hair had gotten so shaggy it started to flop over his ears. Nearly hit his eyebrows, too. Now it's cropped a bit closer to his head, with just a few brown strands falling over onto his forehead. It shows off his face a lot more, too. Makes his eyes pop, like two little brown pools, pulling me right in.

"It doesn't look bad at all," I say, coming back to myself. "It looks nice."

I see the moment the compliment travels through the space

between us and hits Wilson. The faintest tinge of red blooms in his cheeks, and his eyes quickly drop to his shoes.

"Let's talk about your hair," he says. "It's still curly."

It is. This is actually the longest I've gone without straightening it. I make myself busy with the basket and say, "Someone may have changed my opinion on it." It's all I offer. There's no chance I'm fully admitting that Wilson's compliment sort of made me see a part of myself in a new light.

With the picnic basket stocked up, I shut it. "Okay," I say, clapping my hands. God, Julie's teacher theatrics are rubbing off on me. "What else do we have to do?"

"I think that's everything."

"Perfect." I lie down on the blanket, and the world tips upside down. Between the branches of the trees, I see blue slivers of the sky. "You know you easily could have done that without me."

The last thing I expect is for Wilson to join me. When he does, my breath catches. We lie side by side, staring up at the bright summer sky. "Jackie, if you weren't here, I'd still be struggling with the blanket."

I tilt my head to the right to look over at him. I don't know if it was deliberate, but his face is only a head space away from mine. Again, my eyes trace over the soft freckles sprinkled across his skin.

A rush of feelings sweep over me like a tidal wave. I'm shaken with the urge to scoot closer to him, nestle my head into his shoulder, be enveloped in a new sort of comfort. If I close my eyes and block everything out, there's another lifetime where Wilson put this picnic together for me. Where I'm the girl he's waiting for. Where that basket is filled with my favorite foods. Where Wilson got a haircut and changed out of his work clothes to impress me. It's only when I let myself sink far enough into that dream that I realize how badly I want it.

I've spent weeks breaking hearts. Tossing out advice to strangers on how to swiftly exit relationships that weren't fulfilling. A lot of it made me feel like a fraud. How can I possibly advise someone on how to break a heart when I've never allowed myself to get close enough to someone to give them the power to break mine? Now here I am, on the cusp of heartbreak, knowing that the second Kenzie arrives at this picnic, my chance with Wilson is gone. There's no coming back from that.

It may be a bit premature, but part of my heart already feels broken, like it's mourning the *what if.*

But maybe this is what I deserve. I broke them up, and by doing so, I broke Wilson's heart. It only makes sense that the consequence is him breaking mine.

Wilson's words puncture the still air. "I'm nervous."

I open my eyes and find his right there, waiting. His hair fans out on the blanket. I want to run my fingers through the strands. "She's going to love it."

I love it is what I want to say. That if this was all for me, it would be enough.

"That's not what I mean," Wilson says. When his gaze

searches my face, I hold my breath.

"Then what are you worried about?" But I don't need him to elaborate. I can see it plain on his face—the answer is right there, in the way his eyes drop down to my lips again; in the way he let himself lie beside me in the first place. Because any guy hung up on another girl wouldn't be lying here with a different one.

And maybe I'm delusional. Maybe I'm reading so far between the lines that they've completely begun to blur together. Maybe I'm making up an entire language of my own. But for the first time, I doubt if Wilson even wants Kenzie to come today.

Maybe we're both secretly hoping she doesn't.

Then, a face moves in. It hovers above us, blocking out the sky and kicking the blooming moment right out the door.

"Hi," Kenzie says, looking down at the two of us.

"Kenzie!" We yell her name at the same time, our voices heavy with guilt. In a split second we are standing up, fumbling with our limbs, brushing grass off ourselves. Wilson rights himself first, patting down his hair. "Kenzie, hey. You're here. Wow— Hi."

He is bashful and sweet, staring at her with a look of disbelief.

I realize that when he said he was nervous, this must have been the reason—he was nervous she wouldn't come.

I was nervous that she would.

"You told me to come at six. It's six," she says. But her eyes are looking right at me. And her gaze very obviously says *What is she doing here?*

"It's good to see you," Wilson says.

"What's Jackie doing here?"

Yep. There it is.

"I helped Wilson plan this for you." My cheeks are on fire. I feel like the other woman. I want to scream *Nothing happened! We never so much as kissed!* "He did most of it himself," I add quickly. "I just helped with, you know, setting everything up."

Kenzie looks beautiful too, in a flowy white sundress and sparkly eye shadow that catches the sun. I don't even dare to risk a glance at Wilson. In my entire life, I have never felt so awkward.

"The both of you planned a picnic for me?" she says.

"*No.* Wilson planned it. I just helped." The sentence shoots out of my mouth at the exact same second Wilson says, "I planned it. Jackie helped set it up."

Well, I did a bit *more than that, buddy.*

Her eyes are narrowed. She sucks her teeth. "Right."

Oh, she is not happy. I should've run out of here before Kenzie saw me. From her perspective, it must look like *we* were on the date and she's the one intruding.

"And on that note, I should go," I announce. Julie isn't here to drive me home. but that doesn't matter! I will gladly walk. Hell, I'll crawl if I have to. Just get me out of here as fast as humanly possible.

"Thanks for the help," Wilson says. I smile at him. It's really all I can offer right now.

"See you," Kenzie says.

I walk away, and I don't look back.

At some point during the walk to the parking lot, tears begin to sting my eyes. I groan, forcing them not to fall, annoyed by my own emotions. This is exactly what I signed up for: help Wilson win back Kenzie. That's what I did. Now I have to stop being a baby and move on alone.

It's the *alone* part that's getting to me.

I guess somewhere between grabbing lunch at the diner, hanging out in Wilson's office, and late-night drives through town, *alone* morphed into *together*, and I had gotten too used to how that felt.

Now I'm back where I started.

I walk through the parking lot that opens up into the residential area. The streets are lined with new homes, and most of the roads are being repaved. I reach into my pocket to grab my phone to call Julie, when it begins to ring.

It's Wilson.

I answer the call so quickly I nearly drop it. "What happened?"

"She left," he says, his voice not giving any hint of emotion. "Can you come back?"

I don't even respond, I just run to him. Down the sidewalk, weaving through the parked cars—until one car catches my eye. It's Kenzie's baby blue Mini Cooper, and she's standing right beside it, staring at me. Something is telling me to go talk to her, so that's exactly what I do.

She leans against the car, waiting.

I pose the same question. "What happened?"

Kenzie smiles sadly. "It's not going to work out between us."

The relief hits first, then the guilt. "Kenzie—"

"I never wanted to get back together with Wilson, Jackie. I only came here today to see how he was doing and say goodbye before I head home tomorrow."

"You should have told him that," I say, feeling incredibly defensive of him. "He planned all of this for you."

"Did he?"

"What does that mean?"

Kenzie laughs. "Jackie, I hate the outdoors. I'm a city girl, it's the reason I *live* in the city. I don't know why Wilson had this idea that my dream date was a picnic. Don't get me wrong, he knows everything about me. I just think he . . . got distracted by someone else."

I know how that sentence ends. "Distracted by me, you mean."

"I'm not upset. I honestly want him to be happy."

I need her to know that nothing was intentional. That I wasn't trying to like, steal him from her. "This started out as me helping him win you back, I promise. You should've seen how long he spent on that freaking gift basket for you, like it was the most important thing in the world."

Kenzie smiles. Her eyes are far away, lost in some other memory. Maybe of Wilson, but a different version of him. "I don't doubt it. He's a bit of a perfectionist."

"A bit?"

We laugh together. Ten pounds disappear off my shoulders.

She reaches out and taps my wrist. "It was great meeting you, Jackie. Whatever happens between you two, there's no hard feelings."

"Can I ask why you seemed so upset when you arrived today?"

She thinks on it for a moment. "I think part of me was hoping that when I got here and saw Wilson, something would click into place. That love would creep back into me and I'd want to get back together with him. I guess that would be the easiest thing to do. But when I saw you two lying there, it confirmed that we're done. I'm sorry if it came off as being rude. It was only me processing the end of our relationship. And it always kind of sucks to see the person you once loved move on."

Out of everything she said, the selfish part of me clings to the final bit. "You think he's moved on?"

Kenzie nods back toward the park. "Go see for yourself."

So I do. When I cross onto the grass, I spot Wilson without even having to search. My eyes are drawn to him like a magnet. He is sitting on the blanket all alone. "I was lying before. Now this is a truly depressing picnic," I say when I'm standing right behind him.

He huffs out a laugh. "No kidding."

I sit on the blanket, pulling my knees to my chest and wrapping my arms around them. I fidget until I need to break the silence. "Well, since Kenzie won't be eating that food . . ." I hope it'll make him laugh, but Wilson doesn't protest. He just slides the basket to me.

"I spoke to her just now, by the way," I say. "She told me what happened. Are you okay?"

I set out all the containers around me and begin opening them one by one.

"I think so. I really thought . . ."

Wilson keeps talking, but I'm no longer paying attention. My mind is completely stuck on the scene unfolding before me. When I open the first takeout box, it's filled with breaded chicken nuggets. The next one is french fries. After that, two containers of ketchup. A bottle of iced tea. A bag of Cool Ranch Doritos. When I get to the dessert, my brain short-circuits. Wilson picked out a chocolate brownie, chocolate dipped doughnut, and chocolate lava cake.

He's still talking, but I'm back sitting in that ripped leather booth at Angelo's, replaying our conversation about what we'd choose for our final meal. I told him I was a simple girl who wanted chicken nuggets, fries, and ketchup. *Dessert?* he had prodded. My answer was simple: *Chocolate fudge brownie. No— Wait, chocolate dip doughnut. Or maybe a chocolate lava cake. You know what? All of the above.*

The memory blurs with reality. All those foods I told Wilson I loved—the iced tea I had ordered, the Cool Ranch Doritos I mentioned were my favorite that day in his office when he was eating them, too. I knew he remembered the Twix bars, but I didn't know he remembered everything.

"I thought I had planned Kenzie's perfect date," Wilson is saying. "I don't know how I got it so wrong."

It's a good thing I'm sitting down, because another memory crashes into me with enough force to knock me off my feet.

The day I first met Kenzie, when Wilson and I sat together in Monte Jr.'s office, I asked him if he took Kenzie on nice dates. He had said yes. I remember my exact words: *Planning a cute date in Ridgewood must be a pain in the ass. This town is impossible to romanticize. You know what I would love? A cute picnic in a park or something.*

A cute picnic in a park or something.

Filled with all my favorite foods.

That's exactly what Wilson did.

"Wilson." I sound completely breathless. "You didn't plan Kenzie's perfect date."

"What do you mean?"

"You planned mine," I say.

CHAPTER 22

WE SIT IN SILENCE, staring at the evidence splayed out before us. All my favorite foods, ordered and picked up by Wilson and brought here for *me*.

"The evidence doesn't lie," I say. Wilson is taking so long to process this revelation that my stomach is in knots. "You're being very quiet. It's scaring me."

"I don't know what to say." He turns to me with a look of utter shock on his face.

I can't help but laugh. And that laughter helps ease the tension, take away of some of the scariness, the uncertainty.

"Say you have a tiny crush on me," I blurt out. I can't seem to stop smiling.

"I *don't*."

I pick up a fry and use it to point to the food. "The evidence doesn't lie."

Wilson's eyes narrow. "The evidence is a coincidence."

"Oh sure, Wilson. It's just a coincidence that you ordered all my favorite foods, my favorite desserts, my favorite drinks, *and* planned the perfect date that I explicitly told you about a month ago. Geez, what a crazy coincidence!"

He blinks, like my words are finally sinking through his thick head. "You've infiltrated my mind like a parasite."

My mouth drops open before my shock turns into laughter. "That is the last thing I ever expected you to say."

And then Wilson smiles, and relief floods through my chest. I'm not crazy. I'm not imagining it. He knows it, too. "I'm not going to say I have a crush on you," he tells me.

"So you're going to lie? Deny your feelings? Not listen to your heart? *Wow.*"

He shakes his head. But as he does so, he inches closer. "In my defense, your favorite foods are quite generic. I think everyone in this park would be happy with this meal. In fact, I'm pretty sure fries and nuggets are called a *Happy Meal.*"

"Yes, but you planned it specifically for me. Because you like me. Remember?"

"Be quiet and eat your chicken nuggets."

I do just that.

All the food has gone a bit cold, but I'm so giddy, nothing can upset me.

All the pining. All the wishing that this date was for me, and here we are—with a date that Wilson *did* plan for me. Sure, he did

272

so unknowingly. But it still counts!

"The other night at SmartMart—"

I interject. "When you almost kissed me in the parking lot."

Now his mouth drops open. "*You* almost kissed *me*."

"Wilson, be so serious. You were moving *your* face down to *my* face!"

"Because you were moving *your* face up to *my* face!"

We are both smiling so wide our words come out funny.

Somewhere between the banter and the insults, something else grew. Something we were both desperately trying to ignore. Which ended up being a bit counterproductive. By ignoring this for so long, it grew out of hand. Now it's too big to ignore.

"You were *only* supposed to help me win Kenzie back," he teases.

I bite into another nugget. "Well, that ship has sailed. Wait—I still get my promotion. Right?"

He chuckles. "The promotion is yours."

I sigh happily, thinking of a frogless future. "I could kiss you right now."

The words are out before I can tell myself to slam my mouth shut and keep them trapped firmly inside.

"Could you?" he asks, his brown eyes turning to quicksand, pulling me right in.

"I could," I say. "But I don't know if you want that. Considering you dislike me so much."

His face is close enough to mine that if I move even the

slightest, our noses will touch.

"Don't get it wrong, Jackie. I still dislike you very much," he says. "But maybe now I dislike you a little less."

My heart triples in size.

"What a coincidence," I say. "I think I dislike you a little less, too."

Wilson's face has gotten so close to mine that his brown eyes are all I see. I wait for him to pull back, to yell the punch line to the joke that always seems to come. But this time, it never does. This is real. This fluttering in my chest must mimic the fluttering in his chest; I'm not the only person leaning in— He leans in, too.

Now my only thought is how badly I want to kiss Wilson Monroe.

And just like that, Wilson's lips find mine. I once hated so many things about him, but what I now hate the most is that I ever hated him at all.

He's gentle and sweet, all the things I thought he never was. I feel it now in the way his fingers graze my cheeks, the way he cups my face and holds me close to him. He takes over all my senses—I smell his peppery cologne; I hear the steady hum of his breath; I touch the soft strands of his hair; all I see is him. When he pulls away, I've never been left so breathless. We stare at each other in silence, searching one another's faces and coming to the same answer.

Then, we begin to laugh.

"*I'm sorry*," I say, giggling uncontrollably. "I just never thought I'd be kissing you."

There is a permanent blush on his cheeks. "Thanks, Jackie. That's exactly what a guy wants to hear."

I grab a fistful of his shirt and pull him to me. "Come back here, you big baby."

We kiss again. In fact, we don't stop kissing. At some point, the sun dips below the horizon and the sky turns a midnight blue. The food has gone cold, the dessert is probably stale, and I could not care any less. Wilson and I are lying on the blanket, a tangle of limbs, and my lips are swollen from his. It's the last possible way I thought this evening would end, the exact way I hoped it would.

When we are nearly the only people left at the park and it's late enough that I have three missed calls from Julie, we begin to pack up.

Rather *Wilson* begins to pack up. I lie on my stomach, kick my feet in the air, and study his face. The slant of his jawline, the curve of his nose. Those full lips that are the prettiest shade of pink. All the tiny details I spent so long overlooking.

"You really had no idea you were planning this date for me?" I ask.

Wilson is repacking the food. "No idea," he says. "I didn't do it on purpose, at least. Or—I don't know. Maybe a part of me knew? But I wasn't ready to accept it yet."

"I always knew you had a thing for frogs. You freak."

A laugh bursts out of him so forcefully he drops the container of fries. "You'll really say anything, huh?"

I pick up the cold fries while he packs up the rest of the food.

"On a scale of one to ten, how badly are you going to miss me in costume?"

"That's an easy ten," Wilson says. "Making fun of you was the highlight of my day."

I throw a fry at his face. "Just so we're clear, don't think this means I forgive you for putting me in that costume to begin with."

He picks up the fry and throws it right back at me. It thwacks me in the eyebrow. "Don't think I've forgiven *you* for watching TV during working hours."

"So we're both still harboring resentment?"

I scrunch my face up when he kisses the tip of my nose. "Yes," he says, "but maybe a little less than before."

We finish packing up, and I text Julie that I don't need a ride home. I then promptly ignore the winky-face emoji she sends and walk to the car with Wilson. I desperately want to hold his hand, but I'm not sure if we're in hand-holding territory yet. Instead, I opt to walking as close to him as possible without either of us tripping.

As he drives me home, I open all the car windows, lean back against the headrest, and shut my eyes. The scent of Wilson's cologne is carried through the wind, and I have never, ever felt anything remotely close to this. The feeling of happiness—of possibility and excitement—creeps up on me so silently that when it hits, it hits me hard.

When I open my eyes to peek at Wilson, he's smiling as he drives.

"What is it?" I ask.

He stops at a stop sign for three seconds, of course he does, then quickly takes his eyes off the road to meet mine. "I was thinking of that day I found you in the storage room, watching TV on your phone."

I think it's about time I tell him the truth. "About that . . . I wasn't watching TV."

"Then what were you doing?"

"I was FaceTiming my sister Julie, who had just gotten engaged."

"Jackie." I see him struggle between wanting to look at me and keep his eyes on the road like the law-abiding citizen he is. "Why didn't you tell me that?"

"What? Like it would've made you *not* demote me?"

"Of course it would have," he says.

I blink at him. "You mean to say if I had told you the truth, I never would have had to wear the frog costume? I wouldn't have had to *suffer* all this time?"

He takes one hand off the wheel to grab mine. "I wouldn't have told my uncle to demote you if I knew your sister had gotten engaged. I'm not a monster."

"No. Just a bit of a tyrant." Then I groan, smacking the back of my head against the headrest. "I can't believe I could have avoided all this pain, Wilson!"

"It's not my fault," he says defensively. "No one told you to lie to me."

I think back to the months I spent sweating away in that costume. Smiling through pictures. Having my feet stepped on by children, my cheeks pinched. That's a lifetime's worth of pain and humiliation I'm never getting back.

"I'm sending you my therapy bill."

Wilson chuckles in the darkness. "I don't think any amount of therapy can erase those memories, Froggy."

I swat his arm. "That nickname dies tonight."

"I can't agree to those terms."

"Wilson—promise me all frog-related jokes are off the table."

He actually pouts. "But that'll make me very un-hoppy."

He is on a speaking ban for the rest of the drive. I accomplish this by pretending to zipper his mouth shut and throwing the imaginary key out the window. I take frog slander very seriously, and I will not be having it ever again.

I can't stop smiling. Especially as Wilson keeps his mouth pressed shut, making strange humming noises like a ghost trying to communicate with the living world. "What was that?" I say, and he just murmurs some more nonsense.

When he pulls up in front of my house, I pretend to unzip his lips. "You may speak, Willy."

He lets out a long breath. "Whew, thank God. I missed the sound of my own voice."

"I didn't." No matter how many times we may kiss, I don't think the urge to violently insult him will ever fade.

Then we sit in the silent, dark car, hanging in a moment that feels suspiciously like the end of a date. "Well," I say, "I'll see you at work tomorrow."

"Your first day back as a waitress."

This quaint peacefulness fills me from head to toe. A waitress once again. The title I spent so long fighting to reclaim is finally mine. "I'm so excited," I say.

"Three words I never thought I'd hear you say."

I catch myself by surprise when I lean across and kiss him. "Thanks for giving me my old job back."

We say good night and I get out of the car. But when Wilson rolls down his window, I stick my face in one last time for another kiss, feeling almost shy in revealing this new giddy side of myself—like all my sharp edges are beginning to dull.

When he drives off, honking twice, I stand at the end of the driveway and wave. Then I turn around, head toward the porch, and two steps later, I scream. Suzy is sitting on the front steps with her camera out, recording the entire thing.

I groan. She even got the kiss. Dammit. I won't ever live that down.

"Suz, you scared the shit out of me." I collapse on the steps beside her, realizing there is so much I want to tell her.

Suzy stops recording and places the camera on her lap. "Sorry," she says.

In those two syllables alone, I sense that something is wrong.

You don't maintain a friendship with someone for eighteen years without being able to read into every sigh, every word, every glance.

"What's wrong?" I ask. I can already feel that weightless happiness leaving my body.

"How long have you and Wilson been dating?"

I always thought that when the day came and we had a conversation like this, we'd be snickering, laughing, completely giddy. Now she only sounds mad.

"We're not dating," I say. "Well, I don't really know what we are. It kind of happened tonight."

"Tonight," she repeats. "Right, when you were too busy to hang out with me."

I remember her text asking to hang out. Then I realize what this probably looks like from her perspective.

"I went to help him set up the date for—"

"And on Sunday," she continues in a tone that's layered with hurt, "when you told me you couldn't leave the house, and then I saw Wilson pick you up."

I can see the situation spiraling out before me, and I try to reel it back in before I manage to blow up another relationship. "It's not like that," I explain. "Jillian and Julie got into a huge fight that night. Jillian straight up left—we haven't seen her since. We were all so worried, and when you texted me, I couldn't leave."

She fidgets with her camera. "You left with Wilson."

"He needed help planning his date with Kenzie." My words

are rushed, desperate. There must be something I can say to stop this train before it derails.

"Then why are you kissing him in his car?"

My breathing has gone ragged. "There's a lot to explain, but they're done. Like, officially now. And me and Wilson kind of . . . bonded, I guess?"

Suzy snorts. "You know it's more than that, Jackie."

I just want to be in my bed, tucked in, falling asleep, knowing that across the hall is Jillian in hers, and across the lawn is Suzy in hers.

This night was good. It was the beginning of something new. I don't want to taint it. I want to live in that bubble a bit longer. Is that too much to ask?

"I don't know what it is," I confess. Suzy isn't someone I lie to. She doesn't get the sugarcoated version of me, ever. She's the one person who sees everything and always chooses to stay.

"You like him," she says. Hearing it out loud is jarring. "Can't you see how messed up this whole situation is?"

"It wasn't supposed to happen like this."

"You broke him and Kenzie up, Jackie. Do you know what this looks like? It looks like you did it on purpose to take him for yourself!"

The second she puts that out here, I can't unsee it. But the hurt still bubbles up. Is that really what she thinks of me? "That's not true. You know that's not what happened."

"And what do you think Wilson is going to say when he finds

281

out?" She must see the look of shock on my face, because she adds, "Right. You haven't thought that far ahead yet."

Her words are such a blow to the heart, it knocks the air from my lungs. She's right—I haven't thought that far ahead yet. This is the first time it dawns on me that if Wilson finds out about the blog, about what I did to his relationship, he's going to hate me all over again. Now it'll seem like I ruined his relationship twice.

I drop my head into my hands. "I'll figure it out," I say, not believing it myself. "He'll understand."

"And what if he doesn't, Jackie? Because I won't be here when the time comes. I won't be here to help you. I'll be thousands of miles away, with nothing but a documentary to remember you by."

"You said that documentary was for class," I say.

"I lied," she says. "It's not for class. It's for *me*. So that when I'm in a new city with new people, I have this little piece of my best friend that I get to look back on. *That's* why I've been filming you."

That's when the tears start. And I'm not crying over a boy. I'm crying over our friendship. The constant I've had in my life since the day I was born. A constant so present and steady I think I began to take it for granted. But now, threatened with the fact that it might be ending soon, I'm realizing how desperately I need to hold on to this. That I've spent the summer with a pinkie's grip on Suzy, when what I really needed was to use both hands.

"This was supposed to be our summer together," she says. Her voice cracks on the word *our*. "This was our last summer in

Ridgewood before I'm thousands of miles away for four years. And you've managed to spend it with everyone but me."

"That— That's not true."

"You're working two jobs."

"To afford a car so we can have the road trip we've always talked about, Suzy!"

"And when you're not working," she continues, "you're running that blog or spending all your time driving around with Wilson. You ditched our movie night last week to see him, too. How many times am I going to come second to him?"

"Suzy—you're leaving!" Just like that, all my bottled-up emotions spill out. "I'm sorry for focusing on my blog and on Wilson, but you have to understand that I'm *trying* to figure out what's next. I'm trying to find out who I am and where I even manage to fit in here. So that the second you leave town, I'm not left alone. I'm trying to figure out how to exist without my best friend."

"Jackie—"

"You've always been here," I say, swallowing that feeling of my throat closing in. "Our entire lives, we have been separated by no more than ten feet. I look out my freaking window and I see your bedroom. I've realized that so much of my life and who I am is shaped by the people I love. You, Julie, Jillian. I'm like this freaking patchwork of the three of you. And now that you're leaving, it feels like I'm losing part of myself. Like I don't know who I am or who to be without you. Do you get that? I'm sorry for being absent. I guess I've just been trying to come to terms with a world without you, so that it hurts the slightest bit less when you're actually gone."

Tears sting my eyes, and I begin to shut down. This week has been a test of strength, and I'm failing drastically. So many things have been piled and piled and piled on top of me, and I'm nowhere near strong enough to carry all this weight around without collapsing beneath it.

"I can't do this right now," I whisper. My eyes are drooping closed, and I don't want to open them anymore. "You don't understand how long this week has been. Between the fight with Jillian, the constant worrying if she's all right . . . I've been trying my best to balance everything, and I'm sorry if you managed to slip through the cracks, but I can't do this right now, Suzy. I can't handle this on top of everything else. Can we *please* talk about this tomorrow? Can we make this right?"

She fidgets with her camera. "I didn't know you were going through all that."

"I'm sorry I haven't had time to share it with you," I say genuinely.

"We can talk tomorrow," she says. "But you promise it'll be tomorrow? Nothing else will get in the way?"

"I promise."

We both stand up. I feel unsteady on my own two feet. When Suzy hugs me, I nearly fall down. "I know you're trying your best," she says, "but I need my best friend back."

"Tomorrow," I promise her. "Tomorrow, I'm all yours." I

mean it this time, too. No matter what craziness ensues tomorrow, I will be there with Suzy. She's a promise I will no longer break.

I watch Suzy walk home, then head inside myself. When the door shuts behind me, I'm tempted to collapse against it. Somehow, I drag myself up the stairs and into my room. The entire house is quiet, all the bedroom doors closed. Except Jillian's, obviously. She still isn't home.

Before I can snuggle into bed, I realize I haven't checked *iDiary* all day. After what happened with Jill and her promotion, I don't know if I ever want to open it again. But thinking about all those unanswered messages makes me feel guilty, so I go to grab my laptop off my desk and realize it's not there. Right—I left it downstairs on the couch.

But when I head to the living room, it isn't there either.

Panic creeps in. I tell myself to breathe, calm down. It's here somewhere. It has to be.

I head to Julie's room and knock on her bedroom door. When five seconds go by without an answer, I nudge it open and find her asleep. Luckily Julie is a light sleeper, so all it takes is a quick shoulder nudge to wake her up.

"What is it?" she says, rubbing at her eyes.

"Have you seen my laptop?"

She groans, rolling back over in bed and pulling the blanket up to her chin. "I don't know. Ask Jillian."

I must have misheard her. "Why would Jillian know?"

"Mom said she came by today to pick up some clothes and stuff. She probably thought your laptop was hers, like she always does, and took it by accident."

No. No no no no no.

That can't be possible.

I run out of Julie's room and back to mine. I throw the blanket off my bed, the pillows, everything. I look in drawers, in the closet, check every nook and cranny.

My laptop is nowhere to be found.

I'm barely able to force out a breath.

If Jillian took my laptop, it's only a matter of time before she tries to use it.

And when she does, the first thing she'll see is my *iDiary* account.

CHAPTER 23

BEFORE MY SHIFT AT Monte's, I call Jillian about seventy-six times. Each call goes straight to voicemail. I sit in bed, riddled with exhaustion, trying to figure out how exactly I'm supposed to handle this. I don't even know where Jill *is* so I can go and snatch my laptop back. And assuming she is at Camilla's, I have no idea where Camilla lives either.

For once, I take a deep breath and make a Big Girl Decision. I have to prioritize Monte's. Today is my first day back as a waitress, which means my laptop will have to wait for another six hours. I simply have to hope that Jillian somehow doesn't peek, doesn't find my *iDiary* account, and doesn't hate my guts.

This is going to be a long day.

But when I arrive at Monte's, I am so unbearably excited to be a waitress again that the laptop anxiety momentarily fades. My mind is pinned on the higher pay, the tips, the frogless job. Being able to leave work and not looking like a sweaty mess. I checked my bank account the other day, and I'm *so* close to having enough saved up for the car. If I bring in enough tips, it's a done deal. Not to mention that I get to see Wilson again, and that is enough to light me up from head to toe.

"I can't believe you're abandoning me," Anita says, pouting.

We stand in the break room before our shift, Anita in her squirrel costume and me in the waitress uniform: jeans, a white T-shirt, and our green Monte's Magic Castle apron tied around my waist. I smile at my reflection in the mirror, smoothing out a few wrinkles here and there. It's been a long time coming.

"I'm not *abandoning* you," I say, even though I am, sort of.

"You're leaving me alone in the woodlands crew. Next thing I know, you're taking Margaret's job as the princess."

That's ridiculous enough to make me laugh. "I could never be a princess."

"You were a great frog." Anita grabs my shoulders and gently shakes me. Her eyeliner-rimmed eyes stare intensely into mine. "This doesn't have to be the end, Jacqueline. Just get into the frog costume and we can pretend the identity crisis never happened."

I step out of her grip. "Jackie isn't short for Jacqueline, weirdo."

"That's beside the point."

"Look, Anita. Frog Jackie is dead and gone. The quicker you move on, the better." Satisfied with my uniform, I move on to my hair. As waitresses, we are required to have our hair tied up. This morning, Julie helped tie my curls back into a neat little bun. She even did a few braids at my temples to keep my baby hairs at bay. It actually looks pretty cute.

Anita hops off the pity train and takes a seat on the couch. "How did you even manage to convince Wilson to give you your old job back?"

Good thing I was prepared for this exact line of questioning. Before work this morning I sat in bed and planned the entire story in my head. I definitely don't want anyone thinking that my budding relationship with Wilson is what got me the job.

I grab a bag of chips from the cupboard—the ones I picked out with Wilson at SmartMart—then take a seat next to Anita on the couch. I rip open the bag and offer her one. She takes a handful. "Remember Kenzie's breakup letter?"

"I do," she says, crunching away.

"Well, I made a deal with Wilson," I share. "If I helped him win her back, he'd give me my old job back."

Anita looks impressed. "No shit. He actually agreed to it?"

I pop a chip into my mouth. "He was desperate," I say. *And so was I.*

She chews thoughtfully. "Wait— So if you got the promotion, that means he and Kenzie are back together."

"Nope. They broke up for good yesterday." I have to hide the giddiness from my voice. "Turns out they both moved on."

"And he still honored your promotion?"

I nod. "He's a man of his word."

If she can sense that there's information I'm leaving out, Anita doesn't pry. Instead she reapplies a coat of gloss to her lips and smiles. "Good for you, Jackie. Don't get me wrong, I still hate you for ditching me, but I respect the hustle."

I grin proudly. "Thanks."

Then our time has run out, and the clock reads nine. We punch in for our shift, and as we're walking down the hallway to the main area, Wilson's head peeks out from his office door. "Jackie. Do you have a minute?" I tell Anita to go on without me. She shoots me a worried look, but I insist, waving her away.

The moment I step into Wilson's office, he shuts the door behind me.

"Hi," we say in unison. We are both shy and nervous, trying to navigate this new dynamic.

"Nice uniform," he adds.

"Thanks," I say. "Froggy's on fire out back."

His laughter is punctured with that typical Wilson serious-ness. "I think you're joking, but as your boss, I have to ask—*is* the frog costume currently burning behind Monte's?"

"Of course not," I say. "But that costume should be burned. Or at least dry-cleaned, and maybe more than once."

The smile on his face does something unusual to my heart. "Noted."

He is typical Wilson today, the version of himself I have grown most attached to—neat hair, khakis, white shirt. He is so wholly *him* that it makes my breath catch.

He perches on the chair's armrest. I try not to wiggle when his eyes rake me over, head to toe. "Are you sure you're ready to be a waitress again? We can have Dominique train you for a few days—"

"Wilson," I say very sternly, showing him that I mean business. "I was waitressing at Monte's before you even worked here."

"I want you to feel comfortable."

"This is where I feel most comfortable. Didn't Monte Jr. tell you that I consistently brought in the highest tips?"

Wilson grabs my hand and gently tugs me toward him. His eyes are soft, gentle. I feel so elated to be the one he looks at that way. "He didn't," he says.

"Well, I did, and you're just going to have to take my word for it." I know it may seem like I'm lying, but I'm not. I was a great waitress once upon a time. "And what about you? How's that list of changes going?"

At the mention of a to-do list, I see Wilson's entire body shift, like it's adjusting under the weight of his responsibilities. He runs his free hand down his face and says, "I have four interviews this afternoon for cleaners, and we're having new cameras installed by the end of the week. Inside and outside."

I squeeze his hands. I know how hard change is for him, too, but this is a great way to start. "See? I knew you could handle it. But make sure you tell me where all those cameras are, so I know where to avoid."

That makes him laugh, and maybe that's what the two of us

need: his sternness and my inability to take anything seriously. We are like a perfectly balanced scale.

"I'm hoping to have the floors replaced by the winter," Wilson continues. "We're going to have to close for a week or so."

That's music to my ears. "I think everyone could use a week off. Especially you."

He blinks up at me. I don't miss the subtle lines of exhaustion etched into his face. Suddenly, all the authority and the responsibility is stripped away, and I'm staring down at a nineteen-year-old who is keeping a family legacy together and doing a damn good job at it.

"Your dad would be so proud of you," I say. I hope it doesn't cross a line. I hope it doesn't make him uncomfortable or drudge up bad feelings or—

Wilson stands up abruptly, and then he is kissing me. If his arms weren't locked around my waist, I would've been knocked backward. It takes a minute for my brain to restart, and then I am right there, too, meeting him halfway. The feel of his lips, the touch of his hands, the warmth of his breath. It's a feeling that is so new, and I never want it to get old.

"Thank you for saying that," he says, resting his forehead on mine.

"I mean it," I say.

"I'm proud of you, too," he adds. "And I'm excited to see you as a waitress. To be fair, you as a frog set the bar pretty low, so it's only up from here."

I lightly smack his arm. "Just you wait. Soon you'll be implementing a new Employee of the Month program strictly to award it to me."

When Wilson laughs, his face is so close that I catch his breath with my own. "Showing you favoritism is probably a mistake."

"Fine," I agree. "I'll take my rewards in private, in the form of various chocolate bars."

I think that reminds him of something. He quickly says, "Just so you know, my entire car now smells like fried food and chocolate."

"Then perhaps you shouldn't have a crush on a girl who strictly consumes those two food groups."

"Remind me to introduce you to a vegetable."

"I would rather die."

Wilson kisses me again. I hope that door is locked, but it doesn't stop me from digging my fingers into his hair and holding his face to mine. I breathe in his familiar cologne. I remember how a month ago we sat in this room, arguing across the desk. Now the space is the same, but the people in it are entirely different.

When he breaks away, I meet him with a smile. "You're going to make me late for work."

He checks his watch and sighs. "You're right. You should go."

As if it physically pains him to do so, Wilson pulls away. His hands remain on my waist, his eyes locked on mine.

"You are my boss, you know," I say. "You could just allow me to be late."

"I could," he says, "but we both know how much I hate tardiness."

That makes me laugh. "I swear you're nineteen verging on ninety."

"I have to be mature enough for the two of us, Jackie."

Another fantastic point.

Wilson kisses me goodbye, and I'm off, sneaking down the hallway like a ninja, checking over my shoulders to make sure no one has spotted me. It's completely unnecessary and silly, but also sort of fun, so I continue to do it anyway. When I make it to the dining area, I realize I'm the only waitress scheduled today—which means every table is mine for the taking. Normally, I'd be stressed and annoyed with the prospect of actually having to work. Today, I feel hungry. Hungry to make some money, buy myself that Nissan, and, most important, impress Wilson.

When the first three hours of my shift go by, I've only had three customers: two families that showed up with their kids, and one group of teenagers that ordered both an impressive and disturbing amount of pizza.

The real money comes from serving parties—that's where the tips are. Tables like this don't make much, but I still have fun flexing these old muscles. The second I went to greet that first table for lunch, everything came back to me. My old greetings, the way I memorize the orders (mentally linking the food to some part of their appearance, like *cheese pizza for striped shirt*), the dad jokes I used to carry in my arsenal. When the teenagers ask for hot sauce, I bring them two types. "This one is very hot," I say, handing them the first. When I place the second bottle on the table, I finish it off with, "This one isn't as hot, but it has a great personality." It makes all of them laugh.

When my shift ends, it's the most fun I've had at Monte's probably ever. I meet Anita in the break room. "So?" she prompts, taking a chocolate chip muffin from the case. "Was being a waitress everything you wished for and more?"

I think the grin on my face says enough. "Anita, I forgot how fun it was."

She looks at me like I'm crazy, but also like she's happy for me. "Please don't turn into some weirdo who actually enjoys being here. I can't handle any more optimism."

I hook my arm through hers and we head outside to the parking lot. Wilson is locked away in an interview, but I text him a quick goodbye. When we get outside, the heat slams right into me. I search for Julie's car in the parking lot and come up empty. Which is weird. Julie is never late. She knows I finish work at three. She's always here, parked in the first row, waiting with the windows down.

Anita holds a hand up to her eyes to block out the sun. "Something wrong?"

"My sister isn't here." I'm already on my phone, dialing her number.

"Damn it. Your hot sister isn't coming today?"

"No— Not Jillian. Also, *ew*. I thought we agreed you'd stop with that. My other sister, Julie, was supposed to be here." And now she's not answering her phone either. I call two more times, and it goes right to voicemail.

"Come on." Anita takes my hand and ushers me through the parking lot. "I'll give you a ride home."

Which is how I end up stuffed into her car. And when I say stuffed, I mean *stuffed*. The entire car is littered with garbage—plastic water bottles, fast-food bags, too many receipts to count. There are even black eyeliner pencils everywhere. I find two of them in the cupholder and one wedged between the seat. It makes me desperately miss Wilson's car, with its fresh leather scent and freakishly clean interior.

During the drive home I try to call Julie two more times. Both go straight to voicemail, which makes a steady beat of panic creep into my chest. Julie always answers her phone. If I miss one of her calls, she assumes I'm somewhere dead in a ditch and has 911 on standby. For her to not answer, something must be wrong.

When Anita pulls up in front of my house, the answer stares me straight in the face.

Jillian is home.

Her car is parked in the driveway, like it never left.

That must be why Julie isn't answering. She and Jill are either talking through their fight or are so deep into a screaming match that their voices drown out the ringtone.

After thanking Anita for the ride, I creep up my driveway. I try to peer into the windows, but the blinds are closed. Which means I'm going to have to handle this the old-fashioned way.

I unlock the door and step inside to meet my fate—

Julie and Jillian are sitting side by side on the couch, staring at me. On the cushion between them is my laptop. And on the screen is my *iDiary* account.

CHAPTER 24

"YOU'RE HOME," I SAY to Jillian. For a moment, my laptop and the secret they dug up doesn't even matter. I'm so relieved to see my sister sitting there that I ignore the anger in her eyes.

It's Julie who answers. "Jackie, come sit."

On the laptop screen, they have my *iDiary* profile pulled up, showing the last couple of messages I answered. If you scroll down—which I'm certain they have—you can see every piece of advice I've ever given. All the evidence, right there.

"I don't want to sit," I say. Like a storm brewing, I brace for the fight coming. "I don't want to do this again."

"Then maybe you never should have done this"—Jill says, pointing at my laptop—"to begin with. Sit down, Jackie."

My nose begins to burn. My lips quiver. I feel that familiar lump in my throat, the telltale sign that tears are coming.

I take a seat in the armchair across from them. I stare at my knees. My fingers shake. I feel so small, like the stupid youngest sister in need of a scolding.

"Can you even begin to comprehend how humiliating it was for us to read through all these messages?" Jillian says. "To see our most private, intimate moments shared over and over again on your account for entertainment? Like our feelings are some sort of joke to you?"

"Your feelings aren't a joke to me at all. I thought—"

Julie cuts in. "Let her speak, Jackie." Her words aren't fueled with anger like Jillian's. She sounds hurt—deeply hurt. Somehow, it's worse.

"I don't even know what to say," Jillian says. "I can't believe this even *has* to be said. I have to explicitly tell my sister not to blast my personal details all over the internet. That night you came into my bedroom and woke me up, asking me questions about my ex, Hugh. I told you not to share that with anyone. And what did you do? You turned around and published it on your blog not even five minutes later."

I don't know what to say. She's right. I did that and, in the moment, I didn't even think twice.

"You did the same thing to me," Julie says softly. "That day in your bedroom, when you asked me for advice on friends-with-benefits. I told you how hard it was to relive that experience, Jackie. How difficult it was for me to lose my best friend. I was being vulnerable and open with you, thinking my little sister needed my help. But you were just using me for more content."

"Julie— No, that's not why," I begin before Jill cuts me off.

"We told you a lot of intimate details about our lives when you were really young," Julie says. She has her legs crossed on the cushion, fidgeting with her fingers on her lap. "Maybe we shouldn't have shared so much."

"No," I cut in quickly. "Are you kidding? I loved hearing all of it."

Jillian scoffs. "Clearly. You've been what, taking notes for how many years? Waiting for the day you could profit off our pain?"

There are two things I know for certain. The first is that I messed up, badly. The second is that when Jillian is mad, her words aim to kill. What I did was wrong, but I don't deserve to be painted as some monstrous, manipulative person who's been scheming for years.

I manage to remember I have a spine, and I sit up straighter. "That's not fair. I didn't do any of this maliciously. If you scrolled back far enough, you'd see how the blog started and how it spiraled out of control."

"But it's your account, Jackie," Jill fires back. "At any moment you could have shut it down. You could have chosen to stop responding. You could have realized that what you were doing was wrong. I mean, you woke me up in the middle of the night to ask me about a breakup I went through years ago. And here I thought you were just, I don't know, curious? But you were trying to pry information out of me so you could resell my experiences as your own!"

"It was really jarring, Jackie," Julie says now. "To see the way you spun all our past experiences into these quirky little responses. You recycled our stories to make them come off as your own. You lied to thousands of people."

"I thought I was helping them," I say honestly. I really, really did. All those users who wrote in every day—who left comments, sent messages telling me how much my advice helped them. It was like a high I didn't want to come down from.

"Did you think that?" Jill asks. "Because I noticed you monetized your account. From my perspective, it looks like you were only trying to help yourself."

"I've been trying to save up for my road trip with Suzy," I explain. "I haven't earned any money off of the blog. I'll unenroll from the program right now."

"I want to know why you did it," Julie says. "Why you felt the need to go along with this charade and orchestrate this new persona for yourself online. Why?"

This is the part that hurts the most. The shame and the guilt that comes with voicing it. What I want is to run away, lock myself in my bedroom, and keep these feelings to myself. But right now, sitting in front of my sisters, I realize that the *only* way they may understand is if I share that shame with them.

"Because I don't know who I am," I say. I hate the way my

voice shakes, how I have to squeeze my eyes shut so it feels like I'm sitting here alone, talking to myself. "Suzy is leaving, and I was so overwhelmed with trying to figure myself out. She has this passion, this talent, this *thing* she wants to pursue and do with her life. She has a plan, the same way both of you do."

I look at Julie. I force myself to look right at her as I speak, even though it would be so much easier to look away. "Julie, you're a great teacher. You're getting married, you want kids. Your whole life is an answer, not a question mark. And you too, Jill." I turn to her now. "You have a great career. You know exactly who you are. I felt like I was surrounded with all these complete, self-aware people, and I was the one falling behind. When I started that blog, I didn't have plans for college. I was working at a job I hated. When I thought about my future and what I wanted for myself, it felt paralyzing. It was so scary to not know where I wanted to end up a year or two from now."

I take a breath, open my eyes, and find that we're still here, still standing. Even with the words out there, nothing has changed.

"I started *pleasebreakmyheart* by accident," I continue. "It was one silly message I answered, and it spiraled entirely out of control. I had hundreds of people writing in, looking at *me* for advice. Looking at *me* for answers. And that validation—that feeling of having thousands of strangers tell you that you're good at something? It felt like I found what I've spent years looking for. All I wanted was to have a calling, *one* thing I was good at. After so long, I finally found it. I had this blog and the praise that came

302

with it, and it felt so, so good. It felt great to finally be good at something."

When the words are done erupting from my chest, I take another shaky breath. Tears have gathered on my chin, and I wipe them away with the sleeve of my shirt. It might be the most I've ever said to my sisters at once. It's definitely the most personal information I've ever shared with anyone.

When my hands stop shaking and my breathing has slowed down, I peel my gaze away from the floor and look up. On the couch, Jill is staring at me with an unreadable expression on her face. Next to her, Julie is crying.

"This isn't about me," I continue. "The reason why I did it doesn't even matter anymore. You're both right—I shouldn't have shared all that information. Believe me, I regret every message I answered. But I really, really thought I was helping people. If I had even thought for a second it would hurt either of you, I would have stopped. You have to believe me."

"I do," Julie says. "I believe you."

I turn to Jillian. I need her to say something. I need her to be my big sister and tell me that everything will be okay.

"I understand why you did it, Jackie," she says finally. "And I think we're both sorry you were going through all that. But—" When Jillian's voice cracks, a new wave of tears spills out of me.

I watch her pull herself together. I watch her swallow the tears.

"I confided in you about my promotion," she says, her face as hard as stone. "I didn't even tell Julie, or Mom and Dad. I told *you* about it. And you sat there and you sabotaged me. You knew what turning down that interview would cost me, and you did it anyway. Even if your reasoning was justified, you could have talked to me. You could have told me. That was your chance to come clean, to make this right, and you doubled down and let it affect my *career*. Do you not see how hurtful that is?"

"I do," I say, tears soaking my lips. "I'm sorry."

There's a million other things I could say. I could tell her that when Camilla threatened to expose my identity, it scared me and I wanted to protect myself. I could tell Jillian how many days I spent going back and forth trying to figure out what to do, but none of it would matter, because I did it. I cost her the promotion. I affected her career. And the truth is, I don't even think I felt bad. I was only focused on my own pain. I chose myself over her dream job, and I'd give anything to take that back.

Jillian stands up. "I've been staying with Camilla," she says. "I was planning on coming home tomorrow, but I think I need a bit more time now. Just tell Mom and Dad I'm safe."

When she walks by me, I still wait for her to pause. To hug me. To offer me some sort of comfort I know I don't deserve. But like the last time she left, Jillian goes without another word. There's only the sound of her keys jingling, the door closing, then her car pulling out of the driveway.

Julie reaches for a tissue and blows her nose. I go and sit beside her on the couch.

"Please don't hate me," I say. I feel like I'm five years old again. A little kid who's still learning the difference between right and wrong.

"We don't hate you, Jackie. You're our sister. We love you more than anyone else possibly could. But those were our private feelings. You had no right to use them as your own."

I keep wiping the endless stream of tears on my shirtsleeve. "You're right. I shouldn't have done any of it."

She grabs another tissue and wipes at her eyes. "Look, I think everyone needs some space right now."

"Don't leave too—"

"I'm going to stay at Massimo's for a bit," she cuts in quickly. The words gut me. "You really hurt us, Jackie. And I know you probably want to find a way to fix this, but it isn't something for *you* to fix. Right now, maybe just leave us to ourselves so we can find a way to move past this. Okay?"

"Okay," I whisper.

"Can you look after Mr. Chunks?"

"Of course."

Julie looks exactly like Jillian when she grabs her car keys and leaves through the front door.

I stay on the couch a bit longer and cry. The Myers house is now empty, so there's no one even left to hear me. I let myself sink into the hurt. It's what I deserve.

I grab my laptop and opt out of the creators program, ensuring that I don't earn a penny from any of this. When I reach to place the laptop back on the coffee table, I nearly drop it on the floor when I spot Mr. Chunks's head peeking out. I freeze, certain that even the slightest movement will scare him away. His big eyes stare into mine. Then, ever so slowly, he wiggles his giant body out from the couch and plops down on the soft spot of carpet right beside it.

"Hi, buddy," I say. Very gently, I reach down and nudge my fingers into the soft fur gathered at his neck. He instantly begins to purr, craning his neck to the side so I can really get in there.

It's the first time since Julie brought him home that he's stepped out from beneath the couch, and neither of my sisters is here to see it.

My tear drops onto his little nose, and he licks it off.

"You don't hate me, Mr. Chunks. Do you?"

He instantly scurries back under the couch.

Great. Even the cat wants nothing to do with me.

Before bed, I call Suzy. Not matter how badly I want this day to end, I promised her yesterday that we'd talk, and I'll be damned if I manage to let another person down today.

We're both sitting at our bedroom windows with the curtains open, having our usual phone conversation while staring out across the stretch of lawn at each other. She's wearing a sheet mask and braiding her hair. I'm cozied up in an oversize T-shirt with a mug of decaf green tea. I tell her everything about today and wonder when I stopped realizing how important it is to share my life with her.

"Are you going to delete the account?" Suzy asks when I've finished.

"It's the right thing to do," I say, holding the mug up to my chin, letting the heat warm my face.

"Maybe hold off for a bit. You never know if they'll come around."

"They won't," I say with certainty. "And they shouldn't."

I glance at Suzy through the window. She readjusts the sheet mask sliding down her face. "I hate these stupid things," she grumbles to herself. "Look, at least you got a taste of internet fame. How many people can say that?"

"I guess, yeah. It was nice while it lasted."

"What do we do next?" she asks.

Suzy saying *we* tugs at my heart, making me feel less alone.

I wish I knew. "More than the fame, I really did like helping people. I loved the follow-up messages, when they told me how well the advice worked. It felt good, knowing I made someone's life a bit better."

When I look out the window again, Suzy's face has lit up. The mask slides right off. "Oh my *God*, this thing is the worst. But Jackie—I have an idea. Tell me, what's the one good thing that came out of this mess?"

I rack my brain for an answer. All I can think of is Wilson, but I doubt that's what Suzy is referring to. In fact, she hasn't asked about him once.

But then, from the corner of my mind, I pull out another

realization. *The Rundown* didn't only introduce me to loads of great people and great career paths. It made me realize that I really do enjoy helping people—I just said it myself to Suzy. Running my *iDiary* account, speaking with small businesses in town, grabbing lunch for all the girls, making customers laugh with my dad jokes as I take their orders.

For my entire life, that's how my sisters made me feel. Their guidance, their presence, their jokes—all of it made each day easier. Every experience felt more familiar knowing they had experienced it first. By helping people on *pleasebreakmyheart*, it felt like I was finally sending that back into the universe. Like I was helping other young women the same way my sisters helped me.

"I think I found my passion," I say slowly.

"I think so, too."

"And I work at a magazine," I say. "Maybe I can keep doing it. Or a new version of it. I can talk to Camilla about starting some sort of advice column. Maybe Jill and I could even team up on it?"

It doesn't even have to be relationship focused. I could give advice on how to best clean vomit, or how to fall for your mortal enemy. Whatever the advice may be, I just want to keep helping people in some way.

Suzy gasps. "I love that! You can call it like '*Sisters Talking*' or something. Wait, that's really bad. Don't call it that. But something along those lines."

"Suz, this is really good idea," I say. My mind is racing,

thinking of a million different ways to make this happen. This pit of hope plants itself in my chest, and I can feel it growing by the second. "*The Rundown* doesn't have a segment like this yet. It could bring in a whole new audience."

"It doesn't have to be anonymous either," Suzy adds. "This time, you could actually be credited for your work."

The daydreaming comes to a halt when I realize the one big obstacle. "Except Jillian currently hates me and will never go for it. Not to mention that I highly doubt Camilla will green-light this either."

I lean my head against the cool glass.

"Good ideas take time," Suzy says to console me. "Maybe not right now, but who knows where you and Jill will stand in a week? A month? Just promise me you'll pitch the idea to her at some point, because it's fantastic."

I stare down into my tea. I realize I'm holding the pink *Best Sister Ever* mug that Julie bought me for Christmas last year. She bought Jillian the same one but in black. Of course, Jill barely had a reaction to it and simply set it aside. But every night, I saw her fill it with hot cocoa and carry it to her room. She held the mug with two hands, like it was precious enough to cradle.

"I promise," I say. When Jill and I put this behind us, I'm going to run the idea by her and see what she says. A way for us *both* to control the narrative.

"And hey," Suzy says, her tone growing serious. "About yesterday—"

"I'm sorry again," I blurt out. "I shouldn't have ditched you for Wilson. This is our last summer together, and I should've put you first."

"I'm sorry too," Suzy says. "I had no idea you were struggling with all those things. I should have asked. I— Well, I should have been more considerate with how much I was talking about college and leaving Ridgewood."

"You were excited, Suz. I want you to share that with me."

"Yeah, but I could have done it in a way that didn't make you feel left out. I guess . . . Well, I guess even with me moving away, it never once made me question how our friendship would change. Like, I know it will be different, obviously, but I also know it will always be there."

"How can you say that so confidently?" I ask, voicing the question that has weighed on me for far too long.

Dreading the day when her room will be empty, I watch her through the window.

"Because I would never let us *not* be friends, Jackie. Ever. As long as we promise each other that, we're set for life."

"I promise," I say.

"I promise," she says, and those two words are somehow exactly what I've needed to hear for months.

"And for the record, I *am* excited for you, Suzy. I give it like, five years before you're nominated for an Oscar."

"Five? Maybe *twenty*-five," she corrects, but she's laughing all the same.

"You know, we still have a few weeks of summer left . . ." I add.

"We do. And I have *so many* things planned for us, but let's put that on pause. Right now, I need to know what the hell is going on with you and Wilson."

"It's about time you asked," I say, and I tell her everything.

CHAPTER 25

THREE DAYS PASS IN silence. Julie doesn't stop by, neither does Jill. But on Friday afternoon, Wilson calls at five o'clock. That makes me smile. It's the only beacon of light in this entire ordeal.

When I answer, I'm expecting him to say he's finishing early tonight. Maybe he'll ask me to hang out after Monte's is closed. Or better yet, maybe he has another date planned and we can—

"Jackie," he says frantically the moment I answer the call. "I know it's your night off, but can you come in?"

"Why do you sound like you're dying?"

"I think I am," he whispers. On the other end, I can hear a baby crying and what sounds like the door to Wilson's office slamming shut. "Dominique called in sick, we're down a server, and we have a birthday party arriving in thirty minutes. Please. I need you."

Twenty-five minutes later I'm walking through Monte's front

door. I catch Wilson standing at the ticket kiosks, engaged in a serious conversation with a mother who is holding a screaming child against her hip. We hold a second's worth of eye contact, and it's somehow enough to propel me through the next three hours.

The party arrives. It's a group of twenty-two kids and just as many parents, all celebrating a twelve-year-old's birthday. Since the other waiters are busy serving the rest of the guests, I take on the party by myself. There's a brief moment where I second-guess whether I can even handle this, but the moment I tie my apron and step into the zone, I've got it under control. I'm running out pitcher after pitcher of Coca-Cola and ice water. They order enough pizza to send Ridgewood into a wheat crisis, and the birthday boy insists on a "birthday tower of mozzarella sticks." I get creative and ask the kitchen to whip up a triple batch. When they're hot out of the fryer, I grab the baskets we reserve for french fries, line it with our signature checkered paper, pour the mozzarella sticks in so they create a small mountain, and stick a candle on top. For a reason I can't comprehend, it's a huge hit with the guests. The birthday boy screams so loud when he sees it that I actually have to cover my ears.

Then it's time for cake. We have it stored in the kitchen fridge, and I carry it out oh so carefully. I haven't sliced a cake in ages, but the second the knife glides through that blue and red butter-cream—yes, it was Spider-Man themed—we're in business. I get a good sixty slices out of it and hand out plate after plate faster than I can count. When the kids flee the table to hit the arcade, the parents order coffees and a few teas. I bring them out on two perfectly balanced trays and then, for the first time in three hours, I catch my breath.

The dinner rush begins to die down, and some of the other tables free up. A few waiters ask if I need help, but I insist that I'm fine. I want this party all for myself. That way, I'm not expected to split the tip with anyone.

After a few of the guests leave, I wipe down the tables and bring out a second round of cake for the kids who trickle back in. Finally, the birthday boy's parents pay the bill and tip me a fat twenty-two percent, ringing in at nearly $176.00. I stare down at the check with the biggest grin on my face. *This* is why I fought to be a waitress so bad. Froggy money never paid up like this. It never felt this good, either.

After the party leaves and I begin cleaning up, a little squeal catches my attention. I look over and find three girls, no older than eight, huddled together by the claw machine. Trapped in the claw is a shiny pink dolphin. It's getting closer and closer to being dropped into the slot when it falls right back on top of the mountain of plushies. The youngest girl immediately falls to the ground and bursts into tears. The two older ones, who I'm realizing are her sisters, don't miss a beat. One of them sits down beside her and squeezes her tightly. The other sister gets to work. She shoves a few more tickets into the machine and tries again. I watch in agony as the claw grasps the dolphin and drops it right back on top.

Before I understand why I'm doing it, I stop wiping the table and march over there. I always keep a stash of tickets in my apron for this exact reason. The girl manning the game easily steps aside when I approach. I stick three tickets into the machine, and it whirs to life. I maneuver the claw to the left, back a little, then a smidge to the right. I rotate the *tiniest* amount, then slap the big red button. The claw lurches down and grabs the dolphin. When it drops right into the winning slot, all four of us screech with excitement.

I grab the sparkly pink plushie and crouch down until I'm eye to eye with the youngest daughter. "This is for you," I say, handing it over to her.

Her face is red and splotchy, her cheeks so adorably chubby. She takes the dolphin from my hand and immediately tugs it to her chest, burying her face into its soft little body. Then she lurches forward and wraps her tiny arms around my neck.

"Fanks," she says, probably leaking snot and tears on my T-shirt. Still, I hug her tightly.

"You're welcome."

I look up to find her two sisters smiling at me. A second later, the three of them run off, probably to win more games and make more memories to someday look back on.

When Anita walks over to me, I'm leaning against the claw machine, crying my eyes out. As soon as she spots the tears, she looks uncomfortable. It reminds me so much of Jillian that I only cry harder.

"Geez. Was the tip that party left you really that bad?"

That gets a laugh out of me, albeit a wet one. I untie my apron and use it to wipe my eyes. "No. It was actually really good."

"Then why are you crying?"

Because I miss my sisters. Because I miss the days when we were this inseparable, unstoppable force that acted as one another's shadow. We were three unmovable parts of a whole, and it seemed as if we had so much time to stay like that. And now we've grown up, and someday they'll move on—into another house, maybe another state. We have only so many more moments left to be together like this, and I've already wasted too many of them fighting.

When it's clear that I can barely get a word out through the tears, Anita walks me to the front door, careful to keep a solid three feet of space between us so I don't taint her with my emotions.

She holds the door open and pushes me outside. "Get some air, Jackie. Just don't go too close to my car, all right? I'm not in the mood to clean boogers off it tomorrow."

I make it to the back of the building where the dumpsters are. I lean against the brick wall and manage to stand up for a solid minute before I begin to cry. When my legs give out, I slide down, down, down, until I'm sitting on the ground. The sobs break out of me so violently that my entire body begins to shake.

There's a burning in my chest, too. An unmistakable contempt

I feel for myself. All I want is to turn back time. Go back to before I started *pleasebreakmyheart* and allow myself the chance to do everything differently. I'd gladly sacrifice the promotion, go back to being in that freaking frog costume, if only it meant returning home to a house that isn't empty.

I'm searching my apron for a tissue when I hear a pair of shoes scuffling toward me. I look up, and it's Wilson, holding an entire box of tissues. I feel so relieved and happy to see him that I begin to cry all over again. Before I can stand, he is sitting down beside me, pulling me into his chest. And I know how clean his car is, how tidy his office is. Yet here he is, cross-legged on the dirty ground, all in the name of comforting me.

I bury my face into his neck. His hands rub small circles on my back, and the slight pressure feels so, so nice. I focus on that instead, use it to calm my racing heart. He doesn't say a word. He just sits there, holds me, lets me slowly pull myself back together. Somehow, he seems to know exactly what I need.

And yet all I can focus on is the guilt. There is this ten-pound weight on my chest that reminds me of what I did to him. How *pleasebreakmyheart* not only hurt my sisters but hurt him, too. The only difference is he doesn't know it yet.

"Do you want to talk about it?" he whispers, still holding me. He takes tissue after tissue out of the box and dabs at my face. "Did a customer say something to you? I can't promise I'll beat them up, but I'll give them a very stern talking-to."

It's so ridiculously *him* that it makes me laugh, which quickly turns into more tears.

"Jackie." He grabs me again, and we collide together. All I can think is how badly I don't deserve this. That the only reason we got here is because I hurt him, and then I lied to him about it for weeks.

I pull away again and take the tissue from his hand, wiping at my eyes.

"Talk to me," he begs.

It feels like there's a roadblock in my throat. I open my mouth, and nothing comes out. Maybe because the words I truly need to say are too terrifying to put out there.

Before I can dig up the courage for that, I opt for a different truth. "I miss my sisters."

Wilson latches on to that tiny bit of information. "Tell me what happened."

"We got into a fight," I say, my voice hoarse. "I really messed up, Wilson. I hurt them so badly."

He reaches through the darkness and grabs my hand. "Do you want to tell me what you did?"

And before I even know it, I'm telling him everything. About *iDiary*. About *pleasebreakmyheart*. The hundreds of messages and the thousands of followers. I leave out the bit about Kenzie, but I tell him the rest. How I exploited Julie and Jillian, used their secrets so carelessly. How I'm terrified that they may never forgive me.

When I finish, Wilson sits there in silence. "Wow," he says. "I was not expecting any of that."

"Yeah," I say. The tears have subsided, but I can't seem to stop sniffling. "Do you think I'm a terrible person?"

When Wilson smiles at me, it's nothing short of a lifeline. "Jackie, I think you're the best person. Which still feels incredibly weird to say, but I do. And I get why you did what you did, with starting that blog. But I also can see why it hurt your sisters so badly."

I nod. "I hate that I hurt them."

Wilson lets out a long breath. "I can't believe you've had all that going on this entire time."

"Sorry I didn't tell you earlier," I say. "You know, we were kind of mortal enemies up until a few days ago, so."

Wilson knocks his knee into mine. "I really liked being your mortal enemy."

"So did I," I admit, something I've realized in hindsight. "It sort of made coming to work a lot more fun."

A moment passes. I rest my head on Wilson's shoulder. He wraps an arm around me, pulling me close. It feels so good, I wish I could hit Pause and live in this moment indefinitely.

"Your sisters will come around," he says.

"How do you know that?"

Even in the darkness, his eyes find mine. "Because that's what family does, they come around."

"I don't like when we fight like this," I say quietly. "I don't like feeling so separated from them. It's like the rational part of me knows we will be okay, but this other voice in my head reminds me that I may have lost them forever."

"You haven't lost them forever."

As soon as I say it, I want to take it back. I think about Wilson's dad, someone he truly has lost forever. "I'm sorry. That was so insensitive. I shouldn't have—"

"Hey," he interjects, his free hand squeezing my knee. "You say whatever you need to, Jackie. This isn't about me right now."

I breathe out. In the exhale, I give voice to all the thoughts running wild in my mind. "They're my older sisters," I say, feeling tears sting my eyes again. "I need them so badly, Wilson. Like, every day feels so terrifying without them here. I never realized how much I rely on them to just *exist* alongside me, you know? They're this constant companion that makes every day feel less scary because at least we're facing it together."

Wilson doesn't say a word. He only watches me, holds me, lends me his comfort, which is really all I need.

"I think what I regret the most is being so . . . so reckless with their feelings," I continue. "Now it seems so freaking obvious, but in the moment, all I could see was my blog and how it blew up. I was so focused on pleasing some strangers on the internet, I forgot that the people I love the most that were right beside me."

"Did you tell them that?" he asks.

"I did."

"Then that's all you can do, Jackie."

I lift my head off his shoulder and stare at him. "But I shouldn't have done any of it to begin with."

Wilson reaches out and runs his thumb along my cheek, catching another tear. "Of course you're going to say that now. Everyone looks back at their past and thinks, *hey, I really wish I had done that differently.* But isn't that the point? That we can learn and grow? Look, what's done is done, and you can't undo it, so focus on what you *can* do. You apologized, you owned up for your mistakes. Now all you can do is wait for them to come around."

I groan. "I don't want to wait, Willy. I want everything back to normal."

At that, he smiles. "Normal would be you in a frog costume and us hating each other's guts."

I stand corrected. "I want *some things* back to normal."

Wilson leans in and kisses my forehead. "I, for one, kind of like this new normal."

I return his smile. "So do I."

"Do you think . . ." His voice trails off. I watch his eyes flicker up to mine, see that familiar shyness creep into his demeanor. "Do you think this could be our new normal?" he says, blurting the words out.

I start to cry all over again. My hand cups his face, and there's nothing I want more than to say yes. To dive into him and see where the current takes us. But if we agree to this, if we agree to move forward together, we can't start off on shaky ground. If the foundation isn't there from the beginning, it's only a matter of time until the floor gives out entirely.

With my sisters, I never confessed. I waited until they found out themselves, then I closed my eyes and apologized, hoping they'd believe me and come around. But I learned my lesson now, and I'm not making the same mistake twice.

"Jackie." I've gotten so used to the way his voice cradles my name. "You're crying again."

"I lied to you before," I blurt out.

"Okay," he says slowly. "What did you lie about?" Even now, he's so gentle.

I sniffle and Wilson hands me a tissue. "You asked if I had apologized. If I owned up to my mistakes. I did with my sisters. But I haven't apologized to you."

"What's there to apologize for?"

And then the words rush out of me, like they should have weeks ago. "Kenzie wrote into my blog. I had no idea it was her at the time. She wrote in and asked for advice to break up with you, and I gave it to her. It was my idea for her to do it in a letter. I mean, I guess she would have broken up with you anyway, but I helped her do it. And when I found out that it was Kenzie, I should have told you. But I thought offering to help you win her back would be enough to right my wrongs. You have to believe me, Wilson. I had *no idea* it was Kenzie who wrote in. I didn't realize until the day I found her letter in your desk. And then I tried to make it right. I really did."

Wilson moves away from me and stands up. Time stretches on in silence as he stares at me, his mouth slightly open. His eyebrows draw together, and I can see him trying to process everything I said.

"Kenzie wrote into your blog, asking for advice to break up with me?" he repeats.

"Yes. I can show you—"

"No. Please don't."

Wilson begins pacing back and forth. With every step, I feel him getting farther away.

I stand up too and walk to him. I grab his hands, root him in place. "Talk to me."

"You didn't know it was Kenzie," he says slowly.

"I didn't. I thought she was some random girl who needed help, which is why I gave it to her."

"But you knew the moment you read the letter, Jackie. You knew then what you did, and you lied to me about it," Wilson continues. "All those weeks we spent together, planning for Kenzie, and you went along with it."

I stammer over my words. "I'm so sorry," I say.

But no, those words don't feel right.

I try again. "Wilson, I thought I was being helpful."

No. Still wrong.

"When I found out what I did, I tried so hard to make it

right," I say frantically. "That's why I offered to help you win her back. I wanted—I wanted to right my wrongs. I wanted to help fix what I broke."

"But you leveraged your job," he says. When he turns to me, I can see how badly I've hurt him. "Did you really care about helping me, or were you just trying to get your old job back?"

"I think—" I take a breath, hating myself for what I'm about to admit. "I think a little bit of both. When I saw you that day at *The Rundown*, you looked so heartbroken, Wilson. I had never seen you look that way. I really did want to help you, but—I guess I had to help myself too. I selfishly threw in my job promotion. You're right. I shouldn't have made it about me."

Then Wilson takes his hands out of mine, and I know I've lost.

This time, it's a different sense of loss. Not the same ache I feel with my sisters. Not that deep pain that is bearable only because you know that, like Wilson said, family always comes around. But Wilson isn't family. This thing growing between us is so new, so unsteady. It could collapse under the slightest weight, and I'm afraid I've dropped an anvil on it.

"Jackie, you lied to my face for weeks." He runs a hand along his jaw. "God, I probably seemed so pathetic. Moping over my ex to you, when you were the one who gave her the courage to dump me."

I feel like I'm falling apart all over again. I can't stop myself from babbling, throwing out apologies and explanations, but

Wilson just stands there without saying a word. His silence cuts me to the bone. It says so much without saying anything at all.

"Wilson, I didn't know the account was Kenzie—"

"I know that," he says, his voice growing louder. "I get that, Jackie. I'm not mad you gave Kenzie the advice. That doesn't matter. At all. But you should have told me about the blog before we teamed up to win her back. You could have been honest."

"I know, and that's why I'm telling you now. I should have been up-front weeks ago, but I was so scared. For some reason, protecting my blog and my anonymity came before *anything*. I realize now that it shouldn't have. You were more important, my sisters were more important. I messed up. Badly."

There's so much more I have to say, but then Justin peeks his head out from around the corner. I instantly look the other way, not wanting him to catch sight of my tear-streaked face. "Wilson, some lady wants to speak to the manager. Said her kid choked on a mozzarella stick or something," he says.

I'm so shaken I can't even manage a laugh.

"Be right there," Wilson calls back.

When Justin walks away, Wilson takes my face in his hands. I want to hit Pause. I want to hit Pause *right now*.

"I need to get back inside," he says softly, his eyes searching mine. That subtle action alone means everything to me. That, after what has happened between us, he still waits for me to give him the okay to leave.

"I want to keep talking about this," I say, gripping his arms.

"We will," Wilson says, "but not right now. I need to go do my job, and I think we both need a minute to calm down. Why don't you leave early? I'll have your tips ready for next week."

I must nod, because Wilson lets go of my face. He heads back inside, taking all the warmth with him.

CHAPTER 26

I WALK THROUGH THE doors to *The Rundown* Monday morning, and the name has never felt more fitting. This magazine and I are both completely run-down. The scene with Wilson lives permanently at the back of my mind, a constant ache that trickles down to my heart. He hasn't texted, and I don't want to push him, so I've been giving him some space. And Julie and Jillian haven't come home.

It feels like I've reached exile status.

So when I step into the office and see Jillian there, seated at her desk, I nearly collapse on the floor. It's the first time I've felt that there's a chance everything will be okay.

I walk to my desk on wobbly feet. Jillian is my sister, but at this moment she may as well be a complete stranger. "Good morning," I say professionally, taking a seat at my desk.

Jillian glances at me from the corner of her eye. "Hey," she says before returning her attention to the computer.

I mean, lasers didn't shoot out of her eyes and annihilate me on the spot, so a win is a win.

For the next hour I busy myself with online shopping. I had an email waiting from Camilla, asking me to compile a list of links for different office chairs. I need to keep the budget under three thousand dollars, and I email her the list by end of day. It keeps me preoccupied for a while, right until the door to Camilla's office opens and she calls Jillian in. I try to make eye contact with Jill before she walks away, but she deliberately averts my gaze. There's a thinly veiled twinge of sadness to the set of her eyes, and I know they must be discussing her promotion further—or rather, her *lack* of a promotion.

The realization feels like a finger pressing on an old bruise.

I peer behind my shoulder into Camilla's office. The door is open the slightest crack, but not enough for me to make out anything other than the back of Jill's head.

I just want to be able to ask her. To ask Jillian if the promotion is fully off the table. If there is anything—anything at all—that we can do to make it possible again.

Then it dawns on me.

Maybe it's not too late to save Jillian's promotion.

I lower the brightness on my laptop and pull up *iDiary*. Simply having it open in public feels so risky, but this can't wait any longer. After my unread messages load up, I scroll down, down,

down, until I find it—Jillian's second message, where she asked to interview me. I type out a quick response, nothing more than two sentences:

> If the offer still stands, I'd love to. Is it too late to get you that promotion?

I expel all the air out of my body and hit Reply.

I exit out of *iDiary* the second I hear the door to Camilla's office creak open. My heart is beating so quickly, I barely risk a breath. Jill takes a seat at her desk and begins typing on her computer. I wait for some indication that she's seen it: a look my way, a smile, the smallest raise of an eyebrow.

Then it happens.

I feel Jill staring at me. I don't dare to look, but I can physically *feel* her eyes on me. My cheeks burn hot enough to rival the sun.

I wait until she finishes typing and then refresh my *iDiary* inbox.

One new message. And it's from Jillian. Her response is even shorter than mine:

> 6pm. Let's meet <u>here</u>.

The word *here* is underlined. I click on the link, and it takes me to a Google Maps page with directions to our house.

After Michelle drops me off at home, I run inside, grateful that I have a moment to gather my thoughts before Jill arrives.

My parents are out in the backyard. My mom is reading and my dad is lying in the sun with his shirt off. I raid the fridge, thankful for the peace and quiet, then take a quick shower. When my hair is wet and falling in ringlets over my shoulders, I look in the mirror and see this perfect blend of Jillian and Julie. That's the strangest part—I don't see my mom or my dad. It's like I'm entirely made up of my sisters.

And there, nestled between them, is me—the person I am. Different from them, but the same in the ways that matter the most.

At two minutes to six, the front door opens. Jill must have texted my parents and told them to lay off, because—to my complete shock—they don't immediately barrel into the house. They must be giving us space. I can hear the fridge open and close, then the squeak of the leather cushion when Jill takes a seat on the couch.

My hands shake when I walk down the stairs. I cross my arms, tucking them between my armpits. When I walk into the room, I stare wordlessly at my sister.

"Hey," she says.

"Hey."

I resist running over and hugging her.

I take a seat on the opposite end of the couch, gently tucking my legs beneath me as Jill flips open her notepad.

"What changed your mind?" she asks.

When I peer up from my legs, she's watching me.

"Your promotion is more important to me than some blog," I say easily. It's true. Weeks ago, I choose my anonymity over my sister. Now I can't imagine ever making such a foolish choice again.

I don't expect her to thank me, and she doesn't. But before she can get into the first question, I have one more thing to say.

"I'm deleting the blog," I blurt out. "So I guess this interview is an exclusive tell-all. The rise and fall of *pleasebreakmyheart* or whatever you want to call it. Point is, whatever you need from me to get the promotion back on the table, I'll do it."

Jillian closes the notepad. "Are you deleting it because you want to or because you think it's the only way Julie and I will forgive you?"

"Both," I say. I'm moving forward with honesty here, and this is the purest form of the truth. "I can't continue using that account knowing that every single post is going to hurt you and Julie. I won't do that to either of you ever again."

"Are you going to miss running the account?" she asks. Her notepad is still closed. I don't think this question is part of the interview.

This answer isn't as clear. "I will," I say. "I'll miss helping people and the validation that came with it. But . . ." In the moment,

I come to a new realization. "I feel so different from the way I did when I began that account. I have my old waitress job back at Monte's. I love working with you at *The Rundown*. Sure, running *pleasebreakmyheart* helped me unlock this new passion, but now I can find the right way to use it."

I don't mention my idea of starting an advice column at *The Rundown*. It's way too soon for that. But I can't stop myself from hoping that maybe, in a few days, once everything has settled, we can sit down with Camilla and talk about it.

Jillian opens her notepad and clicks her pen. I can see her enter journalist mode. She shifts her body, leans forward, her eyes narrow in on me. "Tell me about the moment you started the account," she says.

The real interview lasts about forty-five minutes. I walk Jill through the entire process: my first post declaring myself a heartbreak expert, the first message I ever received, how the account went viral after @makeupbreakup reposted it. I don't spare a single detail.

When she asks how the overnight fame made me feel, I tell her I soaked it in like a sponge. When she asks how much money I made off the account, I tell her zero dollars. I fire off an answer, and she fires off another question. She's quick thinking, every question deliberate. She pokes and prods but understands exactly when to back off. Now, finally on the receiving end of her interviews, I get to see just how good she really is.

When the interview is done, Jill flips the notepad closed.

Then she says the last thing I ever expected. "Don't delete your account yet."

"Why?" I say, bewildered. I was so certain she would be totally on board with the account being forever forgotten in the depths of the internet.

"I don't know," she says. "Just— For right now, leave it. Okay?"

"Okay."

I look over my shoulder and see our parents still sitting outside. "What did you say to keep them out there so long?" I ask, peering over at Jill.

"I told them if they gave us an hour alone, I'd move back home tonight."

I suck in a sharp breath, my eyes immediately filling with tears.

Jill rolls her eyes. It's the first thing she's done in so long that feels so *her*. "Don't cry," she says. "God, I was gone for a week, and you're turning into Julie."

In the blink of an eye, my sister is back.

As if summoned by her name, the front door opens and Julie walks through. When I spot the overnight bag in her hand, I jump up from the couch.

"Hi," I say. The word explodes out of me so forcefully that Jillian barks out a laugh.

"Hi," Julie says. The moment she spots us on the couch together, she bursts into tears. "I missed you both so much."

Julie and I collide in the middle of the room. She hugs me so tight I struggle to breathe, but it doesn't matter. My tears fall onto her shoulder, and I don't have to look to know that hers are falling onto mine.

Then she pulls back. I grow worried for a second before I see why: Jillian is standing awkwardly beside us, like she's waiting.

My lip quivers. For the first time in a week, it doesn't hurt to breathe.

I don't poke fun at her. Neither does Julie. We probably will in a week or two. Right now, we open our arms and bring Jillian into the hug. Her arms fly around us, and we stand there hugging, crying, Julie slobbering all over everyone. I think we may stand like this for the rest of the night, but then the softest sound pulls us apart.

"Was that . . ."

In sync, we all look down. Right there, standing on the carpet at our feet, far, far away from beneath the couch, is Mr. Chunks. He meows again, his large eyes blinking up at the three of us.

"Well, I'll be damned," Jill says. "He actually does look skinnier."

A second of silence ticks by before we all laugh so hard we are wheezing. Jillian and I are doubled over, barely containing ourselves. Julie has given up entirely and sits cross-legged on the floor, her face smushed into the cat's neck.

"I missed you the most," she tries to whisper.

"We heard that," I say.

Then Julie tugs on both our hands and pulls us down beside her. We sit on the carpet, each with one hand on Mr. Chunks's soft fur. He flips onto his back, purring louder than I thought possible.

"What were you guys talking about before I walked in?" Julie asks.

Jillian explains, then adds, "And Jackie wants to delete the account."

Julie grabs my hand, her eyes growing wide. "Because of us, or because you want to?"

"That's exactly what I said," Jillian says.

"Because I want to," I say. "But Jillian told me to hold off."

"I agree," Julie says. She rubs Mr. Chunks's belly, then quickly pulls her hand away when he tries to bite her wrist.

Collectively, we all ignore that.

"I'm confused," I say. "I thought you both would *want* me to delete the account? Why the change of heart?"

"Change of heart," Jill mumbles. She grabs her notepad and jots that down. "I like that."

Julie ignores her and continues. "Because of what you told us, how this account meant so much to you, Jackie. You said it finally gave you some sort of identity. I don't want to take that away from you."

"Maybe," Jill adds, throwing her notepad onto the couch,

335

"we can find a way to run it with more transparency moving forward?"

I consider their suggestions, then come to a final conclusion. "I know what I want to do."

I grab my laptop out of my bag at the foot of the stairs. My sisters watch as I click into the *iDiary* settings and deactivate my account. Julie screeches. When I look up, Jillian is smiling. I know then and there that she was putting me first. That even if she wanted the blog deleted, she would have put her feelings aside and let me run it if that's what I truly wanted. But now it's my turn— my turn to put them first.

"Julie, I don't need that account to give me my identity. And Jill, I appreciate the offer, but you don't need to be selfless right now. I'm done with that account, I'm done with hurting you both ever again. Can we please, *please* forget it existed and be sisters again?" My voice cracks on the last sentence.

Jill's foot hits mine. "Yes."

"We're still sisters, even when we fight, you big goofball." Julie leans across to hug me, but Mr. Chunks *again* tries to bite her arm the moment it hovers over his body.

"For safety reasons, everyone keep all limbs to yourselves," I say.

Jillian chuckles. "This guy loses a few pounds and all of a sudden turns into a monster."

Jill and I look at each other at the exact same moment, like we're thinking the same thing. "Or maybe he was always a monster," I say.

"And we just never realized it because he wouldn't leave the couch," Jill finishes.

Julie alternates between glaring at the both of us. "Stop bullying my cat."

Just as she says it, he swats his paw at Jill. His nail gets stuck in the fabric of her sock. "Looks like your cat is bullying *us*," she says.

We sit there for another hour, sharing all the moments we've missed out on. Even Jillian shares a tiny bit of information about Camilla—that they started dating two months ago. We don't dare ask about the cheating, but maybe in the future she'll open up to us about that, too.

When it's my turn, I tell them about Wilson. I tell them all of it: the blog, Kenzie, my confession. I tell them how terrified I am that I've lost someone who was never really mine to lose, that even this moment of forgiveness feels tainted by the lingering ache in my heart for him. Because even though my sisters have forgiven me, Wilson hasn't. And a big part of me is terrified that he never will.

"People need time to process their feelings," Julie says to comfort me. "Wilson seems like he's got a lot on his plate, and I bet this is wearing away at him, too."

"Give him some time," Jill says. "And then, make it right."

"How do I do that?"

Julie squeezes my hand. "I think you already know the answer to that."

It takes a moment for me to catch on. As my sisters laugh, I groan.

I peek into my future and see that familiar shade of green.

CHAPTER 27

WHEN THE WEEKEND HITS, my entire family piles into the car for a momentous occasion. On the way to the bank, an argument breaks out the second Julie connects her phone to the car's Bluetooth. When Taylor Swift's *Folklore* album begins to play, Jillian all but jumps through the window into oncoming traffic.

"Stop trying to push your Swiftie agenda onto the rest of us," she says, pouting, her arms crossed.

"If you stopped being a big suck and actually listened, maybe you'd like it," Julie fires back.

Dad drives, Mom sits in the passenger seat. They don't say a word. They just keep glancing at each other and smiling.

I stare out the window, watching the town roll past, thinking of Wilson and everything I have planned to make things right with him.

On a day like today, where there is so much excitement in the air, his absence feels glaringly obvious. It's, like, even happiness feels dull without him here to feel it, too. Which is a very strange feeling—something I've never felt before, this deep desire to share a moment with someone else.

I haven't spoken to him since our last conversation. Too full of nerves to even consider confronting him, I gave my past two shifts at Monte's away. Plus, I sort of needed a moment to stay at home with my sisters. After losing them for a few days, I needed that permanence—that reminder that they won't disappear the second I walk out the front door.

But Wilson has been on my mind every day. All I want to do is text him, call him, see him. I remind myself that the time is coming. Tonight we'll be back on track.

I don't contemplate what will happen if this goes wrong.

When we reach the bank, I leave my sisters to argue in the car. I've come to the realization that not every argument means an ending is near. Especially between family. I hear Wilson's voice again: *That's what family does, they come around.*

My dad and I walk into the bank, and a nice older man helps us. Yesterday, my paycheck from Monte's and *The Rundown* hit my account. When I saw the total of my savings account finally pass twenty-five hundred dollars, there was only one way to celebrate.

The man hands me the bank draft with a smile. "Anything specific you're spending this on?"

My dad squeezes my shoulder and beats me to the answer.

"My daughter's buying her first car."

"Wow! That's a big accomplishment. Congratulations," the man says.

I'm nothing short of radiant. "Thank you."

We pile back into the car to find that Julie has switched over to playing *Reputation*. She's dancing in the back seat. In fact, they're *both* dancing. I take my seat in the third row and say, "What did I miss?"

Julie looks at me over her shoulder. "Jill likes *Reputation*."

"You should've played this album from the get-go," she says. "This is way more my speed."

For the rest of the drive, Julie gives Jillian an in-depth explanation of every song, the meaning behind every lyric, and a detailed history of the people who inspired it. When my dad pulls into the Nissan dealership, the five of us walk inside together.

It takes an hour to fill out the paperwork and a good fifteen minutes for my dad to haggle the price down by a couple hundred. When all is said and done, I hand the salesman my bank draft, my parents pitch in the remaining amount, and we wait while the car is being washed.

"Stop growing up so fast," Julie says, her eyes beginning to water.

"Is there anything that *won't* make you cry?" Jill teases.

Then the employee hands me the keys to my car. I stare at them in disbelief. Being a frog at Monte's, working at *The Rundown*, finally being repromoted to waitress—all these moments flash through my head. All the moments that have led me here, made this possible.

The five of us run outside to the parking lot.

My shiny white hatchback sits parked in the first row. There's a pink bow tied on each side mirror, and a giant one placed on the hood. Julie grabs my left hand. Jill grabs my right one. They squeeze tightly. I squeeze right back.

"Shotgun!" Jill takes off across the parking lot. I unlock the door, and she slides into the passenger seat.

"Guess I'm in the back," Julie grumbles, sulking over to the car.

My parents sling their arms around me. "We're so proud of you," Mom says, pressing her face into mine.

"Your hard work paid off, kiddo," Dad says.

"Thanks, guys," I say.

Before I can run over and join my sisters, my dad gives me the ultimate Dad Talk. "Drive the speed limit," he warns. "At a stop sign, three seconds minimum. When the light turns yellow, you slow down. And when Jill tells you to push it and run the light, what do you do?"

"Ignore her," I answer.

He winks. "You got it."

When I get into the car, Julie and Jillian are already arguing over who gets to control the aux cord. Since my budget was pretty tight, I couldn't afford a newer model, which has Bluetooth. Julie surprised me this morning with the cord.

"Driver gets aux," I interrupt, plugging my phone in and

searching Suzy's Spotify profile. I see that a few hours ago she published a new playlist titled Road Tripping. It makes me smile, and I can't wait to get home and show her.

While the music fills the car, I adjust my seat, make sure everyone has their seatbelt on, then look both ways before pulling out of the parking spot—

"Wait!" Jill screams. I slam on the breaks. We all jerk forward, then back, our heads slamming into the headrest.

I glare at her. "What was that for?"

"Just want to make sure no older women are around for you to hit."

In the back seat, Julie snickers.

"For the last time," I say, pressing down on the gas and easing out of the spot, "I never hit Mrs. Clemens. I gently *nudged* her."

To both their surprise, I manage to drive us home without harming any elderly people.

CHAPTER 28

WHEN WE GET HOME, everyone heads inside but me. Instead, I lean against the car and call Suzy, telling her to come out. A few minutes later she runs out of her house in a pair of pink bunny slippers. I open my arms wide, as if to say *ta-da*!

She halts mid-step on the grass. "Jackie, you didn't . . ."

"I know it's not a yellow Jeep Wrangler, but this is all I could afford."

"Shut up, shut up, shut up!" Suzy runs across the lawn and flings herself at me, nearly knocking me to the ground. "You bought a freaking *car*? Did you buy this today?"

I squeeze her back. "Like an hour ago."

Suzy just stares at me, her mouth agape. "I—I don't even know what to say."

We sit in the car, and Suzy connects her phone to the aux. Her Road Tripping playlist blasts through the speakers, and even though we're parked in my driveway in Ridgewood, it sort of feels like we're flying down the PCH in sunny California.

"So the road trip is on," she says. I can see it so clearly—me missing the right exit, parking in fast-food lots for lunch, pumping way too much gas into this thing. I can't wait.

"I'm sorry if you ever doubted it."

Suzy shakes her head like that's a thing of the past. "Jackie, you worked so hard this summer to give us this. Are you kidding? We've been talking about it for a decade! You're, like, the greatest friend in the history of the world, and oh my gosh, I hate myself. I forgot to get this on video!"

Five minutes later, we reenact the entire thing.

I stand beside my car with my arms wide. Suzy runs out of her house in her pink bunny slippers, this time holding up her camera. We skip the hug for technical reasons, and then we are seated in the car again. Suzy has the camera jabbed in my face, and for the first time, it doesn't annoy me. I'm actually unbelievably happy to know that someone cares enough to capture all of this on video.

When Suz is satisfied with the footage, she lowers the camera. "We've got one week to prepare," she says.

It's like I blinked and summer flew by. "One week? Already?"

"Yup. I can't believe it either. I move in the last week of August, and it's going to take us at least four days to drive there. Probably longer, depending on how often we stop."

"Have you started packing?" I hate the way just talking about her leaving brings tears to my eyes. And dammit, Jill was right—I *am* turning into Julie.

Suzy laughs. "Of course not. I've been binge-watching movies and fighting for my life in that film club forum I showed you at Bee's. God, it's insane how *wrong* someone else's opinion can be."

I wrinkle my nose. "Isn't the point of an opinion that it can't be wrong?"

"Believe me, Jackie, if you read some of these opinions, you'd think otherwise. Someone actually called *The Wolf of Wall Street* a feminist film."

That takes even me by surprise. "Yeah, you're right. Some opinions are definitely wrong."

Suzy toys with the strap of her camera. I can't help but think this is one of the last times we'll be in my car together.

"Do you want to come over and help me pack? Four hands are better than two," she says with a smile.

"There's something else I have to do today. I can come by later tonight? Actually—" I check the time. Monte's doesn't close for another five hours. It's way too early to head over there and see Wilson. "Sure. I'd love that."

We don't say anything, but I know we're both thinking it. I ditched Suzy one too many times this summer. Some for work, some for Wilson. They may have been valid reasons in their own right, but now I'm going to be better at making time for what's important. And Suzy has always been at the top of that list. Tonight, I can make time for her *and* Wilson—like I always should have done.

We spend the next few hours in Suzy's room, drowning in cardboard boxes. Her parents peek their heads in a few times to check on us, and her mom drops off snacks every once in a while. We manage to sort through all her summer clothing and pack up the pieces she wants to bring along.

Her entire collection of DVDs is a lot harder.

"Suzy, you can't bring two hundred DVDs to college. I think my car might actually collapse from the weight. Are DVD players even still a thing?"

She insists they are necessary, so we narrow it down to a solid twenty-five of her most vital movies—just the ones she physically cannot live without. That alone took up the majority of the time. When I check my phone and see that it's nearly nine o'clock, I call it quits.

Suzy walks me across the lawn and back to my car. "Good luck," she says. Somewhere between sorting through jackets and DVDs, I explained the entire situation with Wilson. The lows, and especially the highs. Suzy is convinced he'll come around. I think so too, but there's a lot that has to be said.

A lot that has to be *done*.

My hands shake as I text Anita. The weight of tonight—of what this moment represents—is finally kicking in. Soon I'll be standing in front of Wilson, my heart in my throat, laying my heart totally bare. If he wasn't worth it, I would be hiding in my bedroom right now.

Anita replies that she's on board with my master plan: Take

Back Froggy. It is very much the last thing I thought I'd ever do, but it turns out that having a crush on someone makes you do crazy things.

Twenty minutes later, I pull into Monte's. Anita runs over to my car the moment I park. She taps on the window. As it rolls down, she says, "I'm afraid to ask questions, Jackie. But here you go." She shoves the frog costume into the car, and oh my—the smell that comes off this thing is deadly. I had almost forgotten.

"You're my favorite person in the world," I say.

"The universe!" she corrects, already running back inside.

Right there in the parking lot, I put the costume on over my clothing. It feels like I've gone back in time, but being a frog right now is relevant to the *gesture*. And the gesture says something I need Wilson to know: if it means winning him back, I'll gladly be a frog every day.

When I walk inside, my coworkers all turn and stare at me. I pointedly ignore them, refusing to let my nerves and their stares get the best of me. Then I see him. Wilson stands next to the ticket kiosk, holding his ridiculous clipboard. He's in the middle of jotting something down when his eyes look up and land right on me.

I see the surprise hit him first, then the humor. He begins to laugh. The pen slides right out of his hand, but I can't stop looking at his smile. It's like a freaking magnet, luring me across the floor and to his side. I'm realizing now that it's sort of where I always wanted to be.

"Jackie," he says, the laughter taking his breath away. "What is going on? Why are you dressed as a frog *again*? Wait— Where'd you even get that?" He looks behind his shoulder, slowly realizing that I've planned a heist and stolen the old frog costume right out from under his nose.

"Guess your fancy new security system isn't as good as you thought," I say, smirking.

But this isn't what we need to be talking about right now.

Fully aware that every single person in Monte's is staring at us, I take a deep breath and say the words that have been running through my head for days now. "Wilson, you know more than anyone how much I hate being a frog," I say. When my voice trembles, I take another breath.

"Okay," he says slowly, like he's trying and failing to catch up.

"No, I need to hear you say it. How much do I hate being a frog?"

Wilson crosses his arms, tucking the clipboard beneath his bicep. "A lot," he says. "You complained about it every single day for months. Gave me countless raging headaches."

"Exactly. I hated wearing this costume *so much*. Like, decades from now I will see a frog on the side of the road and shudder with terror." I pause and take a step toward him on wobbly legs. I rip off the stupid frog head and hold it between us like an offering. "But I'll wear it for you, Wilson. I'll wear this stupid costume every single day. I don't care. You are so much more important to me than a job title or a blog post. I don't need the waitressing, or the tips, or even a clean costume that doesn't smell like sweat— Wait, no. I think I might need that, actually." I pause, smiling when Wilson laughs. "But what I really need is to make things right with you. I need you to know how much you mean to me. And if it takes me being a frog again, then I'll do it. I'd— Well, Wilson, I think I'd do anything for you."

Monte's is so quiet, I can hear the steady hum of the arcade games.

My heart beats so loud I hear it ringing in my ears.

I know that behind me, Anita and Justin and Margaret are all staring, wondering what the heck is going on and what exactly happened between me and Wilson when no one else was watching.

Still, all I can look at—all I can focus on—is Wilson. His eyes. His hair. The ironed press of his shirt and the deep brown of his eyes. It's a sight I can never grow tired of. And when that familiar smile begins to tug at the corners of his mouth, my heart stutters into a new rhythm.

Finally, Wilson grabs the frog head from my hands. I'm terrified he's going to place it back over my head, but then he throws it to the ground. Behind us, a child screams. We both begin to laugh.

"I think we just ruined multiple children's innocence," I whisper.

Wilson nods, grinning. "Definitely."

"I mean, *if* we've already scarred everyone here, we may as well just . . ."

He meets me halfway, sweeping me off the ground and kissing me so hard the world sways. There's a whoop. There's a holler. There's something that sounds like gasps, but all of Monte's seems to fade away when Wilson kisses me.

When my feet are planted back on the floor, he says, "No more Froggy. Just Jackie. Okay?"

"Okay," I say breathlessly. I've nearly forgotten what we're talking about.

From the corner of my eye I see a teenage boy in a Pokémon T-shirt standing alarmingly close to us. "Not to ruin the moment or whatever," he says, pushing his glasses further up his nose, "but I'm still waiting on those tickets."

Wilson clears his throat. We are trying so very hard not to laugh.

"Right. Uh— Jackie, I'll meet you outside?"

At ten, I'm sitting in my car, watching my coworkers trickle out. The waitstaff leave first, then a few of the cashiers. It takes another hour before the lights are shut and I see Wilson's silhouette through the glass door. He walks out with Justin, Margaret, and a few members of the woodland crew. They're laughing, chatting, all smiling wide. By the look on Wilson's face, he's having a good time.

I realize that even though I'm not part of this moment, I'm smiling, too. I know how hard Wilson has worked for this, how badly he wanted this connection with his employees. Seeing it happen fills me with pride.

When my coworkers have left and Wilson is locking up alone, I finally step out of my car and cross the space between us. I wait a few feet behind him on the sidewalk.

"Since when are you so popular?" I ask.

Wilson turns around, smiling. Not those old Wilson smiles that were guarded and forced, but the kind of private smile he shared with me when I first tore his walls down.

"Hey, sorry to keep you waiting. There was a whole situation with the ball pit," he says, shuddering. "And believe it or not, it's because of your sister," he says.

He stands at the door. I stand at the edge of the walkway. There are maybe seven feet between us, and I feel every inch of it.

"Let's normalize adding context, Willy."

He smiles like he missed me, too.

"Remember that piece Jillian wrote on me?" he asks. "The interview I did? It was published yesterday in *The Rundown*. You didn't know?"

"I had no idea," I say. With everything that's been going on lately, Jillian must have forgotten to tell me.

Wilson walks toward me, pausing before he gets too close.

"Everyone here read the article," he explains. "I discussed my dad's passing, explained why Monte's means so much to me. I guess once they read it, it sort of altered their opinion of me."

It doesn't surprise me. When I found out, I began to see him differently, too.

"Justin asked me to hang out this weekend," he adds sheepishly.

"You're kidding."

"I'm serious."

"Are you going to go?" I ask.

Wilson shrugs. He tries to play it off, but I can see how much he wants this. How badly he's been craving this approval the second he walked through the door and filled his uncle's shoes. "Maybe," he says.

"You should," I say. "I think you could use a social life."

At that, he laughs. "I'm too busy for a social life, Jackie."

I feel myself loosen up a bit, now that we've gotten our old rhythm back. "Maybe you should free up some time," I say. "Tell me when and where. I'll drive."

"No chance you're driving my car."

"Not *your* car, goof. *My* car."

He notices it then—my white Nissan parked beside his sleek white Lexus. Wilson walks over and runs his hand along the hood. He lets out a low whistle and says, "You bought this? This is your car? Since when?" Even though his Lexus clearly outshines it, there's no trace of teasing or mocking in his voice. He looks genuinely impressed.

I nod proudly. "I got it today. What do you think?"

"It's so you," he says.

"It's a car. How is it 'so me'?"

Wilson leans against his passenger door. I lean against my driver door. We are toe to toe, nearly eye to eye if it wasn't for the height difference.

"It's small, probably drives too fast, and can easily hold its ground against any truck twice its size. Sounds like Jackie Myers."

I want to stand up on my tallest tiptoes and kiss him so hard.

I don't really know what to say to that, so I don't say anything. I'm sort of overwhelmed by his presence. I've gone days without seeing him, and now, having him so close, it's like I've nearly forgotten how to act.

"I know you're probably exhausted and want to head home—" I begin.

"I'm not exhausted," he says quickly. "I can stay."

We both bite down our smiles. "I was hoping we could talk. More than we already talked inside, I mean."

Wilson's gaze lands on his shoes. "I was hoping we could, too."

The parking lot is empty now, and the wind has picked up. The only light is from sporadic streetlights. It covers us in this dim, moody glow. I can see the shadows dance around Wilson's face. See the echo of his eyelashes fluttering against his cheek.

"I'm sorry for hurting you," I say. It's only the tip of the iceberg, but it's a starting point.

Wilson blows out a breath. "I get why you wanted to help me win Kenzie back. I'm not upset about that— I mean, it kind of brought us closer together, so how could I be mad? I just wish you had told me from the get-go. I felt so stupid to have been left in the dark. Knowing that I was pining over Kenzie, and the entire time you knew how over me she really was."

"You're not stupid at all, Wilson. I never thought that. Seeing how hard you fought for Kenzie was sort of what changed my opinion of you in the first place," I admit. "Seeing how much you loved her, how you never gave up on her—it made me realize what a good person you are. How good a *boyfriend* you are."

That seems to take him by surprise. "You— You really think so?"

"I really do," I say quickly. "And when I asked to help win Kenzie back, I should have told you the full story. You deserved that. In hindsight, I'd do it all differently."

In hindsight, I wouldn't do it at all.

Wilson scuffs the toe of his shoe against mine. "Thanks for apologizing." His voice turns teasing. "And thanks for coming here dressed as a frog. I know it's hard for your ego to take a hit."

I pretend to laugh. "Wow. I nearly forgot how funny you are." Then I add, "By the way, I deactivated my blog."

He looks surprised. "Why?"

"It did more harm than good," I say. He nods like he understands. I take his silence as an opening. "I've realized that I do this thing where I assume how people are going to feel. I thought my sisters wouldn't be fazed by my account, when it really hurt them. I thought helping you win Kenzie back would make things right when it only made you feel played. I can't keep assuming. Not if it's going to hurt the people I care most about."

I don't realize how desperately I need physical reassurance until Wilson comes to stand beside me. He leans his body against mine, side to side, my hand fitting perfectly in his.

"You also helped a lot of people, Jackie."

"You don't have to baby me—"

"I'm not," he cuts in. "I spent hours last night going through *pleasebreakmyheart*. I read every piece of advice you gave. All the comments, all the people praising you for how much you helped them? You can't ignore that either."

I'm still stuck on the fact that Wilson read my freaking blog. It's like finding out that your crush read your diary. "I might have helped a *few* people," I admit.

His hand squeezes mine. I only notice I'm staring at the ground when he gently grabs my chin, nudging my face to his. In his eyes, I find a gentleness.

"You helped me," he says. "Even though you went about it in not the greatest way, you helped me, Jackie. You came here the second I needed help with the gift basket. You were there with me the day of the picnic. Every time I needed you, you came through. And if the picnic went the way we had planned, *if* Kenzie and I had gotten back together, what would you have done?"

"I would have let you two be together." The words are out so quickly I barely have to think about them.

"You would have let yourself be miserable—"

"Okay, don't inflate your ego *too* much, Willy. I wouldn't have been *miserable*."

"Heartbroken?" he offers with a laugh.

"Let's say extremely sad."

"Fine—you would have been extremely sad, and still, you

would have let me and Kenzie be together. That doesn't sound selfish to me."

When the wind picks up, he brushes a strand of hair behind my ear. It's not lost on me that my hair is, again, curly. The way he likes it—the way he made *me* begin to like it, too.

"You're right. I'm a great person and should be immediately forgiven for all my crimes," I tease.

"I forgave you the second you put that ridiculous costume on."

"Ridiculous? You mean I *don't* look unbelievably sexy and you can barely keep your hands to yourself?" I take a step closer. Wilson is laughing. "All jokes aside," I say. "I am sorry. And I promise I will never do anything like that again, okay?"

He leans down. "I believe you."

"I wanted to figure this out before I leave next week."

Maybe it's a bit rude of me, but the instant sadness that overwhelms his face makes me feel giddy. It's knowing that he doesn't want me to leave. Knowing that he's going to miss me, too.

"Where are you going?"

"I'm driving Suzy to California for school," I explain. "I'll be gone for like, two weeks or so."

His eyebrows knot together. "And you didn't think to tell your boss that you need time off?"

"Oh." Dammit. How'd I not think of that. "Speaking of— Sooooo, I need some time off."

He holds back a laugh. "I'll make it work."

"Of course you will. I'm your favorite employee."

Right when we are about to kiss, Wilson pulls away. "Dammit. I forgot to give you this." He reaches into his back pocket and hands me a squished Twix bar. The grin that splits across my face could set the world on fire. "I thought that from now on, instead of having you *steal* them from Monte's, I can buy them for you."

"I think I prefer to steal them," I joke.

"Good luck with that," he says. "I told you we had new security cameras installed. Now, nothing happens around here without me noticing."

Our faces inch closer together.

"Remember when you said everyone kind of likes you now?"

"Yes."

"Try not to ruin that, Willy."

"It may come as a surprise to you, but the only person's approval I need is yours, Jackie."

I'm about to fire off some sarcastic remark, but Wilson shuts me up with a kiss. And honestly? I'm content to never say another word. All I need is this, again and again and again.

CHAPTER 29

JILL AND I ARE meeting with Camilla in one hour, and now, at home, the three of us are sitting around the dining room table, arguing over a T-shirt.

"Julie, you're wearing my shirt," Jill insists for the tenth time.

"Jill, this is my shirt. Jackie, tell her it's my shirt."

I lean back in my chair and sigh like a disappointed parent. "Don't bring me into this."

Jillian is rocking her usual morning getup—oversize band T-shirt, men's boxer shorts, smudges of eyeliner around her eyes. Julie, on the other hand, decided to come downstairs this morning *also* in a concert tee. Only it's a Shania Twain shirt we bought years ago at her concert. I bought one. Julie bought one. Jillian bought one. Somehow, there is a fourth T-shirt. And Jillian swears it belongs to her and Julie has stolen it.

"I bought a second shirt at that concert. I always buy two! It's my thing!" Jill says, violently squishing a lemon scone in her fist.

"*I* always buy two shirts, Jill! This is *mine*. This is the second top *I* bought."

I check the time on the stove. "Our meeting is in an hour. We should probably—"

"Shut up, Jackie!" they say at the same time.

"Yup. Sorry." I sink down in my chair and let the fight unfold.

Some twenty minutes later, they reach an agreement: since no one can really remember who bought the shirt, they will share it, like joint custody over a child. Julie will wear it from Monday to Wednesday, Jillian will wear it from Thursday to Saturday, and they will alternate every other Sunday.

"Now that the custody battle has been settled, can we get back to business?"

"Please," Jillian says.

It's Monday morning, and right at nine o'clock, Jillian and I are going to walk into *The Rundown* and pitch our advice column to Camilla. When I finally worked up the courage to share the idea with my sisters, they immediately loved it. We all agreed it was a great way to take what I started on *pleasebreakmyheart* and bring it to a whole new level—this time, with their approval *beforehand*.

Ideally, we want to streamline this as a duo. Jill would be the main writer, and if Camilla agrees to it, I'll be brought on as the assistant writer. Initially I wanted to run the advice column alone, but considering I have no real writing experience, I figured that was too much to ask. I'm hoping Jillian serving as my mentor will sway Camilla.

Plus, Jill said she'd vouch for me. And she is dating the boss, so . . .

"You guys have the idea decided on?" Julie asks. She cuts a scone in half and eats it over a napkin.

I brush the sea of crumbs in front of me into a neat little pile. "Yes. A write-in advice column. Readers send an email, we sift through them, and every week we publish one to three of their questions, giving them an answer to their problems."

"But it's not heartbreak specific," Jill says.

"I think it should be," I say. "I like the idea of keeping it heartbreak-related like my account was. Clearly, there's a huge market for people looking for breakup advice. It could really separate us from other advice columns out there."

"First, I'm so proud of you both that I could cry . . . and I will do so later in the privacy of my bedroom," Julie begins matter-of-factly. "Second, I love that idea, Jackie. I think it's a really, really great point. And this was your idea. So whatever you think is best, we should go with it."

"I agree," Jill adds.

I beam at their approval.

"Then let's move forward assuming that's the game plan," Julie says, clapping her hands like a teacher. "Okay! So what are we still deciding on?"

"A title," I say. The idea is solid, but we can't decide what to call the column.

"Wait—I have an idea." Jill runs out of the room and returns a minute later with her notepad. She flips it open, searches for a page. "Here! I jotted this down the other day when you said it, Jackie. What about 'A Change of Heart'?"

Me and Julie go *ooooooooh*. "I like that," I say. "It definitely fits the theme."

"I like it too," Julie says. "But what about something that's even more specific to heartbreak?"

Jillian closes the notepad. "What do you mean?"

"Uhm." Julie pauses, thinking. "Like, something readers will instantly feel connected with. A phrase or a word that is almost too on the nose, that every woman on the planet has used at some point in her life. A sentence or quip that's used again and again, nearly to the point where it's a cliché."

"Okaaaaaay," I say, following her train of thought. "Well, you two would know this better than me. What are some common phrases said during breakups?"

"'I think we should see other people'," Jill offers.

"'We should take a break'," Julie adds.

"True, but those don't really work as a title," I say.

We think on it for a second longer; then Julie's face lights up. "I've got it. What about 'it's not you, it's me'?"

Jillian immediately shoots the idea down. "No way."

"Why!"

"Because ninety-nine percent of the time it *isn't* you. It's actually *them*."

Then it hits me. The second the words appear in my head, I know I've found our title. "What about 'it's not me, it's you'?"

A gazillion seconds have passed by in silence. Camilla rests her chin on her hand, deep in thought. We are sitting in her office, and I feel like I'm going to jump out of my skin. We just pitched the advice column idea, It's Not Me, It's You, and are waiting for a verdict. Does she like it? Hate it? Never want to hear from me again? I swear, Cami has the greatest poker face known to man. Someone take this woman to a casino, stat.

"I like it," she says finally. Jill and I shamelessly high-five. "Don't get me wrong, there's a few kinks we have to work out. But I really love it, ladies. This could take *The Rundown* into an entirely new direction. Bring in a whole new reader base. It's sort of genius. How did you come up with this again?"

"It was all Jackie's idea," Jill says, winking at me. When she revealed that she'd honor my anonymity with the *pleasebreakmyheart* article and keep it a secret, even from Camilla, it meant more to me than I could ever say.

"That's not totally true," I say. "This idea was a culmination of spending *years* learning and listening to my sisters. If it weren't for them, this column wouldn't exist."

Cami is smiling at both of us. I hope that when she and Jill are ready, she can start coming over again so we can get to know the real her.

"And I'm obsessed with the title. It's quirky, it's cute. It brings such a fun, light element to something that is naturally heavy. It's perfect," Camilla says.

My cheeks hurt from smiling. "I'm so glad you like it. So . . . Is this going to happen? Jill and I can run this column?"

Camilla pushes back from her desk, sitting up a bit straighter in her office chair. "Jackie, I'm ready to take a chance on you. We can discuss the details later, but if you want it, there's a spot here for you here as our assistant writer."

It feels like time has frozen and my heart has stopped beating.

"Are you serious?" I whisper.

Cami laughs. "I'm dead serious."

Beside me, Jill grasps my hand.

I think back to all those days, nights, weeks, months I spent tossing and turning, searching beneath every rock, peeking into every nook and cranny, trying to find some glimpse of myself. Trying to discover who I was, what I'm good at, and, most important, who I want to be. Every moment—every wrong turn, every stumble, every guess in the dark—brought me right here. Without even realizing it, I think I ended up exactly where I was supposed to be all along.

"I'd love to," I say. Tears spring loose from my eyes.

Cami is smiling ear to ear. "Great. Now, there's just one other thing."

"What's that?" Jill asks. She leans forward, like she's ready to shoot down any concern Cami may have.

"Well, Jill, you managed to snag that interview with *please-breakmyheart* that we talked about. Even if we never went through with publishing it, since the account was randomly taken down, I was still impressed by your initiative." Jill and I share a look. Camilla continues talking. "And if you're *also* going to be mentoring Jackie and streamlining this column, I feel like you probably need a new job title, too. How does senior writer sound?"

For the first time in my life, I see Jillian cry. The tears fall down her cheeks and drip onto her T-shirt. She laughs through the tears, wiping them off her face as if she doesn't know where they even came from. "Senior writer sounds pretty great to me," she says.

And that's how *It's Not Me, It's You* was born from *please-breakmyheart*. It went from being a secret I guarded with my life, this thing I password protected, locked behind a vault—an endeavor I embarked on all on my own. I stumbled through the dark and managed to find my footing, but now it's different. There's no more stumbling or going in blind. Now I'm doing this with my sister. It's no longer mine. Now, it's ours.

Somehow, that is infinitely better.

CHAPTER 30

THE MORNING SUZY AND I leave for the road trip, the house erupts into chaos. It's Saturday, though, which means chaos was our only destiny. Dad tried to kick the morning off with a big family breakfast, but he ended up burning the bacon so badly that it set off our smoke alarm. Jillian, seeing this as fate, used the time to chastise my family for eating meat, mainly using the argument "vegetables don't burn like that." When Julie gently reminded her that yes, they do, Jill stormed upstairs—cue her bedroom door slamming shut.

"I'll go check on her," Julie declared before trudging up the stairs after her twin. It was all a bit dramatic, but I'd expect nothing less from a Saturday.

"Do you have everything you need?" Mom asks. We are carrying my bags to the car, loading everything into the trunk.

Across the lawn, Suzy and her parents do the same. My car is so full it might explode.

"Yes, Mom," I say for the hundredth time. All I really packed was some clothing and all my skin- and hair-care products. I figure if there's anything else I desperately need, I'll just buy it along the way.

"You know the directions?" Dad chimes in.

"I have a phone with a built-in GPS."

He shakes his head. "You can't rely on that technology, Jackie. What if your phone dies?"

"Then I use the phone *charger* that I also brought," I say.

My parents and I stand on the porch, huddled in the shade. It's teetering on ninety degrees today, and I already have the AC going in the car.

"Let me grab you a map. Just in ca—"

Jill and Julie walk through the door. "Don't give her a map, Dad," Julie says.

"There's no chance she'll be able to read one," Jillian adds. "You know how this younger generation is—"

"Okay, *rude*," I butt in.

The five of us stand together. I realize this will be the longest I've ever been away from home. Suzy and I calculated it'll take us about four or five days to drive to California—since we plan on stopping at night—and then I have to do the drive back alone. Which is scary for a million different reasons, but I'm ready.

"Hey. We got you a gift." Jillian pulls an envelope out of her pocket and hands it to me.

"It's from both of us," Julie adds.

"You guys didn't have to do that." I tear into the envelope and nearly die on the spot. They bought me a bumper sticker that reads Don't Worry, My Driving Scares Me Too.

The four of them stand there cackling like they are some sort of comedic geniuses.

"It's so everyone knows to leave a lot of room between their car and yours," Julie says, snickering.

Jill laughs so hard she can barely get her words out. "Especially old people. We know you have a track record."

"I barely nudg— You know what? I'm not defending myself anymore." I hug my sisters, throwing an arm around each of them. "Thanks for this."

"You're welcome," the say together.

"Text us when you get there," Jill says.

Julie fails to hide her tears. "Text me at least once an hour. You promise?"

"I promise," I say, smiling at the two of them.

I say my goodbyes, then meet Suzy at the end of the driveway. She's loading her luggage into my car.

"My sisters got me a gift." I peel the sticker off the paper and place it on my bumper.

Suzy immediately begins to laugh. "Shut up. That's amazing."

I close the trunk and turn to my best friend. I still can't wrap my head around the fact that all we have left is these few days. "You ready?"

She nods, tears blooming in her eyes. "I think so."

We face the house, staring up at our families waving at us.

"Should we go say goodbye to our parents one last time?" she asks, sniffling.

"Absolutely not."

We pile into the car, wave back as I reverse out of the driveway, then cruise down the road.

"We're still making that last stop, right?" Suzy asks as she sets up the Road Tripping playlist.

"Yes." We need to stop by Monte's so I can say goodbye to Wilson. We spent the entire last week hanging out every second of every day—well, every second neither of us was working. But even at Monte's, we now seem to be joined at the hip. He even cleared out a drawer in his desk to fill with all my favorite snacks, Twix included.

I'm slowing down at a stop sign when I see a familiar white Lexus getting too close in my rearview. It's speeding behind us, like it's trying to—

"Oh my God. It's Wilson!"

I notice him in the driver's seat, waving frantically to get my attention.

Suzy shrieks. "Jackie, pull over!"

I turn the wheel so suddenly the car jerks to the side of the road. I park three feet from the curb, but I cut the engine and run outside anyway. Wilson does the same. We run toward each other, panting, out of breath, smiling like crazy.

"You were really going to leave without coming to say goodbye, huh?" He shouts as he draws near. His hair is a windblown mess. Why wouldn't it be?

"We were driving to Monte's right now! I was going to surprise you!"

He collides against me, wrapping me in his arms. "I told you about the cameras, Jackie. You can't surprise me."

Then he kisses me, and dammit, two weeks is way too long.

It still baffles me that Wilson—this person I used to deliberately try to get *away* from—has grown into the person who can always bring a smile to my face. The person who makes me the happiest. The person whose hand I always want to hold.

"Shouldn't you be at work?" I ask, wrapping my arms around his neck, straightening his shirt collar.

"I should," he says. "But I think they can manage for an hour. Shit, Jackie. I'm kind of going to miss you."

"*Kind of*?"

He laughs. "I'm *really* going to miss you. When are you coming back?"

"September first," I say. I think of all the things that will be waiting for me when I return. It floods my chest with warmth.

"Cool, cool. Sooooo— Got any plans September first?"

I hate the grin that overtakes my face. "I'm coming home. I just said that, Willy."

He rolls his eyes. "I mean after that. At night. Like, *after* you're home."

I get such a kick out of annoying him. I'm not going to stop now. "Why do you ask?"

He brushes the hair out of my face. We are both fully aware that we are standing in the middle of the road, yet we make no effort to move.

"I want to take you on a date," he says.

"Like a date you accidentally plan for me, or a real date this time?"

Wilson chuckles at the reminder. "A real date," he says easily.

I lean into him. "Then I'll see you September first."

With his hands on the small of my back, Wilson tugs me right up to him. I try to memorize every part of this moment—the way his lips move against mine, how he smells, how his hair feels in my hands. It's going to be the only thought running through my mind until I'm back here, in this town that has begun to grow on me, with these people who have grown on me, too.

We say our goodbyes, and I return to the car, where Suzy is twisted around in her seat, video camera out. She has this sly smile on her face, too. I know she got my entire exchange with Wilson on video. I don't really mind. Hey, it might be kind of cool to look back on this footage someday.

We don't say a word for a while. I drive through town, right past the Welcome to Ridgewood sign. When I see it in my rearview, I smile.

I can't help but think this feels like a beginning. I'm not sure to what exactly, but the feeling is there all the same.

In the passenger seat, Suzy tinkers with the camera. "This documentary is going to kick ass," she says.

"You think so?" I turn my head to glance at her.

"Oh yeah," she says, her smile coming easy. "Your life is definitely a story worth telling."

Acknowledgments

This book came from hundreds of late nights and hundreds of cups of decaf tea. Thank you to HarperCollins for allowing me to do this over and over again. My arm *might* be bruised from all the times I've pinched myself.

Somehow, the scrawny first draft of *It's Not Me, It's You* managed to fall into the hands of my editor, Clare Vaughn. Clare—you instantly deciphered all my Hozier references and understood Jackie, Julie, and Jillian in the way only a sister can. Even now, just thinking about the emails you sent and the notes we passed back and forth makes me smile. I think you were made to dive into this book with me, and it became its very best version because of you. I can't thank you enough for all the love you poured into these characters, and all the comfort your excitement and support brought me. You've truly been the best.

For some reason, books are just better with cats in them. To my real-life Mr. Chunks—Chico, who sleeps beneath the dining room table, snoring his heart out while I work. He also likes to swipe at wrists, and he most definitely cannot fit beneath a couch.

Jackie, Jillian, and Julie are three sisters who fight hard and love harder, the way only sisters can. This book could only be dedicated to Alessia, the sister who lent me clothing growing up, taught me how to straighten my hair, and dueled with me in more yelling matches than I can count. All the best parts of these three fictional sisters were inspired by you.

A huge thank you to the copy editors who catch all my typos, grammatical errors, and inconsistencies. To Andi Porretta, for once again illustrating the cover of my dreams; I've been so unbelievably lucky to experience your art twice now. And to every other person behind the scenes who played a hand in the creation of this book.

My final thank-you is to every reader who picks up this book. More than anything, I hope it makes you laugh.